For Better or Hearse

by

Ann Yost

Jewel of the Night Series

For Better or Hearse

Cover Art by *Kim Mendoza*

The Wild Rose Press, Inc.
PO Box 708
Adams Basin, NY 14410-0708
Visit us at www.thewildrosepress.com

Publishing History
First Crimson Rose Edition, 2012
Second Crimson Rose Edition, 2016
Print ISBN 978-1-5092-1026-8
Digital ISBN 978-1-5092-1027-5

Jewel of the Night Series
Published in the United States of America

She felt like a smashed piñata

as the floor slammed into her hip and funny bone.

"Ow!"

An artificial light flared in her eyes.

"You okay?"

She gritted her teeth and waited for the flare of pain to recede before she opened one eye.

Nick leaned over the side of the bed, his dark hair tousled from sleep, his eyelids heavy, his cheeks bristled with dark whiskers. Gray eyes glittered at her.

"Damn you felt good. C'mon back to bed, honey."

Honey? Honey? She struggled to her feet and planted her fists at her waist as righteous anger ignited the adrenaline in her system. Her words were clean, crisp rifle shots.

"Get. Out. Of. My. Bed."

He squinted at her as if he didn't know what to say, as if it were inconceivable that she wouldn't want to get back into his bed. Her bed. The man was in her bed.

He rolled to his feet in a coordinated move and stood before her unconcerned about his nudity. But why should he be concerned. He was magnificent.

Daisy's injuries receded as she struggled for breath. "Happy now?"

Her gaze fixed on the body part nearest her face, the same part she'd felt pressing against her earlier.

A terrible thought occurred. "Tell me we did not have sex."

He glanced down at himself, a rueful smile on his lips. "I think I can safely promise you we did not have sex. At least, not recently."

Dedication

To Emily and Peter:
May you, too, have a happily ever after.

Chapter One

Happily Ever After still looked like a funeral home.

The cleanup had helped some. The yard looked neater. The shutters no longer tilted at drunken angles. Tall, narrow front windows were detailed in barn red. The paint brightened the aspect of the weathered Victorian affectionately nicknamed the "Gray Lady." Unfortunately, it also made the building look less like a wedding boutique than a haunted house with a hangover.

This morning, though, Daisy Budd had more important things on her mind than cosmetics. Today's Renaissance re-enactment ceremony represented her maiden voyage into the brave new world of wedding planning, and it had to be a slam dunk. The future of her family depended upon it.

The early morning humidity, typical for July in central Michigan, glued Daisy's apricot-colored sundress to her back. The hair she'd straightened with such care only an hour earlier was already tightening into frizzy knots as she inserted the old-fashioned key into the big iron lock on the front door. It opened easily. Too easily. There was no resistance at all.

Daisy sucked in a harsh breath. Under normal circumstances the unlocked door wouldn't have bothered her. Crime was so rare in Mayville the police department had essentially relocated its office to the front booth of the Buttered Biscuit.

But these weren't normal circumstance. Not for Daisy.

The unlocked door was only the latest in a series of unsettling incidents. She'd managed to laugh off the ghostly sounds in the cellar that had sifted upward courtesy of the old laundry chute, but the laughter died when she discovered a bouquet of black roses in her foyer, accompanied by a succinct suggestion that she "Rest in Peace."

And then there were the anonymous letters.

Leave this house while you can. Get out before someone is hurt.

She shivered, despite the rising heat. She'd met with some opposition from folks around town when she'd decided to turn the old mortuary into a wedding boutique, but the two anonymous letters were in a class by themselves. Someone was anxious to get the Budd sisters out of the Gray Lady.

The question was why?

Daisy pushed open the door. She shut her eyes, willing the antique reception desk to be clear, but her heart jerked at the sight of the plain white envelope and her fingers trembled as she scooped it up and shoved it into her oversized straw purse. Dang. She'd believed that if she ignored the stalker, he would get discouraged and give up. Her optimism hadn't been rewarded. Perhaps it was time to go to the cops.

She sighed and forced the worry onto the backburner. Today, of all days, she needed to focus, she thought, as she headed for the curved staircase that led to her office in the former living quarters of the late J. Randolph Bowman. Someone had left the chapel door ajar. She paused briefly to admire metamorphosis of the room where she and her sisters had focused most of their efforts. Dull, gray walls were now angel's wing-white, and lacy Priscilla curtains replaced the heavy, dark drapes. Ancient, stained carpet had been pulled up, and the walnut floors now shone with a high gloss. The black bier at the back was gone, supplanted by a white trellis twined with cream-colored silk roses.

Like Junie said, a bride lucky enough to be married in this room would feel as if she were floating on a meringue. Daisy focused, suddenly, on the large object at the altar. Was she imagining things? Was that a coffin? She squinted, her heart rapping a fast tattoo within her chest. The casket, with its satin-lined, raised lid, looked like a gigantic, empty, jewelry box. Only it wasn't a jewelry box.

And it wasn't empty.

****

Nick Bowman lounged against the thick trunk of a Dutch elm under a For Rent sign. He'd spent most of an hour scoping out the house across the street, his late, great Uncle Randolph's funeral home where Nick's occasional childhood visits had been restricted to the parlor and the chapel. There had never been any reason to study the arrangement of entrances and windows or to examine the cellar that ran the length and breadth of the house.

There was a reason now.

Damn Theo anyway.

Nick put his irritation aside and focused on his task.

Only ten feet separated the wide front porch from the curb which meant anyone strolling down Pine Street could see who entered or exited the Gray Lady. The carport attached to the east side of the structure hid the side entrance, and the backdoor was generally concealed from view by the thick yew bushes that surrounded the back of the property.

Nick rolled his eyes as he recalled his earlier survey of the backyard. Uncle Randolph's well-trimmed lawn remained intact, but the new owner had created a courtyard effect by adding a gilt Cupid statue, benches, and beds full of summer flowers. Today the place was decorated with colorful banners of unicorns and griffins, and several large, wooden tables were lined up, no doubt in preparation for an outdoor feast. Nick continued the inventory.

Ground floor windows with old-fashioned latches and a storm cellar that opened into the main cellar provided any intruder with relatively easy access to the old house.

He could break in with little trouble, but he preferred to gain entrance another way—through finesse and charm. He permitted himself a small grin. His approach invariably worked well with chicks and the Gray Lady's new owner was definitely female.

Nick stepped into the shadow of the elm as a battered red Wrangler roared up the street and careened into the parking lot. The young woman who emerged reminded Nick of a flickering candle and not just because of her short stature, orange dress, and unruly auburn curls. She moved with a quick, light step, like a fast-forwarded TiVo.

Did she make love at that speed?

His lips twisted. He hoped he would not have to find out. He was more than willing to use charm, but he'd prefer not to stoop to seduction. A starry-eyed, small-town girl who would turn a mortuary into a wedding boutique and name it Happily Ever After was not his type.

Nick Bowman made it a practice to stay far away from romantic fools.

The boutique's owner disappeared through the front door, and he detached himself from the tree. It was time to confront Miss Budd. He'd already been in town sixty minutes longer than he liked. He figured he could wrap up this mission in forty-eight hours, twenty-four, if Ms. Budd was as gullible as she looked. And then his debt would be paid, and he could leave this godforsaken place for the last time.

****

Daisy's legs trembled, but she forced herself to walk toward the body in the coffin. Was her anonymous pen pal also a murderer? Had he escalated from threatening letters to bodies? With her mind in a frenzied jumble, it took a few moments for Daisy to recognize the waxy-faced figure in the black bombazine with the delicate ruching at the neckline, but at length she exhaled a sigh of relief. Miss Ora Bunson looked much the way she had each of the hundreds of times she'd sat near this very spot to play There is a Balm in Gilead for Mayville's deceased.

This was not the work of the poisonous note writer but of Miss Ora Bunson's twin, Miss Olive. Daisy's heart slowed to normal.

The moment of relief passed quickly as she identified a new concern. Miss Ora simply could not be present for the afternoon service. Somehow Daisy had to get rid of the body. But how? Call Goodwill?

She slipped her hand into her oversized purse. Her fingers had just closed around her cell phone when a sense of danger caused the tiny hairs on the back of her neck to stand at attention. She had seen nothing, heard nothing, smelled nothing, but she knew suddenly and without a doubt she was no longer the only one in the chapel with a pulse.

Daisy forced herself to turn around to look at the man lounging in the arched doorway. The sun behind him half-shadowed his harsh features, a strong nose and determined chin, a slash of a mouth. He was a shade under six feet tall, lean and rangy with the masked tension of a predator.

Awareness shuddered through her body. His low, rough voice was the only one that had ever turned her blood to lava and her knees to butter.

Nick Bowman.

"Maybe," he drawled, nodding at the coffin, "you should've called this place the Happy Hereafter."

The butterflies in her stomach multiplied as he moved toward her. She noticed his dark hair was no longer neatly trimmed. The thick strands brushed the collar of his khaki shirt, but it was the streaks of silver that grabbed her attention.

Nick Bowman was going gray.

"You get a lot of bodies these days?"

She realized she hadn't spoken yet. She managed a careless shrug. "This is just a protest." She realized she was making no sense, but she couldn't seem to get her thoughts unscrambled. "You know Mayville. Nobody likes change. I imagine that's why you left."

One dark eyebrow lifted and heat surged into Daisy's face.

"So you know who I am."

The recognition wasn't mutual. What a surprise. She grinned to herself as she remembered their one and only conversation on the phone.

Her: Hello

Nick: Hey. Is Caroline there?

Her: Uh, yup.

Nick: Could I speak with her?

Her: Oh. (giggle) Sure.

Not exactly poetry.

She was certain he'd remember Caro.

"I'm Daisy Budd." She held out a hand, and he took it in his strong, warm one. The contact set off jolts of electricity that reverberated through her entire system. It clearly did not have the same effect on him. His expression was blank. She waited in vain for him to put two and two together. "Daisy

Bowman," she repeated. "You dated my sister."

"I did?"

He really was a piece of work. She knew he'd dated plenty of women in the past six years. She'd seen the pictures online of Nick with various tall, tanned blondes hanging off of his arm, but Caro was the most beautiful girl in Clark County.

"Caroline Budd." Daisy winced at the edge in her own voice. "She was Biscuit Queen the summer you left town. Why are you here, anyway?"

"Your front door was open. I wanted to make sure everything was all right."

The force field of testosterone that surrounded him hadn't turned her into a complete idiot.

"You expect me to believe you flew to Michigan just to take a morning constitutional down Pine Street during which you noticed my door was open? Hah. Anyway, it wasn't. I'm sure I shut it behind me." Pretty sure.

He held up his hands and flashed his white teeth at her.

"The mortuary belonged to my uncle. Can you blame me for being curious about the new owner?"

She studied his hard face.

"I don't buy it."

He shrugged. "I'm a guy. You're a pretty girl. I followed you in here by instinct."

Daisy narrowed her eyes. Surely he didn't expect her to swallow a line like that. He stared back at her, his face unreadable, and she felt a sudden jolt of fear. Nick Bowman wasn't here to flirt with her. He had an agenda. And then it came to her.

"This is about buying the Gray Lady, isn't it? I've already told Arthur Sneed it's not for sale. There was no need for your family to send to California for the big guns. You wasted a trip, Mr. Bowman."

His lashes flickered almost imperceptibly.

"Bowman's Biscuits interest in this property has nothing to do with me. And stop calling me Mr. Bowman. My name's Nick, Dolly."

She cast her eyes heavenward. "Daisy," she corrected. "Since you're here, you can take a message to your brother. Your Aunt Isabelle sold me this property in good faith, and I and my sisters have invested a lot of time and money in it. If Bowman's Biscuits needs to expand, they are going to have to do it somewhere else." Adrenaline surged through her system. "And, while you're at it, tell the rest of your family to lay off the anonymous letters and the rest of it. Nothing is going to change my mind."

Even as she spoke the words, she knew they weren't true. The Bowmans were the first family in town. Surely they wouldn't try to frighten her out of the house with anonymous letters.

The expression of honest confusion on Nick's face bore her out.

"What anonymous letters?"

Before she could answer, the metallic notes of Mendelssohn caught her attention, and she fumbled for her phone then answered it in her most professional-sounding voice.

"Happily Ever After, this is Daisy."

"This codpiece is totally unacceptable!"

Daisy winced. When her ex-brother-in-law was really agitated, his high voice tended to scale into a Pavarotti-like register. It also became deafening.

She infused a calming note into her own voice.

"What can I do for you, Quentin?"

"Didn't you hear me? This codpiece is too small. I. Simply. Must. Have. Something. Bigger." He paused between each word for emphasis. "My entire Renaissance history class will be in attendance." He pronounced the term Re-nay-sance. "No anachronisms, Daisy. Everything must be accurate, including my proportions."

Daisy suspected the community college students lured to the wedding by promises of extra credit would be less interested in their professor's dimensions than in the free grog.

"You're a knight," she pointed out. "Your tunic will cover the codpiece."

"Not," he paused again for additional dramatic

effect, "if I lunge."

"Ah. Well, I see what you mean. I'll have Junie take care of it."

"And Daisy, I hope you remembered to get the hand-hewn, oaken benches."

Daisy visualized the five dozen plastic chairs she'd arranged to borrow from St. Mary Star of the Sea down on Elm.

"Everything will be perfect," she assured him. "I've got to go now. Lots to do." She hung up then made a face as she noticed Nick hadn't left. In fact, he'd drawn closer. Too close. His low, rough voice sent shivers up her spine.

"Tell him to get a cup."

She stared. "A cup of what?"

"An athletic supporter. The kind a baseball catcher wears to protect the family jewels."

Daisy blinked. It had never occurred to her to wonder what equipment a catcher wore to protect the family jewels. Heat rose inside her accompanied by irritation. She did not wish to discuss family jewels with Nick Bowman.

She opened her mouth to ask him, again, to leave.

"Merde!" Her younger sister's fluting tones were accompanied by a stampede of hurried footsteps in the hall. Junie always moved at the speed of light. She exploded into the room, her tall, slim figure clad in a hot pink halter top and white shorts the size of a postage stamp. Her blonde ponytail swung freely, as if it had not a care in the world. "My deodorant is so not working. This stuff is worthless!"

The scowl dropped off her pretty face when she spotted their visitor.

"I wouldn't worry about the smell." He grinned at her. "Remember the words of Napoleon to Josephine: "'I'm coming home. Don't bathe.'"

His practiced flirtation irritated the hell out of Daisy. "Was that before or after he dumped her for a younger woman?"

Nick spared her a quick glance, but his attention soon returned to Daisy's sister. Why not? Junie was carefree and fun and as beautiful as Caro.

"Mon Dieu." Junie's expressive eyes filled with female appreciation. "Please tell me you're not one of the altar-bound."

"Never." He grinned at her. "I'm Nick Bowman."

Junie pretended to smack herself on the forehead.

"Zut alors! I've seen you on the Internet. You're even hotter in person."

"You're pretty hot yourself."

Daisy cleared her throat. "Quentin has a problem."

"Just one?"

Daisy frowned at her sister.

"He needs a bigger codpiece," Nick put in.

"Can't he just stuff tissues in his pants?"

Nick flashed his irresistible grin at Junie, and Daisy's stomach clenched. She was well aware that her younger sister was Nick's type, and the reverse was also true. Dark, dangerous, and inappropriate, he registered right in the fat part of Junie's wheelhouse.

"I need you to handle Quent and pick up the chairs at St. Mary's," Daisy said, briskly.

"St. Mary's Star of the Sea? The tuna church?"

Daisy glared at Nick. "Don't you have somewhere to go?"

"Eh bien!" Junie crowed. "He can come avec moi."

The fractured French suddenly turned into a series of short, sharp shrieks.

Daisy sighed. Her sister had finally torn her eyes away from the hunk long enough to spot the corpse.

Mendelssohn sounded again, and Daisy had just enough time to watch Junie launch herself into Nick Bowman's arms before she answered the phone. She covered her free ear with her hand.

"Happily Ever After. This is Daisy."

"Is this Daisy?" The elderly voice was strident. "I called to check on Ora."

"Miss Olive." Daisy kept her voice kind but firm. "You know the Gray Lady is no longer a mortuary. We're a wedding boutique now."

"How utterly ridiculous," the old lady sputtered. "Ora doesn't need a wedding. She needs a funeral."

There was no missing the sense of grief and loss under the tart words, but Daisy knew better than to offer obvious sympathy.

"Mister Foote over in Titusville will do a good job for her."

"Titusville! Impossible!" It was as if Daisy had suggested burying Miss Ora at sea. "Mother and Daddy were buried from Bowman's back in the fifties. Randolph Bowman ordered rosewood caskets for all of us. Lined in powder blue. He promised we would be buried together."

Daisy glanced at the coffin. For the first time she realized that someone, probably the Bunson sister's elderly retainer, Beasley, must have hauled the thing up from the Gray Lady's cellar.

The cellar.

The underground space ran the entire length of the

house but had only one window. Daisy pictured the piles of furniture, boxes and papers, the detritus of past lives that dwelled on its dirt floor, not to mention the leftover caskets. It was a graveyard of memories. She shivered.

"Daisy?"

Miss Olive's voice recalled her to the present.

"I'll tell you what, Miss Olive. If you'll let Elias Foote take care of things, funeral-wise, he is welcome to use the two rosewood coffins." Daisy winced at her own words. She'd made it sound as if Olive intended to be buried with her sister. She hoped the old lady hadn't noticed. She needn't have worried.

"Well." Disapproval dripped from the single syllable. "You shall deliver it yourself, Missmiss, along with Ora. Beasley cut up rough last evening. I don't believe you can count on him."

"We'll take care of it. And we want to hold the reception here," Daisy told her. "Junie can make a special dessert."

"Mercy sakes, Daisy! There's no telling what the girl will dream up. That dreadful cake she brought to the Martha Circle last week! I don't wonder that was what killed my sister."

Daisy winced. Erotic baking was Junie's current creative outlet. Daisy couldn't wait for cosmetology school to start again in the fall.

"She meant to make a relief map of Florida."

"That's what Florence Wainwright said, but Ora and I weren't fooled. There was no panhandle."

"We'll serve macaroons."

"Good gracious! Have you forgotten? Ora is deathly allergic to coconut."

Daisy closed her eyes. "Brownies, then. Goodbye, Miss Olive," Daisy said. She disconnected the phone.

"It wasn't Florida," Junie confided to Nick. She no longer seemed hysterical, but she still clung to his strong frame. "It was a giant phallus. The old ladies weren't supposed to know."

Daisy felt the color rise in her cheeks. She realized she'd discussed male body parts more this morning than she had in months. Years. Nick didn't notice her embarrassment, of course. He seemed enchanted with Junie.

"I'll be happy to help you with the chairs and the codpiece," he said to the younger woman. When he turned to Daisy, his eyes glittered. They looked almost silver in the morning sun. "I can drive the body over to Titusville. I notice the old hearse is still in the carport."

"Merveilleux," Junie murmured.

"No, thanks." Daisy kept her voice cold. Okay, so Nick Bowman wasn't the stalker. Anonymous letters were not his style, and, besides, if he had been anywhere in Clark County during the past few weeks, Daisy would have known. No, Nick Bowman presented a different kind of danger to the Budd sisters, and Daisy did not want him around. "We can handle this ourselves." He lifted a dark eyebrow.

"I believe you mentioned a busy day."

"He's right, Daze," Junie said. "We can't leave Miss Ora here, and there's no time to get anyone else."

Merde. Daisy unconsciously borrowed her sister's favorite phrase in her silent curse. Junie took her brief silence as consent.

"I'll go get the keys." She scampered off.

Daisy decided it was time to issue a warning. "I

appreciate your help, but I want you to stay away from my sister."

A dark eyebrow lifted. "Why?"

Why? Wasn't it obvious? She frowned at Nick. "Because she's dangerous. The last man she got involved with wound up married to her and dead. The two events were not unrelated." That was a bit of a lie, but Daisy was desperate. She couldn't think of anything worse than an affair between Junie and the Bowman family's Prodigal Son.

Nick's hard lips twitched. "You don't need to worry about my safety, darlin'. I can take care of myself. If, on the other hand, you're worried about your sister, don't. I won't be around here long enough to hurt her."

Daisy stuck out her chin. "I'm sure you can take care of yourself, Nick Bowman. And I'm sure I can take care of my sister. Hurt Junie and you'll answer to me."

Nick answered with a slow, seductive grin that turned her inside out. Daisy felt a flash of dismay. In the months since she'd returned to Mayville, Daisy had encountered financial challenges, emotional issues with her sisters, and now a stalker, but she didn't try to fool herself. Every instinct screamed that she was now facing the biggest threat of all.

Nick Bowman.

Chapter Two

By one o'clock the mercury had topped eighty degrees. Nick blinked the sweat out of his eyes and looked at the neat rows of chairs and the bevy of elderly ladies wearing broad-brimmed bonnets as they draped garlands of flowers on the bushes and trees. Dozens of colorful banners hung limp in the heat. The only relief came from the errant spray that spewed from Cupid's arrow.

"Merde," Junie said. "I feel sorry for Mayor Hotchkiss." She indicated the short, stout man covered with a red, ermine robe, his face already the color of boiled beets.

"Why doesn't he take that thing off?"

"He's waiting for the press."

"What press?"

"The Clark County High Cougar Tracks. They may send a photographer. C'mon. Let's set the butterflies up by the archway."

Nick carried the wooden box they'd retrieved from the post office. The butterflies were scheduled to emerge at the exact moment when the officiant pronounced the couple, husband and wife. Or, in this case, lord and wench.

Would any of the butterflies survive that long?

Nick considered it doubtful, but he grinned at Junie. The girl reminded him of a butterfly, light and flighty. Taller than Daisy and reed-slim, her pretty, regular features were set off by a white blonde ponytail. She looked like an adorable extra from Bye-Bye, Birdie.

Her sister, on the other hand, had dressed for the event in the drab brown skirt of a fourteenth century scrubwoman. A white handkerchief obscured the flame-colored, corkscrew curls, but her eyes were wide and intelligent and the color of aged whiskey.

"Why're you staring at Daisy?"

It was an excellent question, and one he had no wish to answer, even to himself.

"I'm looking for a family resemblance."

Junie laughed. "Gran called Daisy a changeling. Caro and I, though, could be twins." She made a face. "Except she's a lot more elegant. But you already know that, right? Didn't you go out with her for awhilea while?"

"Yes."

"She'll be here soon. She picked up Stevie from camp this morning."

Stevie must be the biscuit queen's son. As soon as he saw Junie, he'd remembered Caro. They'd dated for a couple of weeks right before his world exploded. He remembered meeting the grandmother, too, a feisty old lady with the same golden eyes as her middle grandchild.

"Where's your grandmother?"

A shadow passed over Junie's expressive face.

"She died last year. That's why Daisy left her job in Grand Harbor and came home to stay."

That didn't make much sense. "Her job? Was she a wedding planner there?"

"Mais non. The boutique is a pure leap of faith. Gran left us each some money, and Daisy bought the Gray Lady with her portion. She insisted on Caro keeping her inheritance for Stevie, and me for my education.

Nick frowned. He wondered what made Daisy Budd tick, and that curiosity annoyed him.

"Daisy wanted to start a business that would keep us all in Mayville."

"Do you want to stay?"

"Sure. I mean, most of the time. Besides, I owe Daze. She kinda saved my life."

It was hyperbole. Had to be. In any case, Nick didn't want to hear any tales of heroism. Daisy Budd was the enemy. He dropped that topic and moved on to another. "What kind of job did she have in Grand Harbor?"

"She worked at the Gazette. Daisy was their police reporter."

Dammit to Hell. The last thing he needed was a nosy journalist poking into the scandal that connected the Bowman family patriarch to Nazi loot. Shit.

"Junie," Daisy called to her sister. "Nadine needs help with the pasties."

"Okay, okay. I've got to get my dress on anyhow." She gave him a little wave. "See you later, Nick."

Daisy rounded on him as soon as her sister was out of earshot. "Why are you still here?"

He indicated the box. "Butterflies."

"Well, thanks for all your help today, but you must have somewhere else to be."

"Oh, this is undoubtedly the most interesting spot in town today." He let his gaze drop to her peasant blouse. "Nice décolletage."

The whiskey eyes narrowed on him, and she planted her fists at her waist.

"You're wasting the flirting with me. I'm immune."

He stepped close enough to touch the hollow at the base of her neck and dropped his voice to an intimate whisper.

"Don't challenge me, sweetheart. You aren't up to my weight."

A certain unexpected breathiness accompanied his words. Her skin was soft and faintly moist, and Nick had to resist a sudden urge to touch more of it. He lifted his fingers away and spoke before she could order him off the property. "What do you say to a truce? I'm back in town for a few days to tie up some loose ends for my grandfather."

Her face was so expressive. He knew exactly what she was thinking without her saying a word. Where were you when Theo was sick? Why didn't you attend the funeral? What kind of grandson is only interested in his inheritance?

It was easy to resist the urge to explain. Nick had learned the hard way never to explain his actions to anyone. "I'm not here to ravish the local beauties," he added. "And, I told you. I won't hurt your sister."

The clear, hazel eyes met his. "I still need to know why you're in my backyard."

Nick sighed. Trust a journalist not to lose sight of the bottom line.

"Daisy, dear, where do you want these lilies?"

He was saved from making another excuse by the old lady's question, but he knew it was a temporary reprieve.

Nick stared at the old house. It rankled that Daisy considered him a debaucher. Sure he liked women, but he stuck to the type who valued him for his wealth and reputation in the racing community. He did not run around seducing teenagers, for God's sake. Why the hell was she so prickly?

Damn Theo anyway. Why hadn't he taken care of this before he died or, at the very least, left the business to Buzz, Mayville's golden boy? A lump formed in Nick's throat, but he ignored it. He'd given up his family seven years ago. He'd only taken on this mission because of a lull in his schedule.

Nick stuck his hands in the pockets of his jeans and wondered when he'd started lying to himself.

He frowned when he remembered Daisy's odd reference to anonymous letters. Was somebody else aware of the loot? It seemed a pretty big coincidence that the letters should start arriving at this house at the same time he planned to search the place.

Was there another party involved? Had this irksome chore turned into a race?

He walked down to the trellised archway that separated the courtyard from the shallow field and wooded area on the other side of which lay Bowman's Biscuits, Inc. Nick's former legacy. Just for a moment he felt something like regret, but he banished the sensation. He'd built himself a good life on the coast. He'd fulfilled his childhood dream. He didn't need Bowman's Biscuits or anything else in Mayville.

Insects buzzed in the honeysuckle bushes, and the air filled with voices of new arrivals. He turned back to survey the courtyard and the back of the shabby

Victorian house. Seven years ago he'd rejected this kind of small town charm in favor of the anonymity of a glass and steel high rise in Southern California. To be fair, it had rejected him. Or at least Theo had. He reminded himself it had been the right move.

He wished he could search today, but he'd have to exercise a little more subtlety than that. For maximum accessibility he'd have to make friends with the little dragon who guarded her fortress with such ferocity.

He watched her greet her guests. His breath caught at the warmth of the smile on her face. It wouldn't be easy to breach her walls, but he'd already identified her weakness. Daisy couldn't deny her sister anything. Junie was the key. And Junie was already a fan.

A moment later the youngest Budd sister rejoined him. She wore a sky blue gown and pointed cap a la Sleeping Beauty, and her first words were straight out of a Nick's fondest fairytale.

"Could you help me carry a box of costumes up from the cellar?"

His lips stretched into a slow smile. Luck was on his side. "Yeah, I could."

The cellar ran the length and breadth of the house. A long, steep staircase descended to a dirt floor. The faint light allowed by the single window received little help from the naked bulb that swung on a rope from the ceiling and cast eerie shadows over the row of caskets against one wall. Assorted furniture and stacks of boxes covered with sheets created a ghostly effect. Nick noted the presence of several doors and speculated they led to storage rooms or pantries or perhaps a wine cellar, although Uncle Randolph hadn't been much of a drinker.

Somewhere down here there was a piece of priceless treasure stolen from the Nazis. That it had never been found was a testament to the excellence of the hiding place. Few people would think to search the cellar of a funeral home. Even fewer would have the stomach for it.

"This place gives me the creeps," Junie confided.

"You ought to clean it out."

He nodded at the coffins. "You could probably sell those."

"How? On eBay?"

Nick grinned. "I'd be willing to call some funeral homes. If we find a buyer I can deliver 'em in the hearse."

"That'd be awesome," she said. "But, Nick, are you sure you have time?"

He chuckled. "Believe me, if the choice is spending time with my Bowman relatives or moving coffins with you, there's no contest." She flashed her impish smile.

"You'd make a lot of points with Daisy. She's dying to get this place cleaned up." Junie sighed. "She doesn't trust you, you know."

"Is she suspicious of all guys?"

Junie shook her head. "She's usually nice to everybody. I think you're in a special category because you hurt Caro."

He stared at her. Had he missed something here? He'd barely known her eldest sister. They'd had, what, two, maybe three dates?

He reminded himself it didn't matter whether or not Daisy trusted him. He had a job to do, and Miss Junie Budd was going to help him do it. He smiled at her. "Where're the costumes?"

With their arms laden, they stepped outside. The sun's warmth was welcome after the dank air of the cellar. Junie shivered.

"Are you cold?"

"I'm just glad to get out of there. Did I tell you we have a ghost?"

Alarm bells set off in Nick's head. Again. "A ghost?"

"Maybe more than one. Last week Daisy heard some shuffling noises through the laundry chute upstairs. She went down to check it out, but there was nobody there."

"She went down there alone?"

Junie made a face. "Daze isn't afraid of anything."

Except someone who could hurt her sisters.

Nick's gut tightened. Goddammit. Someone else was hunting. Who? How? Had Theo told someone else about the loot?

He'd need to work fast to protect the Bowman family name.

"Nick? Are you okay? You look a little pale around the gills."

"I'm fine. I'll get those coffins cleared out Monday."

"Awesome," Junie said. She spotted her sister. "Oh, there's Stevie."

Nick followed her gaze. A small, dark-haired child dressed in a tiny beefeater's costume had his arms around Daisy's neck.

"Daisy's practically his second mom."

Nick looked away from the pair. He wasn't interested in the Budd family relationships. He changed the subject. "Who is marrying Lord Codpiece?"

Junie giggled. "Cherry Ann Wilfinger. Quentin met her when she took his class 'Tapestries and Tights.' It was love at first sight. She'll be Stevie's stepmother."

"I thought Stevie was Caroline's son."

"Mais, bien sur. Caro was married to Quentin for five years."

The fussy re-enactor married to one of the beautiful Budds? There had to be a story behind that. Not that it was any of Nick's business.

"I've got to greet the guests," Junie said. "Meet you back at the butterflies?"

He grinned at her. "Absolument."

****

"I don't know where you want me to put my scepter." The voice roller-coastered in an annoying whine. "Here?" His honor planted the staff next to his feet and scowled at Daisy. "Or here?" He moved it an inch to the left. "Or here?" He moved it again.

This time, two inches to the right.

Mayor Floyd Hotchkiss was not a happy Henry the-Eighth, but Daisy had to admit the man had captured the English monarch's off-with-their-heads attitude perfectly, although, he looked more like the chief potentate of Munchkinland with his short, round stature and rosy saddlebag cheeks. Too rosy. Despite the soaring temperatures, the mayor continued to wear his heavy crown and velvet robe.

Daisy placed her hand over the mayor's on the scepter's staff. "This," she said, "is the perfect spot." She handed him a bottle of cold water she'd hidden in the fruit ice cooler. The liquid splashed all over the mayor's flushed face as he guzzled it, greedily.

24

"What on earth?" Daisy could barely hear Quentin's outraged shriek over the clanking sound of his armor. The gray tights bagged, and the sun gleamed off the bald spot on the back of his head. She gaped at the enormous bulge between his legs. At least Junie had taken care of the codpiece problem.

Quentin waved his finger in Daisy's face. "Do I have to remind you there was no plastic during the Renaissance?"

Daisy ignored his ire. She hooked her hand around the chainmail that covered his thin arm and guided him away from the overheated mayor.

"You look fantastic, Quent," she pointed out. "Cherry Ann's knight in shining armor." Daisy prayed her sister would be able to close the zipper on the bride's dress. After much debate over her costume Cherry Ann had finally chosen a Juliet-style gown. Even with an industrial-strength corset, zipping up required extraordinary determination.

Daisy gazed around the courtyard with contentment. There were men in tights and tunics, ladies with laced bodices, jesters juggling, and troubadours strumming their lutes. Guests strolled and chatted and sat together on the stone benches by Cupid. The scent of roast turkey legs filled the air as did the freshly baked, honey-drenched pies. Nadine Pfluge, owner and proprietress of the Buttered Biscuit, had provided most of the food, with Junie's help. Daisy hoped she could convince Nadine to continue to cater for Happily Ever After.

She hoped today's wedding would launch the boutique on the road to success. Business was beginning to trickle in, but Daisy needed a flood to cover the mortgage, renovations, and salaries. The Renaissance wedding had a lot riding on it.

"What on earth is Caroline wearing?"

Quentin's irritated voice recalled Daisy's attention to the present, and she glanced at her elder sister. Caro had occasionally been compared with Grace Kelly except the hair that cascaded in silky waves down her back was lighter. A Renaissance gown would have looked sensational on her tall, slim figure, but she'd chosen to wear a crisp, emerald golf shirt and khaki Bermuda shorts. Her hair was pulled into a tight knot at the back of her head. She looked more like a suburban yuppie on her way to the links than a princess bride.

"You know she's not a fan of re-enactments," Daisy reminded Quentin. "But just look at Stevie. He's a perfect miniature tower warder." Her eyes connected with those of her nephew. The boy grinned and waved. Daisy was almost knocked over by the tidal wave of love that swept through her.

"Look, Quent. He's waving at you." Quentin lifted a gloved hand.

"Why don't you go say hello?"

"I'll see him next weekend. We'll be at Mackinac Island just a few days."

Daisy hid her disappointment. She could take Quentin's pomposity, but his indifference toward the little boy never failed to squeeze her heart. She peered at Quentin. There was something wrong. His face was twitching. Moisture poured out of his eyes.

"Where are your glasses?"

"I decided to wear contact lenses for the ceremony. More authentic."

Daisy refrained from mentioning that his wedding

day was probably not the best time to experiment with contacts. Quentin never listened to anybody, and, besides, it was too late. The high school trumpet player she'd hired to announce the bride's arrival let out a series of blasts.

"It's show time," he muttered. He shifted his tunic allowing Daisy a closer look at the huge bulge.

Daisy choked back a laugh. There was an atmosphere of excitement and joy in the courtyard today. It was hard to believe that somewhere a stalker lay in wait, perhaps plotting his next anonymous letter. Or something even more sinister.

The bugle blared again, and Daisy hurried over to stand with her elder sister and nephew to watch the bride arrive on horseback. She squeezed Caro's hand.

"Your first wedding appears to be a triumph."

"Our first wedding," Daisy reminded her.

"Huzzah!" Someone yelled. Soon all the guests were cheering. "Huzzah! Huzzah!"

Daisy squinted against the sun. She focused on the thick stand of trees. A moment later the bride emerged on her white palfrey. The little creature, festooned with ribbons and roses, gasped for breath as Cherry Ann's plump thighs squeezed its sides.

"We should have gotten a bigger horse."

The cheering stopped abruptly, like a baby's cry when he falls asleep.

Stevie's voice rang out. "Look at Cherry Ann! She's not wearing any clothes!"

"Cherry Ann changed her mind about the gown," Daisy said.

"Yeah." Caro's grin reached from ear to ear. "Looks like she went with Lady Godiva."

Chapter Three

Daisy couldn't tear her eyes away from the mounds of majestic, rippling flesh that dripped down Cherry Ann's body like butter cream frosting on cake left out in the sun.

"She's stark naked," someone shouted.

"It's a body stocking," Quentin squealed. He waved his arms wildly. "It's a body stocking!" He clanked through the archway, planted his feet, and extended his hands to assist his bride to the ground. The crowd when Cherry Ann launched herself at her knight and shrieked "Excelsior!"

Quentin wobbled with the impact, and, for a second, it looked as if he would be able to maintain his balance, but the combination of unwieldy armor, the enthusiasm of his beloved, and the effect of gravity overcame his efforts, and Cherry Ann landed on what looked like a pile of scrap metal.

"This moment," Caro murmured, "almost makes up for five miserable years of marriage."

Several guests hurried to aid the couple. After some initial hesitation, Mayor Hotchkiss removed his ermine robe. Quentin wrapped it around his unabashed bride. Red-faced, Quentin screeched at Daisy.

"Where are the butterflies? There are supposed to be butterflies!"

Daisy's eyes caught Junie's eye. Her sister nodded

at Nick who stooped to open the wooden box. Daisy's eyes caught, momentarily, on hard muscles that shifted beneath the khaki shirt. She watched as he got to his feet and glanced in her direction. The ice gray eyes sent a clear message: you may not want me here, but your sister does. She tried to ignore the knot in her stomach.

"One miserable swallowtail," Caro said, as a lone survivor lifted into the air. "We should get a refund." Suddenly Caro's jaw snapped, and her blue eyes narrowed into mean slits. "What," she hissed, "is he doing here?"

The fury in her sister's voice shook Daisy enough that she almost failed to detect the other emotion beneath it. Fear. Daisy studied her sister's white face.

"I should have told you he was in town," she said, apologetically. "He assures me his business won't take long though. You know Junie. She convinced him to help with the wedding.

Caro's peach-tinted nails bit into Daisy's wrist. "Why was he even talking to you? Listen, Daisy. You've got to keep him away from all of us.

Especially Junie."

"I've already warned him about that."

Caro's bitter laugh made Daisy's heart twist. "He won't pay any attention. The guy's lethal. And Junie, well, she's always her own worst enemy."

"I won't let him hurt her. I promise." Daisy wished she'd been able to keep Caro from getting hurt all those years ago.

Caro refused to be mollified. "He has to be here for a reason. He wants something from us."

"The house. He wants the Gray Lady." Despite Nick's denial, Daisy was sure of it. He had decided he wanted to get back into the family, and he figured the Gray Lady was his ticket.

"Give it to him," Caro pleaded.

The suggestion shocked her. "Over my dead body," she said.

Caro's beautiful face was a study in pain. "You don't know Nick. It may come to that."

Daisy squeezed her arm. "We'll be fine as long as we stick together. Trust me on that."

****

The sun was an orange ball balanced on the hazy horizon when Nick finally piloted his rented Malibu up the twisting road to the Bowman Mansion.

The revulsion he'd felt about Mayville had faded during the hours at Happily Ever After, but it had returned in full force tonight. His gut tightened as he parked in the circular drive and stared at the pillared monstrosity before him.

The plantation-style manor house would have graced the banks of the Mississippi. Here, in southern central Michigan where the nearest body of water was Trout Lake, its wide porch, grandiose portico, and massive presence seemed a mirage. Theo had built it in the late fifties as a symbol of Bowman's Biscuits projected prosperity. For the first time Nick wondered if dirty money had paid for this pseudo Tara. A man who could steal valuables looted from Holocaust victims would be capable of anything.

Nick shook his head. Honesty and responsibility had been Pops's defining characteristics. None of this made sense.

None of it added up.

Nick dropped the brass lion's head knocker. The

door opened immediately.

"Welcome home, Mister Nick."

"Finch." Nick nodded at the butler.

The old man still possessed thick, white hair, but the broomstick curved at the shoulders and his face was a roadmap of crevices and gullies. Hell, the guy must be a hundred. Had he stuck around to take care of Theo?

"How's Charles?"

The butler gave a short, glowing recital of the accomplishments of his son and grandchildren after which he announced that Arthur was in the study.

Nick nodded. "He's expecting me."

Memories attacked him in the wide corridors that led through the house. The portraits that lined the walls were someone's ancestors but unconnected with the Bowmans. He and Buzz had spent hours concocting tales about the costumed strangers.

His gaze lingered on the curving banister of the grand staircase. On rainy Saturdays he and his brother had bodysurfed the smooth surface when no one was looking. They'd used the freshly waxed hardwood floor as an impromptu ice rink, too. Pain, sharp and unexpected, arrowed through his heart.

Nick knocked on the door to the study and then entered without waiting for an invitation. The same green-shaded banker's lamp sat on the massive walnut desk and the same smell of old books pervaded the room. An ivory and onyx chess set rested on the window seat waiting for two players who would never return. A boy and his grandfather. The only change in seven years was the occupant of the heavy desk chair.

Arthur Sneed rounded the desk and reached out a hand. The attorney's fingers were as thin as chopsticks, and there were deep, purple crescents beneath the eyes under those pop-bottle lenses.

Theo's illness had taken its toll on his loyal factotum.

"Welcome back," Arthur said.

Nick inhaled the scent of gardenias, and he turned to smile at his Aunt Isabelle. He kissed her cheek.

"Nicky, dear."

Isabelle Bowman looked different. For as long as Nick could remember, she'd worn a series of interchangeable, ill-fitting housedresses that were appropriate for her duties of running the mansion and handling her father's correspondence. Her trim navy pantsuit and jaunty red scarf were a decided change as was the stylish frosted hair. He'd corresponded with Isabelle for seven years, but she hadn't once mentioned her new look. She appeared vibrant and happy. And then he remembered.

"Belated congratulations on your marriage."

Isabelle smiled at Nick and then at her husband. The union between his aunt and his grandfather's attorney made sense from a business standpoint, but Nick wondered about the passion. If there were sparks between them, wouldn't they have ignited earlier in their thirty years of acquaintance? Of course both had been dedicated to Theo and his company. They had that in common.

"Thank you," Isabelle said. "Arthur has been our rock. Along with Alice." She smiled past him, and Nick realized there was another person in the room.

"Hello, Nick," she said, extending a large, hand. Alice was tall and raw-boned, but her straight dark hair swung forward in a stylish cut, and her pale blue summer sheath was complemented with real pearls. Her smile revealed strong white teeth, the canines narrowed into sharp points. "You may not remember me. I'm Alice, Buzz's wife."

Buzz's wife. Had he even known his brother had a wife? He searched his memory as Alice brushed her lips across his cheek, and he smelled something citrusy. A cologne with a bite. A masculine scent. Nick could not imagine his brother with her, and he was woefully aware he'd failed to hide his surprise.

Awareness was apparent in the pale close-set eyes. "Have we met before?"

"Just once. We were all three sheets to the wind." Her laugh reminded him of a hiccup gone wrong.

He forced a smile. "Nice to see you again. Where is Buzz?"

Alice's smile held, but the canines disappeared. "Buzz is in rehab, dear," Isabelle said. "He checked himself in several weeks ago."

"Rehab?" Another shock. His brother had been a social drinker seven years ago. "He's an alcoholic?"

"He developed a problem," Alice explained. "Too much stress."

Nick read the criticism between the lines. The stress had been caused by being left alone to run the company. Nick reminded himself it was not his problem.

"Arthur has taken the reins for the time being," Isabelle explained.

So now the older man was running the place alone. No wonder the attorney looked like death.

"Alice helped nurse Father through the final illness, and she helps out in the office, too. I don't know what we'd do without her."

Isabelle's words died as the outer door opened to admit another tall woman. Judith Bowman's youthful beauty had not worn well, and, with her long striped hair, oversized earrings, and the diaphanous blue-green garment she wore, she resembled an aging flower child.

Nick took her hand and pecked her on the cheek. "Shalom, Shoshanna." She made a face.

"That's all over. Judaism was a little too Wailing Wall for me. I'm called Harmony Lime now. I've found a charming little group in Windy Falls." Judith's defection from another of the major religions was not a surprise. Nick's stepmother routinely jumped from one trend to another. Each time she believed she'd found her true calling and she changed her name, accordingly.

Judith Bowman was the total immersion type.

"A group of what? Fruit worshippers?"

"Wiccans, dear."

"You're a witch?" Why was he surprised?

"A white witch. That's right. Alice and I."

Nick glanced at his sister-in-law. She sent him an expressive look using only her eyes. Nick grinned at her. His impression of Buzz's wife improved.

At precisely eight o'clock, the Bowman family took their seats at one end of a twenty-foot table in the cavernous dining room. Something small, slimy, and unidentifiable appeared in front of Nick. He ignored it and drained his glass of the excellent Chablis. Judith talked. As they worked their way through the hors d'oeuvres, the soup and the salad, food disappeared from her dishes, and yet she never stopped talking. Finally, she lifted her glass to sip the wine, and Arthur seized the opportunity to speak to him.

"When did you get in, Nick?"

"This morning."

"Heavens," Isabelle said, startled. "Where've you been all day?"

There was really no reason not to tell.

"I got shanghaied into helping with the Renaissance wedding over at the funeral home." Four forks halted in mid-air. Four jaws dropped. He understood their confusion. He wasn't exactly the Good Samaritan type.

Isabelle recovered first.

"I can imagine they needed help. Daisy told me they were pulling out all the stops." Nick kept his tone casual.

"I didn't realize you knew Daisy Budd."

"We worked together on the homeless shelter. She's become a one-woman chamber of commerce. She instituted a small loan program for would-be entrepreneurs, and she's helping Nadine branch out as a caterer. She's supported Flowers by Florence. That's Florence Mainwright's new venture. She was the society editor of the Monitor when Daisy's father owned it."

Nick had forgotten the family's connection to the defunct paper. Apparently ink ran in Daisy's blood. Interesting that she'd given it up for orange blossoms and tulle.

"Now, Isabelle," Arthur said, as if they had discussed this topic many times, "no one disputes Daisy Budd's good intentions, but we need that property if we are to expand into prepared foods."

"Expansion?"

Nick knew something about the expansion plans,

but he figured it wouldn't hurt to learn more.

It was Alice who answered him.

"We're losing clients. Our sales numbers have plummeted. I've done some research. It seems that with so many women entering the workforce, there is no one left in the kitchen. Two-income families prefer to stop at the supermarket to pick up prepared foods. Buzz and Arthur have hired a firm to do a feasibility study, but everyone knows the old funeral home sits on the best land for expansion."

"Alice is right," Arthur put in. "We need to overhaul the factory and streamline our books. We need new equipment and new accounting procedures and a professional plant manager. We cannot afford any of that without a significant expansion."

"Father's paternalistic policy made for happy employees," Isabelle said with a sad smile. "They were always allowed to make lots of overtime, and he shut down in November every year for hunting season. But those old ways won't work any longer.

We have to stay competitive in our market." Nick frowned. "What's the bottom line here?"

Arthur shrugged. "Without some major changes, we're looking at heavy layoffs and maybe worse."

"Worse?"

"We can't keep dropping clients. If we keep on as we are, Bowman's Biscuits will have to close." The words hit him in a sucker punch.

Bowman's Biscuits will have to close. It shouldn't mean anything to him, but it did. For a moment, it meant everything.

Damn.

"Nicky? Are you all right?"

He heard Aunt Isabelle's voice but it was Alice Bowman's face he focused on. She gave him an encouraging smile.

"Of course," he said. "It's hard to imagine Mayville without Bowman's Biscuits."

Then why have you stayed away? No one voiced the words, but Nick heard them all the same. Why did you abandon your brother?

Half-brother.

The correction was automatic, but, for once, it failed to clear his conscience.

Isabelle cleared her throat.

"I understand Miss Olive left her sister at the Gray Lady." Judith shook her head.

"That was a mistake. Poor Ora must be free to start on her journey. It's a long way to
Summerland."

Nick pushed back his chair and got to his feet.

"You may be relieved to know she got as far as Titusville today."

Nick was ready for a journey of his own. The evening air felt good after the suffocating atmosphere of Bowman Mansion, but it was the feel of the steering wheel in his hands that cleared his head. Driving had always represented freedom to Nick. He found himself on Main Street.

The decades-old, downward spiral of the automobile industry had crashed into a full-scale depression, and the results showed even in a town where biscuit mix was king.

The empty windows of the former Blackwell's Department Store peered sightlessly at the ragged remains of Main Street.

Winans Pharmacy, where he'd bought his first condoms (For His Lady's Pleasure) was still in business as was D'Agostino's where he'd gotten his first haircut, but Woolworth's at the corner of Main and First had become a now abandoned video arcade. The Buttered Biscuit and Marshall's Market book-ended a vacant storefront that still bore the words, "Mayville Monitor." . On the south side of the Biscuit, a new sign welcomed shoppers, "Books Redux." Nick couldn't decide whether the name was pretentious or merely surprising for the blue-collar town.

Nick looked twice as he passed the Victorian home formerly known as the Mayville Library. The new sign offered customers a chance to pawn their valuables then have their nails done.

Nick didn't recognize the new, red-brick building. but it was well-marked; : The Theodore Bowman Homeless Shelter.

Aunt Isabelle's work? Or maybe this was an Alice project. Buzz's wife seemed to be involved in every aspect of the family's life.

The marquee at the Jewel Box was blank and the building dark. Nick flashed back on the summer nights he'd spent in the theater's balcony, his eyes on the feature film, his hands under some girl's blouse. He couldn't remember if he'd ever taken Caroline Budd to the movies. Her sister's disapproving hazel eyes appeared before his face and he scowled. He didn't need to worry about Daisy. Junie was on his side. First thing Monday morning, he'd get into the Gray Lady's cellar.

He'd find the Nazi loot and return it, if possible. In any case by this time next week he'd be back on the

West Coast.

A chartreuse martini glass caught his eye, and, on impulse, he pulled into the parking spot in front of Mayville's only bar, the Grainery. Beer was the drink of choice in Mayville, and Nick wondered if the joint even stocked gin.

Tonight, he decided, was an excellent time to find out.

Chapter Four

The brilliant blue overhead began to fade as the afternoon slipped toward dusk. The newlyweds departed into the sunset and the wedding guests, particularly the younger ones, abandoned their tights and grog in favor of shorts and beer.

Daisy carried a load of costumes to the cellar. Monday she'd mail them back to the rental company. She peered through the gloom and shivered. First thing next week, she planned to get rid of the leftover coffins that lined one wall like oversized chocolate bars then she'd devote some time to weeding through the flotsam and jetsam of more than a hundred years. She didn't look forward to the task, but it had to be done. She consoled herself with the thought that there might be a few "treasures" buried under the rubbish. She hurried back upstairs. Tonight she wanted to bask with her sisters in the day's success.

The phone on the reception desk halted her progress to the second floor.

"Happily Ever After," she said. "This is Daisy."

"This the Funeral Parlor?"

She sighed. "Not anymore. Happily Ever After is now a wedding boutique."

"I heard this was a mortuary."

Daisy held onto her patience.

"I can direct you to Foote's in Titusville."

"Look, this is Cory Aspen. Channel 6 News."

Daisy paused. "Okay."

"Live at Five, Six, and Seven. In Detroit. I'm on the air every night. You must have seen me."

"I don't have a television set."

"Good God, woman! How the hell do you get the weather?"

"I look outside. If you'll excuse me,"

"Hang on, hang on, Ms. Bowman."

"Ms. Budd."

"What?"

She wished she'd let the call go to voicemail.

"Mr. Aspen, is there something I can do for you?"

"Damn straight. I got a tip about a murder at the mortuary. Some old lady named Onion."

"That was a misunderstanding. One of our elderly residents, Ms. Ora Bunsen died of natural causes." If death-by-pastry was considered a natural cause.

"I heard it was murder."

The man was stubborn. It was a quality that often paid off in the news business. Suddenly she missed her old profession and her hostility fell away.

"Tell you what, Mr. Aspen, if there ever is a murder in Mayville, you'll be the first to know."

Daisy hung up and joined her sisters upstairs on the screened porch off the kitchen. The living quarters in the Gray Lady included three bedrooms and two baths as well as Daisy's office, the large, square kitchen, and the porch. At first she'd thought they would all live there together, but Caro had wanted a separate home for herself and Stevie. Junie claimed she needed her own apartment so that she could grow up, an inarguable goal.

When Isabelle Bowman offered the cabin, Daisy had fallen in love with it. The separate living arrangements worked out well.

"Hey, Daze. We're doing a post mortem."

Junie lounged on the chintz-covered cushions of the glider. Her feet hung over the back, and her ponytail touched the wooden slats of the floor. "My favorite moment was the Troubadors' performance of 'Can't Get No Satisfaction.' Caro's piece de resistance was Cherry Ann's dismount. Merde! I can't even imagine the wedding night."

"Unfortunately," Caroline said, "I can."

Daisy collapsed into one of the well-padded wicker chairs next to her eldest sister.

"My Kodak moment was the planting of the ceremonial sword."

Junie chortled and Caro smiled, but she looked exhausted. The hard-won tranquility of the past few months had fled. Anxiety gripped Daisy's insides as Junie sat up in her chair. "I think Cherry Ann is Quent's perfect match. They say everybody's got a soul mate." She got to her feet. "I've gotta split to get ready for my date."

"Your date?" Daisy and Caro exchanged a stricken glance. "With whom?"

"My boyfriend. You met him last week."

Daisy felt something inside her relax. "The homeless guy?"

"Adrian's not exactly homeless," Junie pointed out. "He's staying at the shelter until things start to jellgel."

"He's waiting for things to jell gel in Mayville?"

Junie shrugged. "He's got irons in the fire."

Daisy knew better than to mention Adrian's

obvious unsuitability. Their best bet was to keep a close eye on matters and wait for Junie's taste to mature.

Junie looked from one sister to the other and grinned.

"Why the silent panic? Did you two think I was going out with Nick Bowman?"

There was no point in denying it. Daisy shrugged. "It seemed reasonable. You spent a lot of time with him today."

"I'll admit he's a major hunk. Definitely a genetic gold mine."

"He's too old for you," Caro said.

"That's what he thinks. He treated me like a kid sister."

The sense of relief that crashed into Daisy seemed out of proportion to the threat. Nick Bowman, for all his reputation, was a decent man. He wouldn't hurt Junie.

"He's gonna get rid of the coffins for us." Junie sounded pleased with herself. "For free, too."

Daisy's eyes darted to her older sister. Caro's already pale face had turned to rice paper. Her blue eyes looked enormous against the translucent skin. Daisy held her forefinger against her lips.

"Night, Junie," she called out. "Don't do anything I wouldn't do."

"Hah!" Junie grinned. "If I followed that advice, I'd never do anything at all."

The front door banged shut. Caroline's voice was terse.

"You can't let Nick Bowman hang around."

"Don't worry, honey. You know Junie. By Monday she'll have forgotten all about this." Daisy made her voice as casual as possible.

Caro shook her head. "That man doesn't do anything without a reason. He has an agenda, and it involves our family." Her lips trembled. "Daisy, I'm afraid."

Daisy got up and hurried to Caro's side. She put her arm around her older, taller sister.

"Trust me. I won't let him hurt Junie. I won't let him hurt any of us. Forget about Nick Bowman. The wedding was a tremendous success. Concentrate on that. We're together, the four of us, and we're on our way."

The summer sky was indigo by the time Daisy turned off the interstate onto the bumpy, unpaved road that led to the cabin. She pulled into the clearing, parked and gazed at Trout Lake. The smooth water glittered like an onyx under a full moon. The air smelled of pine and filled with the ribbits of a frog chorus. Above the lake, the stars burst forth like kernels of freshly popped corn.

Daisy felt all the tension seep out of her. The cabin in the woods had become her sanctuary.

Larry greeted her at the door and glued himself to her ankles until she filled the ceramic bowl emblazoned with the name "Esmerelda." Daisy had found the bowl under the kitchen sink the same day Larry appeared at the door to share her tuna melt. She poured herself a glass of kumquat juice and sat at the small table with the gray Formica top to reread the letters.

They'd arrived at one week intervals, each in a spotless envelope with no stamp or address. Daisy felt a wave of anger as she remembered this morning's missive. The anonymous letter writer had been inside Happily Ever After. She compared the missives. In each case, the message, typed on standard bond, contained the same number of words. Where the messages differed was intensity.

The first, received two weeks earlier, included only a vague, implied threat:

Leave this house while you can.

The second, received the previous Saturday, promised potential bodily harm.

Get out before someone is hurt.

The third one, the one she'd found on her desk a few moments before Nick Bowman's appearance this morning, was succinct. A cold shiver worked its way down her spine as she stared at the words.

Death is coming to the Gray Lady.

A death threat? Was the sender a potential murderer?

Daisy was willing to build a moat around the Gray Lady if it would protect her sisters and nephew, but she couldn't defend them against the unknown. The letter writer was able to get into and out of the old house without being noticed which meant he or she was either resourceful or someone they knew. Daisy shook her head. She knew, and trusted, everyone in town. A fierce anger shook her. This anonymous coward was trying to shake her faith in her community, and she couldn't let that happen.

There really was no choice. It was time to contact the authorities.

Exhaustion struck. It seemed an age since she'd found Miss Ora's dead body in the casket and Nick Bowman's very much alive body in the doorway. Daisy scraped together enough energy to drag herself into the bedroom. By the time she slid between the daffodil-colored sheets, she was half asleep.

****

Nick figured he'd get some hostile looks in the bar. Bowman employed four out of ten people in town, and ten out of ten Mayville residents were affected by the company's fortunes that were rapidly spiraling down. Folks might very well blame him for disappearing into a puff of exhaust seven years ago.

He'd figured wrong. The patrons of the Grainery were the opposite of hostile. They greeted him with handshakes, words of welcome, and questions about his racing career. He obliged them with a few tales and rounds of beer, but he was relieved when they turned back to what he imagined was an oft-visited and favorite topic—past moments of gridiron glory at Clark County High.

When the bar closed at two a.m., Nick stumbled out to the Malibu. He wasn't drunk, but the fresh air, combined with the drinks and lack of sleep hit him hard. Nick knew his body. He figured he had twenty minutes until he passed out.

It was time to find a bed.

He paused at the red light at the end of Main. A right turn took him up the hill to Bowman Mansion. A left led to the interstate. The prospect of an entire night in the mausoleum was unbearable. He opted for freedom. He barreled down I-94 with no destination in mind, but as soon as he spotted the weathered, hand-painted sign half-hidden by reeds, he knew exactly where he was going to sleep.

****

Daisy melted and burned. It was hot enough to blister the paint on the walls. Inferno hot. She tried to

46

push the heat away, but it was always there, like a second skin. Was it coming from her? Did she have a fever? Malaria? Early menopause? Desperate for relief Daisy twisted until a steel bar clamped across her chest. Panic attacked her. She arched backward, and her hips slammed into a new barrier. This one was hard and hot and, in spite of her relative lack of experience, she identified it immediately.

An erection. A big one.

Daisy screeched and launched herself skyward, breaking the hold. She felt like a smashed piñata as the floor slammed into her hip and funny bone.

"Ow!"

An artificial light flared in her eyes.

"You okay?"

She gritted her teeth and waited for the flare of pain to recede before she opened one eye.

Nick leaned over the side of the bed, his dark hair tousled from sleep, his eyelids heavy, his cheeks bristled with dark whiskers. Gray eyes glittered at her.

"Damn you felt good. C'mon back to bed, honey."

Honey? Honey? She struggled to her feet and planted her fists at her waist as righteous anger ignited the adrenaline in her system. Her words were clean, crisp rifle shots.

"Get. Out. Of. My. Bed."

He squinted at her as if he didn't know what to say, as if it were inconceivable that she wouldn't want to get back into his bed. Her bed. The man was in her bed.

He rolled to his feet in a coordinated move and stood before her unconcerned about his nudity. But why should he be concerned. He was magnificent.

Daisy's injuries receded as she struggled for

breath. "Happy now?"

Her gaze fixed on the body part nearest her face, the same part she'd felt pressing against her earlier.

A terrible thought occurred. "Tell me we did not have sex."

He glanced down at himself, a rueful smile on his lips. "I think I can safely promise you we did not have sex. At least, not recently."

Chapter Five

Nick grimaced as he adjusted his jeans. He was damn lucky he could get them zipped at all. What the hell was going on? How had he wound up in bed with Daisy Budd of all people? Christ. He knew he hadn't been that drunk. His temples throbbed as he searched the room for his shirt.

Damn. What a nightmare. He'd meant to stay away from her. Not that he'd crossed the line. The persistent tension in his groin assured him he hadn't made love with anybody. But he'd been close enough to feel her warmth and sweet feminine curves, close enough to get viciously turned on. She'd been pissed as hell.

Well, hell. He'd hoped to sneak through enemy lines using Junie as a shield. Daisy was already suspicious, and now she'd been warned. He knew she'd amass her troops along the border, and it would be a helluva lot harder to get in.

Harder. Drums pounded in Nick's lower body. What was the matter with him? He shouldn't be this turned on. She was the plain Budd sister. He had to pull himself together. Just when he needed all his wits against the Gray Lady's owner, he felt like road kill.

He thrust his fingers through his hair and rubbed the back of his neck, sucked in a deep breath, and followed her out into the cabin's main room. She faced the window over the sink. Her puke pink night shirt hugged her gently rounded hips and revealed shapely legs. Her hair corkscrewed in all directions as if it had lost a battle with an eggbeater.

He braced himself for hysteria, but it didn't come. Instead, she turned and handed him a Betty Rubble glass filled with dog pee.

"It's kumquat juice. Good for whatever ails you." She nodded at the Flintstones' logo. "I figured this was your special glass."

Nick accepted the rank-looking drink.

"Nah. That one was mine." He indicated the glass in her hand embellished with Dino the Dinosaur. A half-smile appeared on her full lips. He watched her throat work as she swallowed the liquid. She had a nice throat. A really beautiful throat. Soft and white.

Nick bit back a curse. In his current hardened state, any female throat would've turned him on.

She sat on one of the 1950's era metal chairs at the Formica-topped table.

"I think we'd better talk."

"You gonna ask me what I'm doing here?"

She shook her head, and the red curls bounced. She looked just like Orphan Annie.

"You figured the place would be empty, right? You'd no way of knowing that I'd rented the cabin from your Aunt Isabelle."

He lifted one eyebrow. The small muscles protested. He must've had more to drink than he'd thought. "You live here?"

She continued as if he hadn't spoken. "A more observant person might have noticed my Jeep in the clearing or my body in the bed, but I imagine you'd been drinking."

He grimaced. She was right.

"I'm sorry, Nick." The unexpected sympathy sliced through him. "It had to be hard on you to come to meet with your family after seven years and to find the mortuary changed. You probably drove out here for some peace and quiet and here I am."

"Goldilocks."

She chuckled. Miss Daisy Budd appeared to have recovered from her encounter with his rude male body.

"Why here?"

"The cabin? No one ever used it. I imagine your aunt expected you'd never come here again. She offered it to me."

"You've got that big house on Pine Street."

"What would you choose? A rambling ex-funeral home or a cozy cottage?"

Her grin lit up her whole face, and something moved in his chest. He felt an answering smile curve his lips. "Touché."

"You, on the other hand, have the entire Bowman mansion in which to bed down."

His smile died. "I'd prefer the cabin."

For a moment they sat in silence. Nick found himself staring at the soft cotton nightshirt that outlined a pair of high, firm breasts. Damn. His zipper pressed against the swollen flesh underneath.

"Nick?"

Her voice was high and breathless and something else. Annoyed? Excited? He stared into hazel eyes as he read the words printed on the cotton.

"For your fairytale wedding, come to Happily Here After."

She made a face. "Caro's idea of a joke."

Caro. The sister he'd dated and abandoned. He heard the tightness in her voice.

"Is that the reason you don't trust me, Daisy? Because I dated your sister?"

She shrugged. "You abandoned your family. You weren't here for Theo's death. Bowman's Biscuits needs your help, but you aren't planning to stay. You mistreated my sister. And speaking of sisters, I know Junie said you could help us clean up the cellar at the Gray Lady, but I'm countermanding that." She ticked off the reasons as if she'd spent plenty of time reviewing them.

"You have something against free help?"

"I've got it covered. I'm sure you have more important things to do in town."

He noted the flash in her golden eyes. There was more going on here than her reluctance to accept help from a Bowman. He'd find out what it was. In the meantime, he'd have to go to Plan B. Just as soon as he figured it out. Her next words took him by surprise.

"You look exhausted." More sympathy?

"You ought to get back to Bowman Mansion and get some rest."

"I told you. I can't sleep there."

The statement was automatic and stark and completely true.

Daisy didn't question it. She met his eyes. "All right. You can finish the night on my sofa. But tomorrow you've got to find somewhere else to stay."

The cushions sagged, and the print was faded and stained on the broken-down, too-short sofa, but he'd take what he could get.

"Thanks."

He limped across the room and collapsed. He did not hear her move, but he felt the soft blanket she tucked around his shoulders, and he inhaled that scent of fresh wildflowers. Daisy's scent.

His eyelids flickered. "Thanks."

"This is the daisy quilt my Gran gran made me," she said. "Don't get sick on it."

****

The cabin needed a fresh coat of paint.

Daisy came to that unsurprising conclusion after she stared at the watermarks above her bed long enough to see the outline of an animal in the stains.

It was a wolf with ghostly gray eyes.

Good grief.

Insomnia wasn't new. During the past couple of yearsyears, she'd tried to carve out a career in journalism in a small town on the other side of the state while worrying about her family back in Mayville, she'd experienced plenty of sleepless nights.

This was not the same generalized anxiety. It was different. Tonight every nerve was wired. Tonight she couldn't sleep because her hormones were Mexican jumping beans. Tonight's trouble could be traced ten feet to the man sleeping on her sofa.

The unfortunate crush of her teen-aged years had morphed into an even more unfortunate cataract of adult desire.

Daisy squeezed her eyes shut. She did not need this right now. Or ever. She did not need this man jumping into the middle of her already out-of-control life.

She did not want him. Or, maybe it was more accurate to say, she didn't want to want him.

Dang.

Daisy willed herself to focus on something else, but each time she closed her eyes, she pictured the hair on his chest and the way it feathered across his muscles to meet in a thin dark line that arrowed toward his groin. She pictured the groin, too, with its flare of dark curls and its jutting erection. Merde!

She was getting as bad as Junie.

She needed an air conditioner. Or a lobotomy.

****

Nick grunted in pain. His neck was bent in two like a chicken ready for the pan. He'd smacked his knee against the coffee table sometime during the night, and his temples throbbed. To add insult to injury, he'd awakened with a particularly painful morning arousal.

He blamed Daisy Budd for all of it.

Daisy Budd and her damned quilt. The scent made it impossible for him to forget the way her soft flesh had tucked into the curve of his body last night.

Nick knew she'd been turned on. Just before she'd exploded like a scalded cat, he'd felt the tight nipples against his forearm and the heat of her body under that nightshirt. She'd wanted him. Of course, that was before she'd recognized him.

And he sure as hell wanted her.

It was out of the question. Wrong woman, wrong time, wrong place.

He stared out the kitchen window at the silhouettes of the tall evergreens around Trout Lake. The sun hadn't yet reached the horizon. In a few minutes, it would flirt with the pine branches as it climbed into the sky.

An unexpected wave of nostalgia rolled through him as he remembered those childhood summer mornings with Buzz and his dad and Pops.

Nick inhaled Daisy's scent, and his body tightened again driving away the old pain. He needed a cold shower, but he wasn't gonna tempt fate by using hers. He folded the blanket, gathered his clothes, and headed for the screened door. The ugliest cat he'd ever seen sat crossed his path. Its tail looked as if it had been attacked by moths.

Nick pushed open the door.

"C'mon fella. Let's both get some fresh air."

****

With the first faint rays of daylight, Daisy gave up the fantasy of sleep. She dressed in a turquoise skirt with an Aztec pattern in yellow, coral, orange, red, and black and a lemon yellow tank top. She fastened the clasp on her squash blossom necklace and added a silver cuff, and she pulled her hair up into a loose fountain out of deference to the heat and humidity of the morning. At least she'd be fully dressed this time when she faced Nick Bowman.

Only she didn't face Nick. He wasn't on the sofa or in the kitchen or bathroom. She peered out the screened door. He was gone, but his car wasn't. She stepped onto the porch. The mirror-like surface of Trout Lake in the morning always made Daisy catch her breath. Today her breath was short for a different reason. A pair of tanned arms powered through the water as if there was no resistance at all.

He finished his workout then swam back toward the dock. Instead of hoisting himself up on the wooden structure, he swam until he reached the shallows and then he stood, tall, broad-shouldered and naked. Poseidon, rising from the water, complete with trident.

Junie was right. The guy was a genetic jackpot.

She had thought herself hidden, but his eyes crinkled at her, and his hard mouth crooked into a smile. Her heart crashed against her ribs even as she tried to remind herself that his male beauty wasn't enough to make up for his neglect of her sister.

She could not allow him to come out to the cabin anymore. While he pulled on a pair of jeans, she practiced the words she'd use to draw boundaries, but she never got a chance to use them. She heard his voice and looked up.

"Thanks for the hospitality." He ducked into the Malibu and within seconds, he'd disappeared down the dirt road.

"You're welcome," Daisy murmured. Larry waved his ragged tail.

Chapter Six

"I want a Romanov theme," the young woman said, with supreme confidence, "and I know exactly how I want to execute it."

Junie choked back a laugh, and Daisy sent her a sharp glance. They simply couldn't make fun of the clients. Stacey Burlingame couldn't be more than nineteen years old, but she took her wedding plans very seriously.

"A Romanov wedding sounds lovely," Daisy said, hastily. "White and silver and crystal? Very romantic."

Stacey nodded. She twirled a lock of her blonde hair. A budding bridezilla unless Daisy missed her guess.

"I want a horse-drawn sleigh," Stacey went on, "and the groomsmen will dress as Cossacks."

"My dear!" Stacey's mother sounded horrified. "That won't do at all. Too war-like."

Not to mention too hot for the unfortunate attendants.

Stacey proceeded as if she hadn't heard. "The bridesmaids will wear peasant clothing, and I want a wolfhound to be ring bearer."

"You want a dog in the ceremony?" This time Junie couldn't repress her reaction. "Quelle horreur!"

"Animals are difficult to control." Daisy raised her

voice to drown out her sister's comment, an unnecessary effort since Stacey wasn't listening to anyone but herself.

"The cake should be shaped like the Russian church with the rounded top."

"St. Basil's Cathedral," Daisy murmured, "with the onion dome."

Junie's eyes brightened. "I can totally make that shape!"

Daisy grimaced as she remembered Junie's recent "tit" cake.

"And," Stacey decreed, "I want falling snow."

"Snow is hard to guarantee," Daisy warned, "even during a Michigan winter."

"Winter? Oh, no! The wedding is June seventeenth," Stacey said.

"A year from the day Dennis finally caved," her mother murmured.

Stacey extended her left hand to display a sparkling diamond the size of a golf ball.

"I'm afraid there is no snow in June."

"Can't you make some? That's what they do at ski resorts."

Daisy shook her head. "No snow."

The mother's relieved smile countered the bride's scowl. Daisy found the physical resemblance between the women somewhat startling. All that separated Eunice Burlingame from her daughter were twenty years and forty pounds. And a few grains of common sense.

"If I can't have snow I want my second choice." Stacey's mouth pursed in a practiced pout. "Lord of the Rings."

Her mother wrung her hands. "Heavens, dear. The wedding party would be full of trolls and wookies."

Daisy decided it was time to take control.

"What would you say to an Arabian Nights fantasy? You could arrive in a horse-drawn carriage."

"The bridesmaids could be the ugly stepsisters," Junie added, helpfully.

Daisy shot her a repressive look. A dreamy look came over the young woman's face.

"You know we could have a mermaid theme.".

"With lots of bright fish," Junie said.

"And water," Mrs. Burlingame noted. "I don't know how they would do the water, dear."

As Junie ran to answer the phone, Daisy explained how they could create the illusion of water with blue fabric and a bubble machine before she escorted them down the stairs. A moment later Junie joined her sister on the front porch.

"Merde. That phone call? A potential client wants a Corpse Bride theme since this is a funeral home."

"Was a funeral home," Daisy corrected her. She refused to be discouraged by the world's reluctance to accept the Gray Lady's most recent incarnation. She faced a slew of mortgage payments and renovation bills. She'd give the people what they wanted. Within reason.

"Call her back," Daisy advised. "Tell her we can do a Corpse Bride. Absolutely."

****

The central offices of Bowman's Biscuits were not impressive for a company with an annual net income of more than a hundred million dollars and a five-hundred employee payroll.

Theo Bowman refused to "gild the lily." A biscuit mix factory, he'd said many times, should look like a biscuit mix factory, no more, no less.

Isabelle glanced at the cement block walls as she made her way up the utilitarian staircase. She'd spent little time at the company's office over the years. She'd never been comfortable here, and that hadn't changed. Anxiety formed a lump in her stomach. She already regretted the impulse that had prompted her to stop by. When she'd proposed a marriage of convenience to her father's attorney, she had not expected to find in the stone-faced Arthur, a virtual geyser of sexuality. It had been most gratifying until it had stopped six weeks earlier. Isabelle wondered if she'd made a mistake to visit him at his office. Why should he welcome the intrusion in his work day when he no longer welcomed it in the privacy of their bedroom. Bedroom? Isabelle wished she could scurry back to the car, but it was too late. Miss Ginger Watson, the company's receptionist, had recognized her. She offered to accompany her to Arthur's office. Isabelle thanked her but declined. She knew the way.

Arthur's long-time secretary, Leilani Harter and she were of an age and friends, after a fashion. Not secretary, Isabelle reminded herself. The modern term was administrative assistant. She and the Harters crossed paths at church and other community events, and Leilani and her husband had attended Isabelle and Arthur's small wedding. Isabelle looked forward to seeing the familiar face, but Leilani's desk chair was empty. Isabelle stood outside her husband's office door, irresolute and awkward. Should she knock? Should she enter unannounced? A sudden shyness paralyzed her.

She told herself to get a grip. She owned a third of the company, and this was her husband's office. She knocked, but there was no answer. Isabelle began to worry.

Maybe Arthur had suffered a heart attack. Maybe he was collapsed on the floor with the useless telephone receiver in his hand. Maybe he was already dead. Her heart jumped into her throat, and she knocked again. Still no answer. Where in the world was he?

Anxiety made her semi-hysterical, and she feared she'd start to scream. Instead, she turned the knob and stepped inside the door. She gaped at the man seated behind his large, walnut desk. He did have the telephone receiver in his hand, but he spoke into it. He looked at her and held up a finger to indicate he'd be another minute. She used the time to recover her equilibrium.

"My goodness you gave me a turn," she said, when he hung up. She waited for him to rise to greet her and was shocked when he remained seated. He indicated the chair across from him and she sat.

Arthur was acting very un-Arthur-like.

"I apologize for the delay," he said. "Stan Milson, down in the warehouse, is concerned about the cancellation of a large order." He frowned. "I told him I'd look into it."

The words barely registered. Isabelle focused on her husband's flushed face. Several thin strands of gray hair were moist with sweat. They clung to his skull. She realized she had never seen Arthur sweat. The always impeccable Windsor knot in his necktie had come undone.

"Oh my god, Arthur," she burst out, "you are ill."

He pulled a fresh, white handkerchief out of his pocket and mopped his forehead.

"No, no, dear, I was working out."

Isabelle glanced at the treadmill she'd bought him for Christmas. Stacks of dusty periodicals and papers rested on it.

Arthur's eyes followed her gaze.

"Calisthenics," he explained. "Not enough time to use the machine."

"Arthur," she said, firmly, "you are not well. I think you should come home and take a nap."

"I'm fine, dear." He was courteous, as always, but there was an unmistakable thread of steel in his voice. "And I've got a hundred problems to solve before closing time. What can I do for you?"

Isabelle thought of the letter in her purse, the one she'd received this morning and, impulsively, had decided to show Arthur. Somehow she couldn't do it. Not here. Not with Arthur in this odd, prickly mood. She sighed, inwardly. He was prickly a lot lately.

"It's not important." She got to her feet. "I won't interrupt you any longer." She waited for him to rise to walk her to the door. Instead he lifted the phone receiver and began to dial. What on earth had happened to her husband's impeccable manners?

"Mrs. Harter," he said, "could you cancel Walter Jacobson? My wife is here, and I'd like to take her to lunch."

The words were all right. The tone was not. Guilt and remorse assailed Isabelle. Arthur carried the wobbly future of Bowman's Biscuits on his thin shoulders. She shouldn't have bothered him.

"No, please don't cancel. I've an appointment

myself. I'll see you tonight, dear." She hastened toward the door without a backward glance. Moments later she slid under the wheel of her Mercedes and stared out the windshield. Something was wrong. By the time she turned up the road to Bowman Mansion, she knew what it was. Arthur had been on the phone with his administrative assistant, but when Isabelle passed Mrs. Harter's desk it was still empty.

He had faked the phone call.

Tears pricked the backs of her eyelids as the grim truth fell into place. No wonder he hadn't been pleased to see her. No wonder he had taken to coming to bed late or not at all. No wonder.

Arthur was having an affair.

With that tart Leilani Harter.

****

Arthur Sneed leaned back in his desk chair and fought a major panic attack.

"That was too close for comfort."

An understatement if ever he'd heard one. He struggled for breath. He was mortified. He'd followed the straight and narrow all his life and now, in his autumn years, he'd lost his way. He didn't need a crystal ball or a séance to know what Theo Bowman would think of him.

Especially since the injured party was Isabelle.

Long fingers drifted across his narrow thigh, and he began to quiver the way he always did when she touched him.

"No more," he said, without conviction. She ignored the order and slid her palm up his thigh until she reached the open zipper and the stalk of thick male flesh. He pictured her on her knees, her mouth closing around the moist tip of his erection. "Oh, God," he whimpered. He gave himself up to another shuddering climax. He didn't know who he was anymore, but he couldn't bring himself to care.

****

The morning clouds drifted and expanded until by mid-afternoon they'd created a gray canopy that resembled Trout Lake before a storm. Or Nick Bowman's eyes. Daisy shook off the image.

Neither Nick Bowman nor his eyes were on her radar screen any longer. She'd successfully banished him. And it hadn't even been very hard. Soon he'd leave Mayville, and she wouldn't have to think about him again which was exactly what she wanted.

The twigs and branches that flew past her office reminded her of a scene from the Wizard of Oz. She hadn't realized the wind had whipped into such a fury.

Junie appeared in Daisy's office, her cheeks flushed from the kitchen and her ponytail askew.

"I think the cauldron cookies will work for the handfast," she announced. "If I mix all the food coloring together, I get something pretty close to black."

"Sounds good. Nadine called a few minutes ago to ask you to stop over at the Biscuit on your way home. She wants your opinion on some choices for Saturday's event." Daisy glanced out the window and watched another branch sail by. "You'd better go now before the storm breaks."

"Tres bien. You'll stay at Caro's?"

Daisy shook her head. "I need to feed Larry. We'll be okay at the cabin."

A sudden crash made both women jump.

"Mon Dieu! What was that?"

"Probably a loose shingle. I'll get the ladder out and check tomorrow."

After Junie left she walked through the house to secure all the doors and windows. She'd reached the back door, purse in hand, when the phone rang.

Dang.

"Happily Ever After," she said. "This is Daisy."

"Debbie Popple here. I need a favor from you."

Debbie, a curvaceous, forty-something divorcee who owned her own real estate company had brokered the deal between Daisy and the late Randolph Bowman's estate. She was tall, buxom and confident, and her hair, a few shades darker than Daisy's, was styled by a salon in the Detroit suburbs. Most local women, including Daisy, patronized the only salon in town, Hair by Denise, on Main Street.

"I'll cut to the chase." Debbie's voice was as crisp as a ginger snap. "I want you to set me up with Nick Bowman."

Daisy blinked. "Set you up? I don't think he's in the market for a house." Except Daisy's house; the Gray Lady.

"This isn't about real estate," Debbie said, impatiently, "this is personal. I want you to introduce us."

"Personal? You mean you want to date Nick Bowman?"

"Naturally I want to date him. Everyone wants to date him. He's rich, eligible, and he's smokin' hot." Thunder crashed overhead and she jumped.

"Uh, Debbie, what've you heard about the weather?"

"Tornado warnings until ten for the tri-county area. A funnel cloud's been sighted near Livonia. Stay inside until further notice. You should turn on your TV." Debbie rattled off the information like a professional weathercaster, and the words struck fear into Daisy's heart. Larry was alone. He would be frightened.

"Listen, I've got to go."

"What about Nick?"

Good grief.

"Why don't you call him? I'm sure he'd be glad to meet you."

Debbie dismissed the idea. "Too obvious. You've got access, and you know what we say in the real estate biz, location, location, location. I know he spent the night out at your cabin."

Daisy grimaced. That had to be a record even for Mayville's efficient grapevine.

"Relax, Daisy. Your halo is safe. Everyone knows you never misbehave, and, in any case, you're not his type."

Daisy couldn't argue with that. "Right."

"So, can you fix me up?"

A shutter banged against the house, and Daisy jumped. She had to get home.

"I'll mention it if I see him." It was a safe enough promise. She never intended to see Nick Bowman again.

"Don't just mention it, hon. Sell it. Sell me. Tell him I've got lots of experience and an excellent technique. Believe me, it's true."

Thunder crashed and lightning slashed the sky outside the windows. Inside, the air conditioner stopped humming and the lights went out. The storm charged into high gear like a two-year-old's tantrum.

"Look, Debbie, I've got to go." Without waiting for the other woman's response, she disconnected the phone. The Gray Lady's ancient electrical system demanded careful handling, and Daisy knew she had to flip the breaker switch to avoid a power surge when electricity was restored. The problem was, the fuse box was in the cellar. The dank, dark, scary cellar. Dang.

She located the heavy-duty portable flashlight under the kitchen sink and made her way down two flights of stairs. Daisy prided herself on her practicality but the storm, the dark and the cellar made her feel like a gothic heroine. She half expected a bat to tangle in her hair or a vampire to rise from one of the coffins. She shivered.

She moved across the dirt floor as quickly as possible. Sweat dampened the back of her blouse, and her legs quivered. She flipped the main electrical switch then made a beeline for the stairs and daylight, but she stumbled and the flashlight beam threw wide. Daisy's stomach twisted as she stared at the black candle on top of a coffin.

More than anything, she wanted to take the wooden steps two at a time. She reminded herself this was her house, her business. Her future. Her sisters' future. She couldn't run. She forced herself to touch the strange candle. Her throat constricted with fear. She was certain no one had been down here all day.

Except that someone had.

The wax was still warm.

Her heart crashed against her ribs. She shone the light on the object and discovered there was more to fear than the black candle. The dish in which it sat was filled with carcasses. She peered at the bodies of the dead butterflies and bit back a cry.

Was it a statement by the stalker or a protest?

She'd banned Nick from the Gray Lady. Was this childish but eerie display his revenge?

Her fear receded, replaced by anger. She'd get to the bottom of this, and when she identified the author of this harassment, she intended to go after him with everything at her disposal.

She would permit no one to harass her family.

No one.

Chapter Seven

Nick slumped in the driver's seat of the Malibu. He'd parked on Michigan Avenue behind the Gray Lady. On a clear day he'd have a great view of the back of the house through a static veil of green. Today's storm-blackened sky and the dancing leaves reduced the visibility to nearly zero.

He'd lived in this town for more than twenty years and didn't need a weathercaster to tell him these were ideal conditions for tornadoes. For once, that was a good thing. Nick intended to turn the rotten weather to his advantage. No one would be out tonight. No one would know if he broke into the old mortuary. He'd have hours to explore the damn cellar. All night. All he had to do was wait for Miss Daisy Budd to leave for the day. With any luck, he'd have completed his mission by dawn, and by late morning, he could be on a flight out of town.

With any luck. Nick snorted. Lately, luck had deserted him.

He squinted through the rain-spattered windshield, and his heart jerked when he saw her. A gust of wind whipped at her hair and her skirt. She clutched that oversized straw purse to her chest, but there was nothing to protect her from the bucketing rain. Her soaked blouse clung to her chest, and he caught a glimpse of high, well-formed breasts. Nick's body tightened with need. He ignored it.

He'd figured out right away that Daisy Budd wasn't for him, and, as she'd made clear last night, he wasn't for her.

She managed to get into the Jeep. Nick pulled away from the curb. He'd figured he'd follow her to her sister's house just to make sure the coast was clear. He did not intend to be interrupted tonight.

The little red vehicle took a right on Pine then another on Main. The torrent had already flooded the street which was bereft of both cars and pedestrians. Daisy's tires created deep furrows of water as she made her way to the right hand turn on Third Street, the one that led to her sister's house on Fillmore.

Only she didn't turn on Third. Nick frowned. Where the devil was she headed? In another two blocks, they'd be at the end of Main where she would have no choice but to turn right to drive up to the Bowman Mansion or left to hook up with the interstate that led to the lake. He cursed as the left hand blinker flirted with him through the rain. Surely she wasn't heading to the cabin. The small wooden structure covered in tin and surrounded by trees and water provided poor shelter in a storm. A tornado or a rogue bolt of lightning could reduce the place to a house of sticks.

Was the woman insane?

He pictured the warm hazel eyes and the answer came to him.

This wasn't about sanity. This was about the damned cat.

He sat at the crossroads and watched her lights wink in the distance. His cell rang and he picked it up.

"Yeah?"

"Hello, Nick. This is Isabelle. Could you come to dinner tonight?"

Under no circumstances. He had an agenda that did not include family.

"Thank you. I have other plans."

He heard a little sob and couldn't believe his ears. He'd never known Isabelle to cry.

"Aunt Isabelle? What's wrong?"

"Oh, Nick. I can't talk about it over the phone." She sobbed. "I don't know what to do."

"All right," he soothed. "I'm on Main Street. I'll be there in three minutes."

He parked in the circular drive in front of the mansion and sprinted up the covered front porch steps. The wind screamed across the blackened sky. Worry about Daisy ripped at him. He shook it off.

For once Finch was not at his post. Instead, Isabelle met him at the door and took him into her small parlor. He inhaled her familiar scent of gardenias and, at her insistence, dropped into one of the spindly French chairs. She sat opposite then reached out to him, and he covered her cold hands with his warm ones, .

"What is it?"

She sniffed. "We're having grilled wild tuna served on a bed of soba noodles."

Nick shook his head. Aunt Isabelle might be in the middle of a crisis, but she'd still managed to order a gourmet meal.

"I meant what is it that's worrying you."

"I know." She withdrew her hands, sniffed, fumbled in the purse on the desk and withdrew an envelope. She handed it over and he scanned it.

"An invoice for fifty thousand dollars from

someone named Spuds Langston," he said, half to himself, before he caught the name on the bill. His eyes shot to his aunt's face. "What could Buzz have bought for half a grand?"

"I haven't a clue," Isabelle replied. "All I know is that we can't possibly put our hands on that kind of money. Not right now."

Nick stared at the statement. It said, "For services rendered."

"Have you shown it to Arthur?"

Tears welled up in Isabelle's faded blue eyes.

They slipped down her pale cheeks.

"I tried." She sniffed. "I went to the office today and, oh, Nick, this is simply beyond the pale. It seems Arthur is, well, carrying on with Leilani Harter."

Nick stared at her. He could not imagine Arthur carrying on. Not even with his wife. Never with Leilani Harter, a respected wife, mother, and grandmother.

"Aunt, Mrs. Harter taught Buzz and me in Sunday school."

"I know." Her face crumpled. "That makes it even worse!"

"It isn't possible."

Isabelle covered her eyes with her hands. "When I stepped into his office he didn't rise." He looked at her, blankly.

"The man has impeccable manners. He always rises when a lady enters the room. And that's not all. His clothes were disheveled, and he was sweaty and flushed." She let out a little moan. "His tie was undone."

"Maybe he was overheated."

"He said he'd been exercising, but he hadn't. The

treadmill I bought him was covered with papers." She let out a little sob. "And that isn't even the worst of it. He lied, Nick. He pretended to be on the phone with her in order to get rid of me."

"What makes you think it was a lie?"

His aunt's lined face looked ten years older than it had only days earlier.

"He couldn't have been talking to her on the phone. She wasn't at her desk."

"Maybe he'd called her cell." Isabelle appeared to consider that.

"No, no, I don't think so. They were discussing his calendar."

"Well there's got to be some other explanation.
Ask Arthur."

"I can't," she moaned. "I just can't." She buried her face in her hands.

"I've known Arthur Sneed all my life, Aunt Isabelle. He is the soul of courtesy and honor. Pops trusted him. You know that."

"But why was he so... moist?" Nick groped for a comforting answer.

"Push-ups?"

She sniffed. "He did mention calisthenics."

They were interrupted when the door to the small parlor opened, and Nick's sister-in-law appeared. He was surprised she hadn't knocked. She looked surprised to see him.

"Oh, I didn't mean to interrupt. I have a few questions from Harmony Lime about the upcoming Wiccan festivities."

Nick knew his aunt would be gracious to the intruder. For once he didn't mind the interruption. He was out of suggestions to explain what Isabelle saw as Arthur's suspicious behavior.

"Please come in, Alice," Isabelle said. "How can I help you?"

Nick half-listened to some nonsense about elderberries and newt's eyes while he fretted about Daisy. Damn the woman! If a tornado hit the lake, she'd find herself in hell. Or Kansas. He cut off his sister-in-law as he got to his feet.

"I'll speak with you later," he said to his aunt and escaped into the foyer before she could press him to stay for grilled tuna. Almost immediately long fingers with black nails wrapped around his arm. Nick ground his teeth and forced a smile.

"Judith."

Tonight his stepmother wore a black gown studded with silver suns and moons. Wardrobe, he remembered, had frequently figured in Judith Bowman's spiritual choices.

"Harmony Lime," she reminded him. "My dear, you must come see my newest passion."

He listened to the rain beating a crazy tattoo against the sides of the sturdy mansion and fought a sense of helplessness. He had no business worrying about Daisy Budd. The woman was old enough to take care of herself. Besides, tonight was a perfect opportunity to find the treasure. Reluctantly he followed his stepmother down the corridor and into a room he vaguely remembered as a sun porch but which was now, apparently, an arboretum. Rows of clay pots filled with plants basked in artificial light and an earthy scent filled the air.

"You've become a gardener?"

"Oh, no. I've hired someone to tend the plants. My interest is mixology. The potions and brews in my Book of Shadows require special herbs so I grow them here. I've got a wicked love potion. Would you like to try it?"

Nick stared at Judith's still-beautiful face. She was a kook and totally self-absorbed, but, to her credit, she'd never treated him any differently than her own son.

"I suppose," she said, with a little sigh, "you think I'm a flake, but I'm not really. I just have a short attention span."

The unexpected humor was his undoing.

"I think you're beautiful and adventurous." He realized he meant the compliment.

She flashed a brilliant smile. "Life's a journey, Nick, dear. If we stop seeking, we stop evolving." She waved her be-ringed hands. "Your journey has come full circle. It was time for you to come home."

His warm feelings evaporated. Judith must have heard why he'd left at some time or other, but perhaps, like so many things, it had flitted in and out of her brain. He glanced at his watch.

"Is there something I can do for you?"

Her face sobered.

"There's something you can do for all of us. The family needs you, Nick. Buzzy's in over his head.

You have to stay."

"It's out of the question, Judith. I'm sorry."

"Theo raised you as his own grandson," she reminded him.

Sure he had. Right up until he'd cut Nick off at the knees. "I have my own life. My own career."

She shook her head and her long hair swayed. "Your life is here. I've read it in the stars. Besides, you still own a third of the company. And besides," she went on, ignoring his lack of response, "this weekend I'll introduce you to the high priestess and Grand Dragon of my coven. They are to be handfasted at the mortuary."

"Wedding boutique," he corrected her. Then he clamped his jaw shut, appalled. Why on earth did he care what people called Daisy's establishment?

"Of course. Happily Ever After. Such a fanciful name."

He thought about her latest fruit-inspired identity. The woman knew fanciful.

"I have to go."

"You know, Nicky," Harmony Lime said. "You are conflicted about something. Your aura is becoming muddy."

He flashed her a sardonic smile.

"Somehow, that doesn't surprise me."

****

The Jeep rocked and slid as rain crashed into it, but Daisy didn't slow her pace. She hoped Larry wasn't too frightened. If only she'd brought him to town with her. They could have stayed in Caro's cozy house. The only safe place in the cabin was the windowless bathroom.

The power was out when she got to the cabin. No surprise there. Daisy used a flashlight to locate Larry under her bed then she coaxed him out with a bowl of tuna fish onto which she'd crumbled an Oreo cookie. After she toweled off and changed her soaked clothing, she settled down to read by flashlight.

Several hours later she awoke when she turned on

her side to get more comfortable and felt something cold and hard beneath her cheek.

Porcelain?

Ah, yes. The howl of the wind against the cabin's corners and the clatter of rain on the tin roof reminded her she'd chosen to spend the night in the bathtub. She shifted and grimaced as her bones protested. In spite of the nested blankets, the tub was unforgiving. Still half-asleep, she expected only darkness when she opened her eyes, but a single candle flame danced on top of the vanity. It revealed a dark form perched on the closed toilet set. A human form. The hair lifted on Daisy's neck even as she recognized his uniquely masculine scent.

"Nick?"

"Right here."

"Here?" She struggled to sit up. "You're in the bathroom with me?"

"Safest place in a storm. But you already knew that." She squinted at him and noticed an odd bulkiness around his neck.

She sat up with a groan. "Is that Larry?"

"Yeah."

She blinked the sleep out of her eyes. "What are you doing here?"

"I was busy today. No time to find another bed. I figured you were too kind to throw me out in the storm."

She eyed him a moment.

"I think you came out here to see me."

He shrugged, and the cat's relaxed body moved up and down. "Maybe I came to see Larry."

She knew she should question him, make him

reveal his agenda, but she couldn't make herself do it. She was glad to have company in the storm. And, recklessly, she was glad that company was Nick Bowman.

"C'mon out of the tub," he urged. "The storm has eased up. You're safe now." He reached out to help her up and the contact made her blood race. Her face felt hot, and she was grateful for the dark. Suddenly her absent defenses kicked in.

"I don't want you hanging around the Gray Lady," she said, stiffly, "or around here."

Considering that she had not withdrawn her hand from his, the words sounded childish and ridiculous.

"You want me to leave?" No. No. Never.

"You can stay here tonight," she said, ungraciously.

"Thanks."

Daisy pulled away from him and stalked out into the cabin. She needed some distance from his overwhelming masculinity. She found the Daisy blanket and threw it at him. "You can have the sofa, again."

He looked at her. "I thought we might use this time to talk."

She didn't want to talk. She wanted to slide her fingers up under his T-shirt. She wanted to feel the hard muscles there and in his shoulders. She wanted to press her restless body against him.

"About what?" She knew she sounded irritable.

He used the lightning reflexes that had made him such a great Formula One driver to haul her into his arms.

"The English Patient."

Her skin felt like a straightjacket. In contrast, her core melted. She couldn't seem to think.

"You know, the film that featured sex in a bathtub."

Sex. She fought an almost overwhelming desire to press herself against him. She had to remember he was the enemy.

"I have a better idea. Let's talk about what you want from me."

It was a perfect opening for a move, almost a proposition itself. She wondered if it had come from her subconscious. She wanted him. Despite his past cruelty to her sister and the present threat to her property, she wanted him. She'd always wanted Nick Bowman. She felt his stillness in the dark, but he did not come closer and the back of her throat ached. He was going to let the moment pass. He did not want her.

"Why don't you have a seat on the sofa. I'll get us a drink."

By the time they occupied opposite ends of the sofa, the wind had died down. The rain against the tin roof sounded like a slot machine paying off. Nick let out a sigh that grabbed at Daisy's heart.

"Tell me what you're really doing in Mayville," she said, in a low voice. "Tell me what you want from me."

She couldn't see the bleak expression in his gray eyes, but she knew it was there as he turned to look into the empty stone fireplace. The single candle flame cast shadows on the hard planes of his face and highlighted his long, dark, lashes.

"All right. Long version or short one?"

She shrugged. "I've got all night."

He didn't speak for a moment as if he needed the time to collect his thoughts.

"I always expected to take over Bowman's Biscuits," he said, finally. "I was told, and believed, I'd be Theo's successor in the dynasty."

Daisy nodded. Everyone in Mayville understood the old man's wish to keep the prosperous baking mix company in the family and of Nick's intended part in that plan. When Nick overturned the applecart seven years earlier, he left the town in a state of shock.

"At Theo's urging, I earned an MBA, and Buzz studied marketing. We expected to run the company together. That last summer we resumed our childhood friendship. We fished and talked and, well, sewed some wild oats.

That last summer. The summer of Caro's broken heart. Daisy leaned forward and braced herself for the story.

"One night we brought some girls out to the cabin, drank too much, and didn't return to town. Theo was furious. He'd always insisted that we not give the town any reason to gossip about us. He hauled us into his office the next morning and we went, hung over and ready to defend ourselves, but we didn't get a lecture about moral standards."

Nick paused, and Daisy waited while a feeling of trepidation worked its way up her spine. She resisted the urge to touch the arm flung over the back of the sofa.

"It didn't exactly go as anticipated. Pops lost his temper. Called me too immature to run a hundred million-dollar company. Told me to go race cars for a while. I fought him. Reminded him of the years of walking the straight and narrow compared with one night in the cabin with a couple of random girls."

Random girls. Is that how he thought of Caro? Her heart hurt for her sister.

"I told Pops, in my most condescending voice, that as the oldest grandson, I was ready for my role in the company. I told him," Nick's voice cracked, "that he was too old to run it."

All thoughts of Caro left her head. She heard the self-condemnation in his voice, but she heard something else, too. Pain. She found she couldn't wait any longer.

"What did he say?"

Nick's voice was flat.

"He told me it was a lie."

"What? What was a lie?" She realized she was holding her breath.

"He told me I was not the oldest grandson. I was a step-grandson. It turns out his son, Hamilton, married my mother when I was eighteen months old. Buzz is my half-brother. There is no Bowman blood in my veins. Not a drop."

Daisy's heart curled into a fetal position. In her world, family relationships meant everything, and she couldn't imagine how much Theo's words had hurt. She reached out to touch Nick's cheek and realized she'd moved the length of the sofa. He stiffened, and she dropped her hand. Nick didn't want sympathy. Not from her. She refused to be offended. This wasn't about her.

"So you left. And you stayed away."

"Turned out the old man did me a favor."

"You mean because you were free to pursue a

dream?"

"Family slows you down. Hell, it turns you into molasses. Somebody always needs something. You should know better than anybody. Your sister tells me you came home to take care of her."

Daisy's jaw dropped. "I wanted to come back to Mayville. I love my sisters."

He stared at her. "And your career? She said you always wanted to be a journalist. Like your dad."

"Dreams change."

"Not that much. From reporter to wedding planner is quite a leap."

She shrugged. "I like business and I like family. Happily Ever After allows me to combine the two. Caro's a wonderful dress designer. When the Gray Lady became available it seemed like fate."

His gray eyes were unreadable.

"What's the real reason you started the business? Your sisters are grown."

Under other circumstances she might not have told him. But he had just confided a dark, painful secret and in the small hours of the night, with the rain tap-dancing overhead, it seemed as if they were the only two people in the world. She sat back and prepared to share her story.

Chapter Eight

"After high school, Junie enrolled in a cosmetology school in Detroit. She went to a bar one night and met a man who swept her off her feet.

They eloped a few days later." Nick stared at her, intently.

"Turned out the guy was part of some Vegas crime operation. She figured out her mistake pretty fast, but he wouldn't let her go. Neither would the mob. They figured she'd seen too much. She and I talked by phone and devised a plan to use me as a decoy while she sneaked out of the hotel and took a cab to the airport. A few days later she got a call from police. Her husband died in a suspected mob hit. If she'd still been with him, they'd have gotten her, too."

"Jesus."

"At almost the same time, Caro was divorcing Quentin, and she needed a job. The timing was right to come back home. I'm not sorry."

He looked at her for a long minute. "Have you always tried to protect your sisters from their mistakes?"

"No, of course not. It's just, well, family sticks together."

"Have either of them tried to rescue you?" She smiled at him. He really didn't understand. "They rescue me every day. Without them I'd be alone in the world."

"Not necessarily. You could have a family of your own, a husband, kids."

Daisy shook her head. Talk about marriage would lead to talk about love, and that was too darn close to her feelings about him. She realized they'd strayed from the topic. "I understand why you left, but I'm still puzzled about why you returned." He looked away from her.

"I got a posthumous letter from Pops. He'd instructed a Detroit attorney to send it after his death. He asked me to come back to Mayville long enough to take care of a loose end."

Daisy could only imagine how it would feel to get a request from the grave.

Nick's eyes narrowed on her.

"Don't give me that sympathetic look. This is just business. It turns out that years ago when Pops and his wife lived in the Gray Lady he hid something in the cellar. Later he moved into Bowman Mansion and Randolph turned the house into a mortuary. In the letter, Pops asked me to find the item, which had been stolen, and to do my best to return it to the rightful owner."

Daisy's mind locked on the salient fact.

"There's something stolen in the Gray Lady?"

Nick shrugged. "It's a perfect hiding place. What's more off-putting than the dark, gloomy cellar of a funeral home?"

He had a point. Unfortunately.

"What is it?"

"I don't know exactly. He and Randolph brought it back from Germany." Nick's pause created an unintentional dramatic effect. "He said it was 'Nazi loot.'"

"Oh my God."

Nick's breath seeped out in a long sigh.

"Something called a blue diamond.' I don't know whether it's a painting or sculpture or if it really is a gem. I just know it's priceless and, apparently, radioactive." His eyes narrowed. "And I know one other thing. Someone else is after it."

She stared at him as the pieces clicked into place. Was this the reason for the anonymous letters? Daisy told herself she'd think about that later. At the moment, the only thing that mattered was Nick. "You're on a quest," she said.

"What?"

"Your grandfather set up a quest for you. You know, like King Arthur and the Knights of the Round Table. He challenged you to protect the family's name in spite of all that's happened. He offered you a challenge, Nick, and you accepted it. He wanted you back in the family."

"Bullshit. He sent for me to clean up a mess so Buzz wouldn't get egg on his face."

Daisy shook her head. "You know that's not true. He trusted you, Nick. It's a peace offering. He wanted to apologize for hurting you years ago."

"D'you see everything through rose-colored glasses? No apology was necessary. I'm not his grandson. And Theo could've found me any time during the past seven years. Why wait until he's dead?"

"I guess that's something you'll want to find out."

He cursed again.

"They need you, you know. Word is the company's

lost customers since Buzz took over." Nick's face darkened. "Not my problem." She studied him.

"I wonder."

He jumped to his feet. "Unlike you, I don't feel it's necessary to meddle in everyone else's business. Live and let live. The bottom can fall out of Bowman's Biscuits for all I care. I'm not sticking around."

She didn't argue with him. She wondered if Theo Bowman had been right to rake up all the old, hurt feelings. She put her palm on top of his closed fist. A moment later he shocked her by turning his hand upside down and closing his fingers around hers.

"Want to comfort me, Sunshine?"

She should pull her hand away. His touch sent gerbils racing through her stomach, and his scent filled her head. It's just chemistry. But it felt like so much more. It always had with Nick. Even during the years before they'd spoken. She gave him a reckless grin and the words tumbled out.

"You asking me to go to bed with you?"

He tightened his grip and did not smile. "No. I want you to give me access to the Gray Lady's cellar."

Of course. He'd come out here tonight to soften her up not to seduce her. She'd let her fantasies take over again. What a fool. With an effort she pulled herself together.

"You really don't want the house, do you?"

"Just access."

She nodded. At least she could give him what he needed. Daisy knew this would be the last time they'd talk in such an intimate manner. She still wanted to know what had happened seven years ago and this was the moment to find out.

"Nick, about my sister. You never meant to hurt her, did you?"

He frowned. "I told you I wouldn't hurt Junie."

Too late Daisy realized she should have kept her mouth shut. Caro would not appreciate a revelation of those long ago feelings to someone who could barely remember her.

"She's a little impulse. Junie, I mean. Sometimes things just happen."

He squeezed her hand and she realized he was still holding it. "Junie is safe with me."

****

Hours later Nick kicked off the Daisy quilt. It smelled too damn much like the woman for whom it was named, and that fragrance had kept him tight and hard and sleepless. She'd shocked him with the reference to sex. Hell. Maybe he should've done what all his hormones urged him to do. Maybe he should've kissed her and let things take their natural course. He wanted her badly enough. Unfortunately, he seemed to have developed scruples. He breathed deeply and willed the tension to leave his body. This made no sense. Daisy Budd wasn't even his type. But he responded to her warmth, her earnestness, her soft curves like a Pavlovian rat. She was capable of great passion in building her business and protecting her sisters. What would that passion be like unleashed on him? His blood zoomed south and his body tightened with need. Damnation.

****

Daisy kicked off her blankets. Again.

She'd spent the past several hours flopping from side to side. Occasionally she tried her back and then her stomach. She could find no comfort. Her body still felt hot and tight from those moments on the sofa. She'd wanted to taste his kiss. Just once. Merde as Junie would say. Who was she trying to kid? She was twenty-six years old, and, if past was prologue, she wouldn't be attracted to anyone else for another twenty-six years. The fact was she wanted Nick to make love to her.

Unfortunately, he was only interested in her cellar. Except that, for a few moments, she'd felt a connection, as if, given half a chance, he'd like to make love with her, too. She screwed up her face. It wasn't like she was asking for happily ever after with Prince Charming.

She just wanted one dance at the ball.

But it didn't look as if it would happen.

A rumbling sound rolled through the cabin.

Daisy pulled her pillow over her ears.

Dang. Even his snore was sexy.

****

The tinny notes of a cell phone roused Nick from his half-slumber. He heard Daisy's sleep-roughened voice and the rest of his body roused, too.

Well, hell.

It had to be one of her sisters. Since she was doing much more listening than talking, his money was on Junie.

Nick got up and moved into the small kitchen. He measured coffee into the familiar, dented percolator and pasted a smile on his face moments later when he heard the bedroom door open.

She wore a lime-colored, sleeveless blouse that tied at her waist and showed off a pair of well-defined, lightly tanned arms, a pair of pink cropped slacks and pink tennis shoes encrusted with rhinestones. A perfect outfit for a dyed-in-the-wool romantic.

"You're a symphony in pink," he said.

"Watermelon. "I'm a symphony in watermelon.""

He grimaced. "Don't remind me of fruit. Have you heard my stepmother's new name?"

"Harmony Lime? Sure. We're doing a handfasting for her coven this week."

He didn't really want to talk about Judith.

"I get the sense you like bright colors."

She laughed. The light sound got under his skin and slid into his pants.

"When you grow up sandwiched between two biscuit queens, you learn to distinguish yourself any way you can."

He studied her flushed cheeks, small nose, and wide golden eyes. Her flaming corkscrew curls were already fighting the confines of her barrettes.

"You don't need to compete with your sisters," he said. "You're unique."

She grabbed the sink in a mock faint. "Take me now, sailor."

"It would be a mistake." He said the words quickly, knowing he had to say them, wishing it were otherwise.

Her flush deepened and she shrugged.

"You made coffee?"

"And I cooked breakfast," he said. He handed her a bowl filled with Count Chocula.

"A useful man in the kitchen."

Nick poured her a cup of coffee and tried to remember the last time he'd waited on a woman and the answer came easily: never. "You got a call."

She nodded.

"Junie's worried. Her boyfriend never showed up for their date last night."

"Maybe he listened to the tornado warnings."

"He never checked in at home, though."

"Home?"

She made a face. "He lives at the Theodore Bowman Homeless Shelter."

He frowned at her. "You're letting her date a drifter?"

"She's twenty. I can't tell her to not to date someone."

"Unless it's me."

Her eyes widened. He couldn't decide which of them was more shocked by his curt words.

"That was a joke."

"Oh." She licked a drop of milk from her full lower lip, and sexual awareness surged through him.

"All I want," he lied, "is a decent night's sleep."

"Maybe," she drawled, "you ought to find a bed."

He wanted it to be her bed. "Yeah." He jumped to his feet. "You ready to go?"

A clear blue sky greeted Nick and Daisy when they stepped into the clearing, but there were signs of the storm. Despite the way the Jeep wheels were mired in mud, Daisy slid under the steering wheel.

"It's stuck," he said.

"I'll get it out."

He sighed. Sometimes a cockeyed optimist had to learn things the hard way.

He returned to the porch and settled in one of the Adirondack chairs.

"Nick? Aren't you going to get in?"

"I've got some time."

She shrugged, got in under the wheel, and gunned the motor. Mud flew and the tires dug deeper into the soaked earth. Stubborn woman.

"Need help?"

She didn't answer. She gunned the motor again. The tires dug a deeper groove into the mud. She continued to bury the vehicle until he got out of his chair, circled the cabin, and returned to the car.

She looked at the two-by-fours.

"What're those for?"

He held them up for her inspection before he wedged them under the vehicle's back wheels. An instant later he opened the driver's side door.

"Switch places."

"I've got it."

He couldn't believe she was arguing with him.

"Daisy, if you want to get to work before Christmas, get out of that car. Now."

"But it's my car," her words escalated into an incoherent shriek when he succumbed to an irresistible urge to scoop her into his arms. She wiggled and protested as he carried her to the passenger side and stuffed her in the car.

He backed away, annoyed and aroused.

A moment later he extricated the Jeep and slogged down Trout Lake Road.

"You might want to figure out what to tell people."

"Tell people about what?"

He glanced at her. Was she that naïve?

"I spent the night at your place. Again."

"No one will know, and, in any case, no one would believe we fooled around. I'm not your type."

He glanced at her. "You're not?"

"That's the word on the street."

Nick wished he could convey the wisdom to his bothersome libido.

"Omigod! Look at the tree."

He pulled to the side of the road. Damn. Where the hell was his head? He'd forgotten all about the fallen tree. He'd been forced to leave the Malibu out here last night and now they were knee-deep in mud. They climbed over the thick trunk.

"Go ahead," Daisy said, with a cheerful smile, "work your magic."

He made a choked sound. "I appreciate your confidence, but it'll take a truck and a winch to get this baby out."

"That's okay." She took her cell out of the oversized purse. "I'll call for a ride."

"Daisy?"

"Yeah?"

"You're gonna need a story."

"Hmm."

Twenty minutes later a silver convertible arrived with a stylish redhead at the wheel.

She spoke to Daisy but kept her cool, blue gaze on Nick.

"I happened to be at the Biscuit with Junie. She's got some lip-shaped scones in the oven, so I volunteered to pick you up." She turned to Nick and batted her synthetic lashes at him. "You sit up front, Sugar."

"Nick, meet Debbie Popple," Daisy said as she stepped onto the convertible's running board and climbed into the backseat.

"Ah. I believe I saw your calendar in the Biscuit.

'Debbie sells Mayville?'"

The real estate agent licked her lips. "Debbie sells whatever your little heart wants.

****

The commute to town had never before bothered Daisy. Normally she rolled down all her windows and cranked up her tunes. This morning, though, as she listened to Nick respond to Debbie's broad flirting, the trip seemed endless. She finally sat back and called Parker Wilson at the service station. He told her he'd use the county wrecker to get the tree off her road and Nick's car out of the mud. No charge.

She started to relate the good news, but at the sound of Debbie's wickedly seductive laugh, Daisy clamped her teeth shut. She reminded herself she had no claim on Nick Bowman. Thank God they hadn't gotten physically involved.

Main Street, when they finally reached it, looked like a battlefield after a skirmish between the oaks and the elms. Leafy branches lay on sidewalks and across the road.

The town's public works department which consisted of Wilmer Osgood and a handful of volunteers, scooped debris into trash cans which they dumped into the pickup with "Mayville Public Works" printed on the side.

Nick failed to consult her when he agreed to Debbie's suggestion to stop for coffee at the Biscuit, and, sick of being ignored, Daisy excused herself and set out on foot for Happily Ever After.

The brisk three-block walk helped clear her head. She went right up to her office and called Miss Florence, who assured her the flowers for the hand-fasting had survived the storm.

"I brought the Queen-of-the-nights inside, and I covered the tiger lilies. Everything sailed through without a bruise. It's been a delightful challenge to come up with the right posies for a handfast. I have to thank you again, dear. Flowers by Florence is, quite simply, my dream come true. Oh, I understand the Bowman boy got stranded at your place last night."

Daisy marveled at the grapevine's efficiency. She reminded herself Nick's overnight was hardly a secret.

"He'd driven out to the cabin to check on it. While he was there. a tree came down and blocked Trout Lake Road."

"No need to explain, dear. I know you are not the type for hanky-panky."

The comment irritated her. She had to stop living like a nun. In fact, she was danged tempted to find some willing male and indulge in a one-night stand. Just for the heck of it.

"On the other hand," Miss Florence said, "my niece's daughter, Gailee, well, she's a different story.

Perhaps you'd mention her name to Mister Bowman."

Daisy knew Gailee. She was about Junie's age and worked as a nail technician in Titusville. She was also a single mother.

"I don't believe he's looking for someone to date, Miss Florence. He won't be here very long."

"Nonsense. That old goat always intended to bring Nick back. Just in time, too."

"You've heard about the problems at Bowman's Biscuits?"

"I was referring to the dynasty. The family needs

an heir, and Buzz's marriage appears fruitless." Daisy did not know what to say to that. "Gailee is a sure thing. And, you know, she makes her own pickles."

Miss Florence wanted Nick Bowman to marry Gailee? Daisy pictured suave, urbane Nick Bowman with Gailee and her pickles.

"If the subject comes up, I'll mention your niece," she promised.

A moment later Caroline arrived with a bag of fresh biscuits. Her exquisite face wore the pinched, pale look Daisy remembered from earlier years. Her sister did not beat around the bush.

"Nadine said Nick Bowman slept at the cabin."

"He did. On the sofa."

Caro's eyes narrowed to slits. "Of course on the sofa. The question is why was he there?"

Daisy buried her irritation. It was important to soothe Caro, but how could she do that without revealing his secret? "I can't tell you, but rest assured it has nothing to do with you or any of the family."

Caroline's mouth tightened. "How long will he be in Mayville?"

There was no chance to answer the question. A familiar shriek echoed through the big house, accompanied by frantic footsteps on the stairs.

"OMIGOD! OMIGOD! OMIGOD!" Junie's words arrived in the kitchen before she did. "It's Adrian! OMIGOD! It's ADRIAN!" Her ponytail swished and tears poured from her eyes. Sobs and gulps punctuated her report.

"Call an ambulance," she yowled. "He's in the fountain!"

Chapter Nine

Daisy stared at the man face down in the shallow water of the Cupid Fountain. He wore a red and-orange Aloha shirt and sandals. Khaki shorts ballooned around his pale legs and long hair floated near his head like seaweed. Daisy knew immediately an ambulance would be no help at all. She glanced at her younger sister whose face was buried in Caro's shoulder.

"This is why he never showed up last night," Junie wailed. "And why he never came back to the shelter. He fell into the Cupid Fountain and drowned. What a cruel accident!"

Adrian, or whatever his name was, had certainly drowned. But was it an accident? Or was this the death predicted in the anonymous letter? Daisy wrapped her arms around her waist as a shiver coursed down her spine.

"This is my fault," Junie cried. "I didn't think he'd come with the tornado warning and all. I tried to call to postpone, but his cell wasn't working. Oh, I've turned into one of those creatures who lure sailors to their death!"

"Sirens," Caro murmured. She patted her little sister's back.

Daisy with horror stared at the body. She'd allowed herself to get distracted by her regrettable attraction to Nice Bowman when she should have been investigating the ominous happenings at the Gray Lady. This was her fault.

"Daze, you'd better call 9-1-1," Caro said, in a quiet voice.

Junie lifted her head. "You think they can revive him?"

Daisy retrieved her phone and punched in the emergency number.

"This is 9-1-1. How can I help you?"

"Miss Myrna? Why are you still on duty?"

Miss Myrna Whitcomb, an octogenarian photographer whom Daisy had hired to work at Happily Ever After, also worked the night shift for the Mayville Police Department. Daisy checked her watch. Miss Myrna should have been off two hours ago.

"Oh, hello, Daisy, dear. Arletta's girl went into labor, so I agreed to pull a double."

Daisy frowned. At eighty-plus years of age, Miss Myrna needed her sleep.

"How are things at the mortuary, dear?"

"Not good, Miss Myrna. I need you to send Jimmy over."

"Jimmy's at the Biscuit, dear, with the chief. You know Winthrop. You can't disturb his breakfast unless it's a dire emergency."

Winthrop Sharkey had served as Mayville's police chief for the past thirty years. The job suited him perfectly. What little crime there was in Mayville went largely ignored, and Sharkey spent all morning, every morning in his designated booth at the Biscuit.

Daisy knew the drifter's death would present a serious affront to the chief.

"This is a dire emergency. We've got a body at

Happily Ever After."

Miss Myrna paused.

"Is it Ora, dear?"

"No, no. Someone else. A man. In the fountain."

"My land! That must have given you a turn. Is Nick Bowman still with you?"

Daisy swallowed her exasperation. Thank the Lord there was never a real emergency in Mayville.

Almost never. She infused steel into her voice.

"Miss Myrna."

"All right, Daisy. I'll page the chief."

Miss Myrna, Daisy knew, had the Buttered Biscuit on direct dial.

****

Winthrop Sharkey looked like what might happen if a snake swallowed a mongoose. Well over six feet tall with thin, elastic arms and legs, he sported a gut that had long since defeated the efforts of his belt and could only be held in check by a pair of thick suspenders.

His passion for food was rivaled only by his dislike of work. Luckily his second-in-command had Mayville's criminal population under control.

Jimmy Crossfield, red-haired and freckled with the lithe body of a former high school wrestler, was both conscientious and smart. He was also a friend. He'd been Daisy's date to their senior prom.

The two officers stood by the fountain and stared at the body while Junie's hiccups broke the stillness of the summer morning.

"Who the hell is he," Sharkey finally asked.

"My boyfriend," Junie sobbed. "Adrian Smith." She told the tale of the aborted date.

"Where did you spend the night?"

The question, naturally, came from the ever alert Jimmy.

"At my apartment."

"She lives above the carriage house next to Caroline Budd's place," the deputy told his chief.

Sharkey stared. "So you didn't see this, uh,

Adrian last night."

Junie blinked. "That's what I said."

"Chief needs to clarify everything for the report,"

Jimmy soothed. He'd grown used to running interference for his boss.

"I knew something was wrong," Junie whimpered. "So I called Daisy."

Sharkey perked up. "Was she with the deceased last night?"

"Oh, do you have to call him that? Of course she wasn't. I always call Daisy when things go wrong."

Sharkey looked at Daisy. "Did you see this fella last night?"

"No, chiefChief. I live out at the cabin on Trout Lake."

"Not safe near the water in a storm."

Daisy nodded. "I hung out in the bathroom."

Sharkey grunted and fell silent. Daisy suspected he'd run out of ideas.

Jimmy broke the silence. "We should probably fish him out."

The men laid him on the flat stones that surrounded the fountain.

"That looks uncomfortable," Junie wailed.

"I don't think he'll mind," Caro said. "Let's go inside and get a cup of tea."

Sharkey's long face revealed a wistful expression, which Jimmy correctly interpreted.

"Before tea we need somebody to call it," Jimmy said. "And you'll need to authorize an autopsy."

"No call for that." Sharkey frowned as he, no doubt, contemplated the amount of paperwork involved in an autopsy. "Fella drowned."

"There may have been foul play,"

Sharkey shot his deputy a look of disgust. "Aw, hell."

"He's so pale," Junie whispered.

Jimmy moved toward her and took her arm. Everybody in Mayville knew about the deputy's crush on the youngest Budd sister.

"Let's get that tea," he said. "I'll call the M.E. when we get inside." He led Junie into the house.

Daisy's pulse quickened. She wanted to get a closer look at the body, but she needed some time.

"Caro, offer the chief some of those fresh biscuits, will you? I'll watch the body until the medical examiner arrives."

The chief hesitated. Daisy realized he felt some compunction about abandoning her with the corpse. She needed to make it all right for him.

"You could get statements from Caro and Junie," Daisy suggested.

"You be okay here, gal? Don't let nobody touch anything."

"No problem."

Daisy wrestled with her conscience over the direct lie but not for long. She needed to know how Adrian's death tied into the anonymous letters. She needed to know if there was a serious threat to her family and business.

She knelt by the body as soon as the back door swung shut. The prospect of sliding her fingers into the pockets of the sodden Bermuda shorts was distinctly unappealing, but she forced herself to do it. The leather billfold she found contained a laminated driver's license registered to Hiram "Spuds" Langston. Adrian Smith was an alias. She made a mental note of the Chicago address.

The hair stood up on the back of Daisy's neck, and she shoved the wallet back into the pocket before Nick rounded the corner of the yew bushes.

She stood as he strode across the courtyard.

"What the hell's going on?"

As always, his masculine presence took her breath away. Her heart slammed into her ribs.

"Junie's missing boyfriend. We found him in the fountain."

"Well, hell."

He knelt and removed the billfold again while Daisy entertained herself by admiring the way the ripples of muscle moved under his black cotton T T-shirt. She saw those muscles tense for a microsecond.

"What? What is it?"

He didn't answer. Instead he stood and waved at the men dressed in the identifying vests of the medical examiner's office. Jimmy returned a moment later.

Nick wrapped his fingers around Daisy's upper arm and hauled her away from the body. His touch sent ribbons of sensation coursing through her body and her knees felt weak. Dang. What was it about Nick Bowman that reduced her to a mass of quivering ganglions?

Just then the screened door burst open, and Junie flew across the courtyard and into Nick's arms. She related the story, accompanied by a new spate of sobs, into the soft cotton of his shirt. He stroked Junie's back, and Daisy looked away, horrified by the lightning bolt of jealousy that attacked out of nowhere. She caught a glimpse of Jimmy's grim face and the hostile body language of her older sister, and she knew she wasn't the only one affected by the scene.

Eventually Junie calmed down. "I want to do a memorial service for Adrian," she announced.

"Of course," Nick murmured.

"Something natural. Native American or Druid. I'm fairly certain the Wiccan ceremony requires a newt and a couple of doves."

"I think I can hook you up," Nick said.

He'd assured Daisy he had no use for his family, but the comment indicated he knew all about Judith's interest in Wicca. Was Theo's plan working? Would Nick choose to stay in Mayville?

She hoped not. It would be torture to live here in the same town with him. On the other hand, she wanted him to re-establish some kind of relationship with his family. She let out a soul-deep sigh, but, of course, no one noticed.

"Can you do it now, Nick?"

The warm smile he bestowed on her sister caught at Daisy's heart.

"Sure, princess."

A moment later they'd disappeared behind the hedge. Daisy turned to gauge Caro's reaction, but her sister had gone back inside.

Jimmy helped the medical examiners lift the body

onto a stretcher and into the van.

"They'll do an autopsy, but it won't be conclusive. Drownings wipe out most of the clues."

"How could it have been an accident," Daisy asked.

Jimmy shrugged. "He could've been drunk or stoned. Hit his head and blacked out."

"Stoned?"

"I heard rumors he's a dealer," Jimmy said.

Daisy closed her eyes. "When will she stop dating losers?"

"She looked pretty cozy with Bowman just now."

"He's not a threat." Her own words surprised her.

"What makes you think not? He's a chick magnet."

"He said he wouldn't hurt her. I believe him." Jimmy threw her a skeptical look.

"Did the M.E. give you a time of death?"

"Between eleven-thirty and midnight. Why?"

"Curiosity. The guy drowned in my fountain."

Jimmy's arm came around her. A friendly arm, warm and comforting. It did not incite either goose bumps or shivers.

"It wasn't your fault, Daze. Just a coincidence."

She knew she should tell him about the letters but she hesitated. Once the police came into it everyone in town would know, which meant everyone in the state would know including all the brides-to be.

Daisy decided to wait until she had a chance to do a little investigating on her own.

Half an hour later she headed for the homeless shelter on Main Street.

Half the people in town were in their yards cleaning up debris. She waved but didn't stop. Let them find out about the body from someone else.

The homeless shelter looked deserted, but Daisy tried the door handle just to make sure. She found Alice Bowman at the front desk. The woman wore a tailored outfit consisting of a taupe silk blouse and cream linen pants fastened with a gold belt. Alice dressed well, but she had six or seven years on her twenty-eight-year-old husband and they showed. She looked up over the pair of granny glasses perched on her nose. Her half-smile hid her alarming canines. Daisy smiled at her.

"Daisy. Are you here to see Isabelle about the hand-fasting?"

"No. You may not have heard, but the storm last night claimed a victim. Your resident, Adrian Smith, turned up in the cupid fountain this morning. It seems he drowned."

"Gracious, how horrible."

Her words were right, but her tone was unruffled. Alice Bowman's eccentricities matched those of the rest of the Bowman household, and yet, Daisy had always felt sorry for her. Even after seven years, she seemed like an outsider, not just to Mayville's first family but to the town itself.

"I figured I should see if there was a next-of kin."

"Of course." She pulled out a register. "There should be some information in here. Let's see. Adrian Smith, between jobs, permanent address in Detroit. That's all."

The address was probably as fake as his alias, but Daisy dutifully took it.

"Do you mind if I look through his belongings?"

Alice removed her glasses. Without the plastic barrier her eyes seemed closer together as if the frames had kept them from sliding toward her nose.

"I can't see any reason why not. Follow me."

Daisy followed the taller woman down a hall to a large, dormitory-style room. Next to each twin-sized bed was a small bureau, a bedside table, and a lamp. If a resident could erect imaginary walls, he'd have a cozy little space. The room was as neat and tidy as an army barracks except for the rumpled sheets in the far corner.

"Mr. Smith was our only guest," Alice said. "The only one we've had all summer. I guess Isabelle is right to fear the shelter will be underused."

Daisy nodded. Maybe if she didn't chat the other woman would return to the front desk. She didn't want a witness when she rummaged through the dead man's belongings.

"What a shame the accident had to happen at Happily Ever After."

"Mmm."

"It could be bad for business. But then, perhaps he was drunk. Or on drugs. You could hardly be blamed."

Daisy flashed her a half smile but did not reply. She didn't want to think about the loss of life in her fountain. She wanted Alice to disappear so she could start her search. A moment later, fate, in the form of a telephone call, rang and Alice excused herself.

Daisy knelt to peer under the bed where she found a duffle bag full of clothes. She opened it and recoiled. Phew! She held her breath and sifted through underwear, socks and aloha shirts only to find nothing but soiled laundry.

The dresser drawers were empty, as was the bedside table drawer except for the Gideon Bible tucked inside. Daisy wondered how many of the hundreds of thousands of gifted Holy Books were ever read. She leafed through it, not expecting to find anything at all, but she felt a surge of anticipation when the book naturally fell open in the book of Mark at chapter ten. She stared at the words scrawled on a post-it note.

124 Pine Street, Mayville, Mich. B.D. Blue diamond?

Her address. The words blurred before her eyes, and she felt a stab of fear. Her address. The Gray Lady.

Spuds Langston had not just drifted into town. Neither had he been interested in Junie.

Spuds Langston had come to Mayville because of the Gray Lady, and Daisy was certain she knew the reason why. The man had been after the Nazi treasure. She paused, lost in thought. How did the anonymous letters figure into this? Had Spuds been their author? She heard Alice's approaching footsteps so she slipped the paper in her pocket, closed the Bible, and returned it to its drawer.

"Daisy, when I told Isabelle you were here she said to offer you the beds from the shelter. I gather the Wiccans find it more romantic to sleep at a former funeral home than in a modern homeless shelter." Alice smiled.

"That would be great. I'll pick them up on Friday."

"That's covered," Alice said. "Isabelle said to tell you Nick can bring them over."

Nick and beds. Daisy felt a jolt of pure lust swiftly followed by a pang of regret.

Dang.

****

Junie found Harmony Lime both enthralling and

comforting. Nick decided it was safe to leave them alone together so he arranged to liberate his car from the mud and have it washed and delivered to him at the mansion before he returned to Happily Ever After. The murder would delay his search of the cellar, but more than that, it brought up some worrisome questions. Langston had almost certainly been after the blue diamond. Had he been working alone or with a partner? Had that partner killed him? Had he or she already found the treasure, or did he represent a threat to the Budd sisters?

Yellow police tape stretched across Gray Lady's front door, and Deputy Jimmy Crossfield sat in one of the wicker chairs on the front porch. He appeared to be filling out paperwork.

"House is sealed until further notice."

Nick detected a frosty note in the man's voice. Nick recognized jealousy when he heard it. So Junie had a redheaded suitor. Nick got back in the sedan, phoned the medical examiner's office, and was put through to the head man who assured him he would report the autopsy results as soon as they became available. In Clark County, it paid to be a Bowman.

Nick looked out his car window at the sun dappled pavement. He had a choice to make. He could break into the Victorian tonight and find out once and for all if the blue diamond was there, but he couldn't do that and keep an eye on Daisy Budd at the same time. And he'd have to keep an eye on her. She was a reporter at heart and she was, understandably worried about her sisters and her business. As soon as his back was turned she'd investigate her way into trouble. He had no choice. He had to get the answers himself—and fast—

and he had to keep her safe, which meant he had to spend the night at the cabin. Nick groaned.

That, he knew, wouldn't be safe for either of them.

He turned the ignition key and revved the motor, then he pointed the Malibu toward the office of Bowman's Biscuits. He needed a computer.

Arthur Sneed, hollow-eyed and skeletal, looked like a malaria victim. Something had to be done about this damn company before it killed Isabelle's husband. The attorney summoned Nick into his office.

"There's something I'd like to show you." He handed the younger man a bound report.

"Could you look that over? It's the study we commissioned for the overhaul."

"Forget it," Nick snapped. He'd gotten tangled enough in Mayville concerns. The company, Theo's company, was none of his business.

"No strings attached," Arthur said. "Buzz contacted me this morning. He'll be back in a couple of days. You've got a good mind, Nick, and, like it or not, you own a third of the company. I'd like your input."

Shame filled Nick. It was utterly unfair to stick Arthur with the responsibility for Bowman's Biscuits. The man already shouldered too much responsibility. He took the report, but it burned his fingers. Theo's company.

"I'll look it over."

Chapter Ten

Most of the homes in the streets nearest Main had been constructed just after World War II to provide homes for returning soldiers and their new wives. Caroline's house on Fillmore was no exception. The Cape Cod's deeply slanted roof and twin dormers gave the sturdy little house a homey look. Rhododendrons lined the front walk, and there was a wooden porch in the back.

During the year she and Stevie had lived on Fillmore Street, Caro had made bright curtains and slipcovers for her home. Daisy's heart always warmed when she drove up to the house. She found her sister at her drafting table focused on a new dress design, absorbed, as always, in the work she loved.

Daisy pulled a chair up to the round oak kitchen table and opened her laptop. She searched for any information about Spuds Langston, a resident of Chicago.

By the time Stevie arrived home from an afternoon outing with a friend, Daisy had decided her next move. She believed Langston had come to Mayville in search of the loot, but there was something more than greed involved here. Why would an outsider leave the hateful letters and the dead butterflies? And then there was Spuds' suspicious death. The man had had a partner but who? Daisy intended to find out.

There was no help for it. First thing in the morning, she'd head for the city of the big shoulders.

Caroline's tongue peeked out of her mouth, a sure indication she was lost in creative thought.

"Let me take Stevie to the Biscuit for dinner," Daisy said.

"Mmm."

Daisy smiled. It was as much response as she would get, and it was all she needed.

****

Nick spotted his prey the minute he stepped inside the Biscuit, not a difficult task as the restaurant consisted of six booths, six tables, and a lunch counter, all visible from the door.

She wasn't alone.

Nick paused for a moment, arrested by the picture of the animated young woman and the small boy. The child's face glowed, no doubt as result of capturing his aunt's complete attention. Nick recognized the feeling. Daisy Budd had a rare ability to make a guy feel like the only star in her sky.

Nadine glanced at him as she stepped out from behind the counter to deliver two plates of the special to Daisy's table. Nick gestured to indicate he wanted the same. The tables were full, and, although no one looked directly at him, he knew he held the attention of all the diners except Daisy and her companion.

"Hey," he said, interrupting them. He grinned at the boy. "Mind if I join you?"

The momentary irritation on the child's face turned to delight. A racing fan or just a kid who missed his father?

Nick slid into the seat across from Daisy.

110

****

Daisy knew he'd arrived because of the telltale hairs that stood up on the back of her neck. Also, she'd seen him come through the door. She didn't look directly at him, but everything inside her tightened, and the air was suddenly full of electricity. Daisy frowned at her reaction. She felt like a five-year-old who'd spotted Santa for the first time.

As Nick crossed the room, her heart beat faster and her adrenaline surged. She couldn't seem to think. In that moment she would have given her right arm not to feel the intense attraction. She wanted her control back. She wanted her life back.

She wanted not to want Nick.

Naturally arrogant, Nick made no apology for interrupting the téte-a-téte. He slid into the booth next to Stevie, grinned at the child, and got a sweet smile in return. Good grief. The Budds were all putty in the man's hands. Even the young ones. Resentment washed away some of Daisy's sensual haze. She reminded herself to keep her head.

"You're the race car driver, right?"

Nick nodded. "Formula Ones."

Stevie wrinkled his nose. "Formula? That's for babies."

Nick flipped his paper placemat, pulled out a pen and using swift, bold strokes, drew a detailed picture of his racer.

The man had serious artistic talent. Who knew?

"Wow," Stevie said. "Can I keep it, Mr. Bowman?"

"Nick," said Nick. "Sure."

He answered all the child's questions with a

patience that shocked Daisy, and he told stories of his experiences on the track. He didn't romanticize it, either. He described the fumes and the fire and the danger of crashes.

Daisy fought a sense of profound admiration. Nick had lost his home and his future, but he'd pulled himself together and pursued a dream. Just the way Theo had. The old man must have been proud of his grandson's hard work, his courage, and his persistence.

Suddenly, she knew she'd been right about Theo. He hadn't disowned his step-grandson. He'd set him free so Nick would have a chance to find success on his own terms. The old man must have expected the Prodigal Son to return. How sad it had happened too late.

But perhaps it had to be that way.

"Did you ever get hurt?"

"Just a few broken bones. I've been lucky."

"Did you get a cast? What color?"

"Orange." He made a face. "A cute nurse talked me into it while I was still groggy from the operation."

"Cool. Can I ride in your car?"

Nick smiled at the boy. "My car's out in California. I've got a couple of races scheduled for this summer. I'm thinking about hanging up my wheels and devoting my time to the business."

"You're going to retire?" The involuntary question came from Daisy.

"Thinkin' about it."

"But it's so cool," Stevie interjected.

Nick shrugged. "Seems like it's time."

When had he decided that? From his bemused expression, Daisy suspected he'd surprised himself with the statement. Maybe Mayville was having an effect on its long, lost son.

"You interested in one of those fresh-baked cookies up in the case?"

Stevie nodded in response to Nick's question.

"They're called snickerdoodles," he explained.

Nick pulled out his wallet and drew out some bills. "Can you tell Nadine this is for our three dinners and three snickerdoodles?"

"Sure, Nick."

"Mister Bowman," Daisy corrected.

"I mean, Mister Bowman."

"Nick is fine," Nick told the child as he scampered off his bench and headed for the counter. "He reminds me of myself at that age."

Daisy stared at him, much struck by the observation.

"What did you find at the homeless shelter?"

Her eyebrows rose.

"Alice told Aunt Isabelle who told Junie who told me when I picked her up this afternoon."

"The grapevine." They said the word in unison.

Daisy yelled, "Jinx!"

"What's that?"

"Shh. You lost the jinx. You can't speak at all until someone says your name three times." He squinted at her.

"Hey. I don't make up the rules. But I enforce 'em." She grinned at him.

Stevie reappeared with a plate of fresh cookies.

"Nadine sent extra for you, Nick," he said.

Nick held up one finger so that only Daisy could see it.

"She said you used to like 'em back when you lived in Mayville. Did you live in Mayville before, Nick?"

Nick held up a second finger.

"I used to live in Titusville with my dad. Now me and my mom have a nice house, and I wish Daisy could come live with us. Not Junie. She's too noisy for every day, but she's fun. Do you like Daisy, Nick?"

The man beamed at the child and leered at Daisy. "Yes. Yes, I do. And Nadine's right. I like snickerdoodles, too."

The cookie was halfway to his mouth when the front door slammed open. Caroline, pale but beautiful in a white summer sweater with matching slacks, trembled with rage. All conversation ceased as she approached Daisy's table with all the banked anger of a gunfighter with a score to settle.

She grabbed her son's hand and pulled him off the bench, but her focus and her words were for her sister, and they broke Daisy's heart.

"I trusted you." A moment later the door shut behind Caroline and the little boy. Daisy's throat ached with the effort not to cry. She started to get up to go to Caro when she became aware of strong fingers around her wrist.

"What did I do," he asked, in a voice too low for anyone else to hear, "to make her hate me so much?"

Daisy shook her head. How could he not know Caroline had loved him?

"We dated a few times. It was casual. She acts as if I stole her firstborn."

"Let me go. I need to talk to her."

"Wait until tomorrow. You don't want to have it

114

out in front of the boy, and she needs time to calm down. So do you."

Daisy felt his warm hand cover her cold fingers. She wanted to tell him to let her go. The words wouldn't come. Her vision blurred.

"Don't cry," he said, softly. "You'll work it out with your sister."

She wanted to tell him the tears weren't for Caroline. At least, not just Caroline. She clamped her jaw shut.

"I'll drive you back to the cabin," he said.

Her heart fluttered. She wanted him to spend another night with her, but it would be a huge mistake. "That's not a good idea."

"It is if you want to get home. The Jeep's still out at the lake. Remember?"

Well, dang. "All right, then."

The tree trunk was gone. Nick drove up to the clearing and parked the car. Then he hiked back to the Jeep while she went inside to feed Larry and await her doom. No, her fate. She wanted Nick. It looked like she was going to get her wish, at least for one night. She didn't know whether to be happy or sad.

Daisy showered and changed into a clean oversized T-shirt and thought about the man waiting for her in the tiny living room. In the past twenty-four hours, he'd shown her a new side. He wasn't just a womanizing race car driver. He was a survivor, a man who had learned to reinvent himself, a man who had the patience to talk to a child and the empathy to soothe a hurt woman.

He was, also, a man her sister had loved. After he'd left that summer, Caro had fallen into a depression.

While Gran, Daisy, and even Junie watched and worried, she'd married Quentin. Stevie's appearance brought them all joy, but Caro had never really regained her placid cheerfulness. Was it all because of Nick? But he said they'd only dated a few times. Was that long enough to fall in love? Daisy considered her own reaction to Nick, and her lips drew into a thin line. She knew the answer all too well.

The Wedding March shrilled from the cell phone in her purse. She stepped to the bed to answer it and felt a rush of relief when she recognized Caroline's voice.

"Daze? Don't hang up on me. I want to apologize. I know I overreacted."

"No, you were fine," Daisy lied.

"I think it's a mistake for you to spend so much time with Nick. He's dangerous, honey. I'm afraid he'll hurt you the way he hurt me."

"Caro." Daisy forced herself to ask the question. She had to know. "Were you in love with Nick Bowman?"

Caroline took too long with her evasive response. Daisy's chest felt tight.

"We'd only gone out a few times. But after that night in the cabin he just disappeared. No phone call. Nothing. It hurt. He has no heart, Daisy.

Please, please don't let him get close to you."

Too late.

"He'll only be in town a few more days and like everybody keeps saying, I'm not his type. I'll be fine."

"Stay away from him, Daze."

"I can take care of myself." A moment later, though, when she stepped into the empty living room, she knew she'd be able to keep her promise.

Disappointment swamped her. Nick had returned to town. He hadn't wanted to spend another night with her. Undoubtedly, that was for the best.

It took several hours of tossing, turning, and arguing with herself before she really believed that.

In the morning, Daisy dressed in black slacks, a black silk T-shirt with a bright red blazer and black sneakers. She planned to enter Langston's office through the front door during working hours, but she intended to be ready if a night stealth mission was called for. She threw a change of clothes into an overnight bag, left plenty of water and cat food for Larry, and stepped out of the cabin and into the predawn morning. She'd just reached the Jeep when she heard his voice.

"Where do you think you're going?"

She swung her oversized purse and caught him in the mid-section.

He grunted. "Good God, woman! What've you got in there? An anvil?"

She froze. "Nick?"

For the first time the hair on the back of her neck had let her down.

He wrapped her up in his arms and held her close. The steady, comforting beat of his heart played against her ear. After a few minutes, the fight-or-flight response tailed off, and she forced herself to move away from him.

"Why are you here?"

He gave her a weary smile as if he appreciated the irony of the question. She wondered how many times he'd heard it since he arrived in Mayville.

"I spent the night in the Malibu."

She glanced at the car parked next to her own.

"Why?"

"Why'd you think?" He sounded cranky. She noticed he put one hand against his ribs. Good grief! Had she bruised him with her purse? "Remember the murder? You're alone out here."

"But I wasn't in danger."

He didn't bother to reply.

"Let's go. We'll take the Jeep."

"What? We'll take the Jeep where?"

"To Chicago, Daisy." His brow cleared and his eyes gentled.

She stared at him and mentally admitted defeat. She couldn't out-think this guy.

"Either we drive together or I follow in the Malibu." He yawned. "I choose the first door. I haven't slept in a bed in three nights."

"Whose fault is that?"

"Yours." He opened the driver's side door. "Hop in."

"Why don't you stay at the cabin and get some sleep?"

She wondered at her last ditch attempt to resist the outcome she wanted. Pride, probably. He fixed her with a look.

"Get in. And wake me when we get there."

He slept for six hours and awoke without prompting when the Chicago skyline appeared on the horizon. He yawned and stretched like a big, lazy, sensuous cat.

"Looks like we've reached the Emerald City."

Chapter Eleven

Nick had gotten the requisite forty winks, but they'd been troubled ones.

The fact was, he'd been troubled throughout his visit to Mayville. He simply could not shake off the sense of trepidation he'd felt since the body had been discovered at Happily Ever After; a body that was NOT Miss Ora.

Clearly, Theo had told someone else about the mysterious blue diamond, and that someone had put both Nick's investigation and the Budd sisters at risk.

A pain shot up his forearm, and he forced his fingers to unclench. He'd known Daisy would insist on investigating the murder herself. She had a proprietary interest in anything that happened at the Gray Lady, and the woman was no fool. She'd undoubtedly put two and two together and figured there was a connection between the drowning and the Nazi loot. Nick told himself he'd had no choice but to accompany her to Chicago, but he knew it was more than that.

He'd had enough of fighting the unexpected attraction. He knew his resolution to keep his hands off Daisy Budd would not make it through this trip, but he no longer cared. At least, not enough to resist. He wanted her and he knew she wanted him and they were both adults. He'd resigned himself to the prospect of fireworks in the old town tonight, and, on the whole, he wasn't sorry.

He just hoped that, when this was over, she wouldn't be sorry either.

"Nick?"

Her voice sounded husky, and his blood heated. He wanted to skip the investigation and go find a room. Or, better yet, pull off into a parking lot and go at it right there. Patience.

"Yeah?"

"I should probably tell you about the letters."

The recital only took a few minutes, but when she'd finished, he'd forgotten all about sex. Mostly. Goddammit. Something very wrong was going on here.

"You okay?"

"Just some second thoughts. We're gonna find a motel and drop you off. I'll check out Langston's office alone."

"Not a chance." Her voice was very firm. "While we're on the subject, how do you know Adrian's real name?" She answered herself before he could speak. "Never mind. It was a silly question. You're a Bowman in Clark County. By the way, I Mapquested the directions. They're in the glove box."

"Don't need 'em. Take this exit."

She glanced at him.

"I went to grad school here. I know the city."

They drove through a south side neighborhood down on its luck. The massive brick homes built at the turn of the last century for large, wealthy families were now apartments and small offices, carved up like Thanksgiving turkeys. The large structures gave way to shabby row houses, many of them vacant. They found Langston's street address, but there was no sign on the door.

"I'll park one street over," she said.

"Park in front. We can keep an eye on the Jeep." And it would make for a faster getaway.

They mounted the three steps of the front stoop and crossed a porch, and Nick's sense of unease increased. Daisy fumbled with her big straw purse and extracted a credit card.

"This isn't Bloomingdale's."

She shot him a disparaging look then tried to slide the piece of plastic into the crack between the door and the sill.

"This is how you're planning to get in?"

"Yup."

"That why you wore a cat burglar outfit?"

Color bloomed in her cheeks, but her eyes laughed up at him.

"Somehow it seemed more appropriate last night when I planned my wardrobe. I thought I might be doing this at night. Alone."

"Ah." He wanted to watch her struggle with the door. He wanted to tease her and joke with her and pull her down on the scrubby grass in Spuds Langston's non-existent front yard. Wrong time, wrong place he reminded himself. He drew a set of skeleton keys out of his pocket.

"Allow me." An instant later they walked down a dark hallway which led to a narrow staircase. There appeared to be only one office. The frosted glass on the top of the door revealed the unreadable remains of gilt letters.

Spuds Langston had run a modest operation by any standard. Nick used the skeleton key again. This time he pulled Daisy behind him before he turned the knob. No sense taking chances.

The dingy windows robbed the afternoon sun of its brilliance, but it was clear the room was almost empty. A single metal desk sat in one corner and a pair of battered file cabinets stood next to an incongruous fireplace. A stained percolator and a hot plate rested on top of the cabinets.

The emptiness of the room did nothing to decrease his sense of wrongness.

"C'mon," he said. "Let's get this over with."

She paused and looked at him.

"What's wrong?"

"Something's not right." He waited for her to dismiss the unspecific fear, but she just nodded. After Theo blindsided him seven years earlier, he'd honed his instincts just as he'd protected his heart. He looked at Daisy's wide eyes and wished he'd brought a gun.

Daisy seemed to read his mind.

"It'll be okay. I'll check the filing cabinets," she said. "Why don't you take the desk."

"Yes, ma'am."

A moment later he heard the rattle of a drawer followed by a disappointed gasp.

"Empty! There's no way to tell if this is even Spuds' office."

"Somebody's cleaned out the desk, too."

The two side drawers contained nothing. Nick opened the top drawer and picked up a number two pencil with teeth marks on it. He gazed at the paperclips, rubber band, and rusted scissors, but he picked up the business card and stared at the name. Buzz Bowman.

He remembered the bill addressed to his brother from Spuds Langston. It almost made sense. But why the hell had Buzz purchased "services" from a down-and-out P.I. destined to become a murder victim?

"Nick? You okay?"

He put the card in his pocket. The sense of danger he'd had from the moment they crossed the threshold nearly overwhelmed him. He had to get her out of here.

"Let's go."

He hooked her arm with his fingers and pulled her toward the door. He wasn't able to keep the anxiety out of his voice when he barked at her. "Move, woman."

The noise on the other side of the door sounded like cat scratches. Dammit to hell. He thrust Daisy behind him, opened the door, and confronted a child.

The kid was maybe fourteen, Daisy's height and dressed in baggy cutoffs and a Snoop Dogg T-shirt. He should have been at band camp instead of holding a gun on a couple of housebreakers. Shit.

"Who are you?" His pre-adolescent voice cracked. Daisy spoke before Nick could.

"You want to know our names? Since when do muggers ask for identification?"

The boy's curly eyelashes flickered, and his none too-steady hand tightened on the gun.

Great. Armed and nervous.

"Take it easy, pal."

Dark eyes stared at him. "I asked you a question."

Nick blocked Daisy and prayed she wouldn't make any sudden moves before he got the situation under control. It was no big surprise when that prayer fell on deaf ears.

"We came by to see Mister Langston," Daisy said.

She stepped out from behind Nick and the gunman's hand jerked.

Nick's gut clenched when the barrel turned on Daisy. Daisy.

"Don't mess with me, fuckers. Put your hands up."

Nick raised his hands. "Daisy," he ordered, "do as he says."

She ignored him. "I've got money in my purse and you can have it," she said. "But you really shouldn't wave your weapon around. Most accidents with guns happen to the people who own them. You could get hurt."

Nick kept his eyes on Snoop. Right now their biggest threat was an accident. The kid didn't want to shoot, but that didn't mean he wouldn't.

"Get behind me," he growled.

Daisy's incessant talk provided some distraction. He inched closer to the boy. Another couple of feet and he could knock the revolver away from mini-Rambo.

"Tell me your names, or I'll blow your boyfriend's face off."

Daisy's response was prompt.

"We came all the way from Michigan to speak to Spuds Langston. And he isn't my boyfriend. He used to date my sister."

Nick gritted his teeth.

"Ain't nobody 'sposed ta be here."

"Are you the caretaker? Does Mister Langston pay you to watch the place?"

The boy turned to Nick. "Can't you make her shut up?"

Another eighteen inches. Maybe twenty.

"Probably not."

"I take it you like Snoop Dogg," Daisy said.

"Shut up!" The boy sounded desperate. "Tell me your names, or I'll shoot." He swiveled and stepped back, the gun firmly trained on Nick's chest. Well, hell.

Daisy's shriek could have shattered glass.

"Officer!"

The gunman slammed his hands against his ears, and Nick saw his opening. He grabbed the kid's wrist, but he was too late. Daisy's huge straw purse exploded against Snoop's face. The boy cried out in pain and rage and squeezed off a shot.

An instant later he screamed in pain, dropped to the floor, and clutched his thigh. The gun skittered across the uncarpeted floor.

"She made me shoot myself," the boy howled. "Goddamn bitch!"

"Nick! Call 9-1-1!" Daisy stripped off her jacket, dropped to the floor, and pressed the fabric against a geyser of blood. The bullet had hit an artery.

"I'm sorry," Daisy told the victim, "I didn't intend for you to get hurt, but it's a good lesson in gun safety."

Nick called emergency. Blood seeped from the wound despite the pressure. He ripped off his gray T-shirt.

"Go down and meet the ambulance. I'll take care of this."

Snoop writhed on the floor, alternately cursing Daisy and moaning. His cries escalated when Nick tightened the tourniquet on his leg. The gray fabric turned red but more slowly. Nick knew Daisy wouldn't approve of his tactics. He waited until she was out of earshot before he spoke.

"Shut up and listen to me. I want a name. Who paid

you to protect this office?"

The boy's filled with tears. "Am I gonna die?"

"No. Did Langston pay you to hang around here?"

The dark lashes rested against the smooth, sweat-streaked cheekbones. God, the kid was young.

"Yeah. Mister, you gotta call my mom."

"I will. What did he want you to do?"

"Huh? What?"

Any minute now the kid would go into shock. Nick tightened the makeshift bandage to keep him conscious. "What's your mom's name? Where is she?" The kid provided the information.

"All right. Langston. What'd he pay you for?"

"Gave me a phone. Told me to get names from anybody who showed up. Nobody came though till you and the redhead."

Snoop's voice faded, but Nick heard the approaching siren. Thank God they were in a high crime district. "Give me the phone."

"No."

"I'll pay you for it." With one hand he grabbed some bills from his wallet and slipped them into Snoop's pocket where he found the phone.

"Tell Mom I'm sorry I skipped class."

"Where d'you go to school?"

He didn't need the information. He just wanted to keep the kid conscious.

"Thurston Middle."

He continued to hemorrhage, his face ashen. Shit.

The boy passed out as the EMTs pushed in the door. Nick filled them in on the situation while they worked. One technician slid an oxygen mask on the kid and the other started an I.V. He was on a stretcher and into an ambulance in record time.

"Where're you taking him," Nick heard Daisy ask the driver.

"Chicago Memorial. Cop'll want to talk to you." Double shit.

"Give him some money," Daisy ordered.

The kid had threatened them with a gun, and she wanted to subsidize his summer?

"Taken care of," he said, in a low voice. He gripped her upper arm and piloted her outside and over to a young cop.

"Listen, Officer, my wife's sick. Let me get her home. I'll meet you back at the station."

"I can't let you do that."

Nick sized him up. Young, handsome, shiny wedding ring. "Morning sickness."

"Oh." Understanding dawned in the officer's eyes. "Sure. It's the station at Twelfth and Gatley."

He tipped his hat. "Hope you feel better, ma'am."

"She will," Nick replied. "In nine months."

"Your names?"

"Brad and Kathy Naylor," Nick said. He stuffed Daisy into the passenger side of the Jeep. "Thanks, Officer. Kathy likes to barf in peace."

****

Nick drove to the nearest corner, turned and turned again.

"We've got to contact that young man's mother."

"As soon as we get some distance from the cops."

"Brad and Kathy Naylor?"

"My neighbors in L.A."

"Are they nice people?"

"I don't know, Daisy. I saw their name on the

mailbox."

"Oh."

He drove to the edge of town and turned into the driveway of a Holiday Inn Express.

"They have a complimentary breakfast," she said. He shot her a look and she made a face. "Not that it will matter to us. We can leave as soon as we make sure the boy's all right."

"Go in and register. Please."

Squirrels raced up and down her spine.

Register? As in spend the night?

"I can't go anywhere without a shower and clean clothes."

Her eyes dropped to his chest. His breathing caused his muscles to lift and flex. It was mesmerizing.

"Daisy."

"Just admiring the view."

The gray eyes widened and glittered. What on earth was she doing? This was no time to embark on a passionate one-night stand. Except it was the perfect time. She swallowed hard.

His eyes narrowed, suddenly. "Do you have any idea," he said, through gritted teeth, "how close you came to getting shot?"

"He pointed the gun at you. He would have shot you."

"He wouldn't have shot anybody. I had the situation under control."

"How could I know that? You're a race car driver not James Bond." Suddenly she remembered the skeleton keys. "Or have you done this before?"

A guilty expression crossed his face and disappeared.

"I'm a guy. You should've known I'd protect you."

She crossed her arms across her chest. "That sounds macho, but that hasn't been my experience.

The men in our lives haven't protected us at all."

"You and your sisters."

She nodded. "I've gotten used to protecting them. You should have trusted me to take care of you."

"I'll let you take care of me, baby. Later."

The sudden drop in his voice, the huskiness sent her senses spinning. Was he talking about sex? Was this really going to happen?

"Daisy?"

"Hmmm?"

"Can you run over to that store and get me some clothes?"

"Okay."

"Check in first, okay?" He gestured to his blood streaked jeans. "I look like something out of SAW IV. The desk clerk would call the cops."

She grinned at him.

"Maybe they'd send Officer Morning Sickness."

****

He knew he shouldn't take her to bed tonight.

He knew he'd never make it until tonight.

Damn. Was it the danger-fueled adrenaline? He didn't think so. He'd wanted her from the first, back when it made no sense. Back when he'd considered her not his type.

She wasn't any type at all. She was unique. Optimistic. Unpredictable. He watched the red water run into the drain. The cold spray was effective on the bloodstains, but it had zero effect on his arousal.

He got out and dried off, ruefully aware the

terrycloth around his waist did nothing to hide his excitement. She was laying out his clothing on the bed. The vision made him even harder.

She turned and sucked in her breath when she saw him.

"I hope these fit," she said, finally.

He had no intention of finding out anytime soon.

Her voice fell to a whisper. "I need a shower, too."

He counted to sixty by tens before he joined her.

Chapter Twelve

The cool water felt good on her hot skin. Was she doing the right thing? She'd waited a long time for the right guy without even realizing it. Nick was Mr. Right for her. Daisy knew that, for him, she was Ms. Right Now, but at the moment, that seemed good enough. She wanted him and she knew, in the very depths of her heart, she would never forgive herself if she gave up this chance to have him. No matter how much it would hurt later.

And it would hurt a lot. Nick Bowman wasn't marriage material _ not for Daisy Budd. But a one-night stand? Why not? Everybody did it. Some people, like Debbie Popple, did it frequently.

She leaned against the tile of the shower stall and closed her eyes so she didn't see him come in and, for once, she didn't smell him, either. When he pulled back the curtain and stepped into her space, her heart exploded.

Nick rested his palms against the wall on either side of her. She was surrounded by his impossible masculinity. His eyes framed by black, wet lashes were very gray and focused. She couldn't get any air in her lungs as she watched his lips lower to hers, and then it didn't matter because she was breathing him.

After a few seconds she broke the kiss. "Daisy?"

"Oxygen," she squeaked. "I need oxygen."

His slow, sensuous smile melted what was left of her insides. He cupped the back of her head, and she felt the strength of his fingers in her hair.

"Trust me. I can provide everything you need."

He took her mouth again, and she circled his waist with her arms and slid her palms up the firm, well-defined muscles of his back. Without much experience she didn't know what she was supposed to do, but she knew she wanted to get as close to him as possible. She wanted to feel every inch of him. Her fingers glanced over a few ridged scars and, in one spot a patch of too-smooth skin. A burn. From a car accident? Her heart stuttered, but there was no time to focus on pain from the past.

There was too much pleasure in the present.

She was sandwiched between the tiles at her back and his hard chest. He ground himself against her, and she gasped at the hot breath on her neck and the rough sounds in her ear. She slid a hand down his flat abdomen and found the incontrovertible proof of his desire.

"God," they breathed, simultaneously.

"Jinx," she whispered, automatically. He clearly didn't want to play.

"Baby, your hand feels so good." He kissed her hard and deep. After a moment he lifted his head then licked the shower water off the hollow at the base of her neck and the top of one breast. She gasped.

His wicked tongue moved lower until he finally closed his lips around one hard-tipped nipple. At the same time, he used his thumb and forefinger to caress the other breast. The sensation triggered explosions of desire through her entire body. She writhed against the tiles and clenched her fists. He cursed and retrieved her hand.

"Too much too soon, baby. I want this to last."

And then his big hand smoothed down her midriff and over her stomach until it reached the super sensitive spot between her legs. She marveled at how easily he'd found it, and, just for an instant, she thought of the dozens of other women in his life. And when he slid a finger inside her, she couldn't think at all.

"You're soaking wet."

Wet and throbbing. He stroked her harder and faster. She felt something coil inside her until it was so tight she thought she'd burst.

"Please," she whimpered. She twisted against him. "Please."

"It's okay, baby. I'll take care of it. I know what I'm doing."

She believed him. She threw back her head and hit the tiles.

"Ow!"

"Damn." He cupped her buttocks in his strong hands and lifted her. "Put your legs around my waist, honey. I can't wait."

She felt the sharp thrust, the overfull sensation, and the tightness, but his skillful stroking diverted her. The tension became almost unbearable, and she held her breath.

"Breathe, Daisy," he murmured. "I don't want you to pass out until after you come."

Her orgasm hit like a meteor out of the sky. She shrieked and dug her nails into his shoulders. From a distance, she felt him stiffen as he gripped her buttocks and groaned into her neck. They rode the storm together and finished with her body still pinned against the wall, her legs around his hips and his head on her breast. Tender feelings flooded her as she listened to the snare drum beat of his heart and stroked his back as he gulped for air.

"That almost killed me."

"Is that a complaint?"

"God, no. I don't know about sex in a bathtub, but it sure as hell works in a shower stall."

Sex. She was glad he'd used the word. She needed to remind herself this was a one-night stand.

Tenderness did not belong here, just raw animal sex.

That was enough.

****

The magnificent afterglow was extinguished by guilt.

What the hell had he done?

The first time shouldn't be in a motel shower. Not for a woman like Daisy. He'd probably bruised her spine on the unforgiving tiles, and he hadn't even bothered to ask whether she was protected.

His stomach heaved. He'd been religious about birth control with all those women who were on the pill. He prayed Daisy was in that number but figured it was unlikely. Her passion was infinitely exciting but new and raw. He recalled the tight inner muscles and the way they'd milked him. His blood rushed south. Hell. He could take her again right now. He pressed himself against her and suppressed a groan. He couldn't. He'd already tied a noose around his neck and hers.

The least he could do was not tighten it.

Her hand found him and he shuddered.

"Nick?"

He fought the urge to plunge into her welcoming body.

"Daisy, is there any chance you're on the pill?"

****

She grimaced. If she forgot this was a casual affair he'd be sure to remind her. He waited for an answer and she felt the shift in his tension. He was more than turned on. He was worried.

"Yes. There's an excellent chance."

It was the most bald-faced lie she could remember, but she didn't regret it. The pride that had been sadly missing in the shower kicked in. She had no intention of trapping him in a loveless marriage.

He must have sensed her withdrawal because he took her hand and led her out of the shower, grabbed a towel, and dried her off in a business-like way.

"I shouldn't have been so blunt," he said. "I've never failed to use birth control, but you had me forgetting my own name. I had to make sure. You'll make a wonderful mother, someday, Daisy, but I don't want a family."

She nodded. "You won't get one from me."

Relief filled the gray eyes. She bit back tears and forced a smile.

He slid his hand inside the towel and found the magic spot between her legs. She could see his arousal, hard and heavy.

"In that case, how about round two?"

She met his eyes while she stroked him. He made a sound and scooped her up. An instant later she was on her back. He came up over her and she welcomed him.

She'd turned into an idiot.

It was dark when she awoke. She turned to look at him. His hands were stacked under his head.

"Want to get some food?"

He turned toward her. "Was Happily Ever After Caroline's dream, too?"

Needle pricks of guilt and pain attacked her. Caro. Daisy could imagine her elder sister's reaction to this. "It was the right solution for all of us."

"That isn't what I asked."

She swallowed around a lump in her throat. She didn't want to talk about Caroline. Not now. Not here.

"Did she ever want to work for a design house in Chicago or New York?"

"That wouldn't work for Stevie."

"People raise children in cities."

"It's hard to do it alone. In Mayville she has Junie and me. And Quentin."

"He seems to have limited interest in his kid."

Daisy didn't want to talk about Quentin or Stevie, either.

"Junie's a free spirit," he went on. "Is she bored in Mayville?"

"Of course not. She's got friends and work. What else is there?"

"Fulfillment. Independence. Adventure."

The words hurt because there was truth in them. "No one is completely free, Nick."

"I am."

She wanted to remind him that he'd come home in answer to Theo's summons. She wanted to point out that in L.A. he might be free, but he was alone. But he wouldn't want to hear any of that, and it wasn't her business, anyway.

"Junie needs to grow up before she leaves home."

"Maybe she can't until she's allowed to make her own decisions, her own mistakes."

He found her hand and laced his fingers through it.

"I know you've provided them with stability and love, Daisy, but at some point, you have to let go."

She shook her head. She'd tried letting go. It hadn't worked. She refused to try to explain that to the anti-family man. She rolled to her feet and realized she was naked and cold. He moved with incredible speed and she was pulled into his heat.

"I don't want to make you sad, honey. Sometimes an outsider can see more than those on the inside."

It was on the tip of her tongue to ask him whether he always psychoanalyzed his one-night stands. Instead she focused on how he'd characterized himself.

An outsider.

Not a surprise. Theo had not only kicked him out of the family seven years earlier, he'd assured Nick he could never belong. He had no reason to cherish family or trust it. Nick Bowman had decided to live life as an island. The thought made her sad.

"A person can't have everything," she said, gently. "Our mother left years ago, then our dad died. Gran gave up her retirement years to raise us. We have seen the importance of family first hand. It's worth some sacrifice to us."

He held her close and kissed the top of her head, their friendship, such as it was, restored.

The Chicago deep dish pizza and the moonlit walk on Lake Michigan with Daisy rounded out the evening. Daisy's eyes closed in the Jeep, and she figured they'd crawl into bed and pass out the minute they got back to the motel room.

She was half right.

They made long, slow, sweet love until they were moist, panting, and limp. The morning came too soon. A part of Daisy wished they could stay where they were forever. She tried to imagine sixty years in a cinder block motel room and she giggled.

She watched Nick step into his new jeans, zip, and button them. She sighed.

"We have to talk about this situation."

She paused in the act of brushing her hair. He wanted to talk about the relationship?

"Langston sent my brother a bill for fifty grand. That ties him to my family. His death ties him to the Gray Lady. I think we can assume Langston was searching for the blue diamond." Ah. That situation.

"Buzz is implicated."

Daisy shook her head. "That makes him sound guilty. I've known your brother a long time." Theo's younger son was shorter and stockier than Nick. He'd played football at prep school and in college. His blue eyes radiated warmth and friendliness, and everybody in town liked him. "Buzz wouldn't be involved in a murder."

"You never really know people, Daisy. That's something you'll learn."

She shook her head. "Leaving aside Buzz's character, it wouldn't make sense for him to hire Langston then kill the guy before he found the loot. Besides, he's in rehab."

Nick scrubbed a hand over his five o'clock shadow. He scowled.

"Whoever killed Spuds must've sent the letters and left the dead butterflies," Daisy went on. "There's more going on here than pure greed. Someone is angry and, I suspect, hurt." She sighed.

"I think it's time to go to the police."

"Not yet."

She studied his face. "Why not? Because of the negative publicity for Bowman's Biscuits? You know, Nick, for a guy who doesn't believe in family you're very protective of yours."

He shot her an annoyed look, but she merely raised her eyebrows.

Chapter Thirteen

Daisy was uncharacteristically quiet as they consumed the complimentary rolls, juice, and coffee, and Nick had time to reflect on the dream. He'd had it occasionally since he'd left seven years earlier but never after a night of sensational sex.

Of course he'd never had that kind of sex with anyone else. The realization shocked him.

The dream was a true story. Pops, tall, slim and with a full head of thick gray hair, walked out onto the dock. He wore a red flannel shirt, jeans, and boots, and he had his arms around his two much smaller companions whose clothing echoed his. Nick inhaled the scent of pines and cold morning air and felt the leap of excitement. He was with the two people in the world he loved, and it was the happiest day of his life.

Suddenly everything changed. Each boy caught a baby trout. Buzz claimed he would gut and grill his catch, but Nick couldn't bear to kill the shiny, silvery creatures. His stomach lurched as the tiny fish twisted and turned, desperate to regain their freedom.

And then Pops told the boys to release their catch.

Intense relief mixed with soul-deep shame inside the elder grandson as Pops overruled Buzz's protest. Nick remembered the exact words.

"They're small fry. We'll let these fellers get more meat on their bones before we eat 'em." He'd looked at

Nick. "And we will eat 'em. That's what they're here for.

"That's their job. Everybody's got a job, son. Our job is to take care of Bowman's Biscuits and the family."

Bowman's Biscuits. The family.

Nick had always known his importance in both until the morning Pops had caught and eaten him.

"You okay?"

He looked into the melting golden eyes of the woman next to him. Daisy banished the cold and the bleakness. He wanted to pull her over the console and hold onto her. He didn't, of course. The one-night stand was over.

"I'm fine."

****

Daisy wanted to make her way behind the mask. She wanted to tear away his pain and cynicism. She wanted to make him feel warm and connected but she could see his resistance. He kept his face forward. He wouldn't let her in. She reminded herself she'd been expecting this. Last night had been last night. She had no future with Nick Bowman. But she wasn't ready for the present to end. Not yet.

She stared out at the countryside and watched the weather deteriorate. Overcast skies eased into a solid gray canopy and finally, by the time they hit the western border of their own state, the wind rippled through the crops. It bent cornstalks almost to the ground while above them lightning danced and played in the charcoal sky.

Daisy watched Nick's fingers tighten around the steering wheel. A muscle moved in his hard jaw, and a faint layer of perspiration covered his upper lip. The dreary sadness of the first part of the trip had disappeared with the advent of the storm. The tension outside the Jeep was reflected inside. Tension and sexual heat.

Nick wanted her. She experienced a surge of happiness and a sense of feminine power. He wanted her. The storm was turning him on. She corrected herself. The storm and her.

Every nerve ending seemed to be waiting for something. She shivered with sensual awareness. He noticed.

"Cold?"

"No." She deliberately waited a beat. "Hot."

He sent her a quick glance but rain dashed the side of the Jeep in a harsh gust and he fought to control the wheel.

"Sorry," he muttered.

The apology was for his lapse in concentration on the road. She deliberately misinterpreted it.

"I'm not."

Thunder clamored and lightning played with the tops of the trees. Rain splattered the car like a garden hose gone berserk. Nick kicked the wipers up to their maximum speed, but the blades couldn't keep pace with the rain. She wondered that he could see to drive. The sinews popped up on his powerful forearms as he battled the steering wheel.

"We should pull over," she said.

He didn't take his eyes off the road. "I'm a professional driver, remember?"

The undercurrent in his voice wasn't irritation. She noted the bulge in his lap. The storm couldn't cure that.

She placed a hand on his rock hard thigh and the car slipped. He cursed.

She conducted a short debate with herself. She didn't want to die on I-94. On the other hand, the temptation to push him was strong. She leaned over and covered his crotch. He jumped.

"Mother of God! What the hell are you doing?"

She didn't think it was a serious question. She tightened her fingers and felt him swell. He cursed again. A sense of delicious power sliced through her.

"You're making my panties wet," she murmured. "Holy Christ."

The rain on the roof reminded her of their night in the cabin. She'd wanted him then, too. The windshield wipers swished and slashed in a rhythmic dance. The inside of the vehicle was dark and as private as the cabin.

Daisy concentrated on her task. She molded and shaped the male flesh under the denim. She loved to feel it ripple and pulse under her hand. She watched a drop of sweat makes its way over stark cheekbones. She reveled in his soft curses.

She knew it was dangerous, but she couldn't bring herself to care. He belonged to her, in this moment. She called the shots. She wanted more. She reached for his belt.

"We'll wind up in a tree." His voice was hoarse, raspy.

"No, we won't. You're a professional driver, remember?"

She dipped her fingers into his waistband, and he sucked in his breath to give her more access. This time when she worked his buckle he didn't protest. She unzipped slowly, carefully, tantalizingly. When the cloth separated his heavy erection leapt into her hands, and he made a strangling sound.

"No more."

She ignored the plea. This sex play was completely different from what they'd done last night, but it was equally erotic. Moisture seeped between her legs and dampened her slacks. She stroked the turgid flesh lightly then with her fingernails. He shuddered and jerked.

Daisy was Magellan, DeSoto, Christopher Columbus. An insatiable explorer. She wanted more. She slipped her fingers underneath to fondle his testicles. They shifted in her palm, marbles in a protective bag. A needy whimper came from one of them. Her. She loved touching him. She wanted him inside her.

"Pull over."

"Bad idea."

He meant because they'd tacitly agreed to leave their one-night stand in Chicago. Grief barreled into her, but she thrust it aside as the rain exploded against the windshield.

"I can't see" he muttered.

She glanced at his face. His eyes were squeezed shut.

"Pull over," she repeated. "This isn't safe."

****

Holy shit.

He didn't get it.

This wasn't new territory. Okay, it hadn't happened on wheels before, at least not with a storm raging outside, but hell, he'd been touched lots of times.

Not like this.

Daisy's touch was magic.

He was employing every ounce of his considerable control to keep from erupting in her hands. Or maybe that's what she wanted. He knew she was loving this. She was loving him. It made the experience more intense. And much more dangerous. He heard her say pull over, and he was shocked.

Hell, he'd forgotten he was driving. He blinked at the windshield. Shit. Zero visibility even for a man with exceptionally sharp eyes. At least they were alone on the road. He spotted the overpass seconds before they reached it. He braked, expertly, and slid into the dry protection under the bridge. God. He wanted to haul her over his lap and bury himself so deep that neither one of them would ever forget. He reached for her, but she was faster. Her fingers surrounded his aching shaft she brought him into her warm, welcoming mouth. "Jesus!"

She paused, uncertain, but he didn't think he'd survive if she stopped. He wrapped his fingers in her curls and held her head in place. She licked and sucked with more enthusiasm than skill.

"So damn good."

He pulled at her hair and suppressed a groan. He needed to come, but he tried to hold off. He never wanted this to end.

The urgency got the upper hand, and he felt the familiar gathering as his body prepared for a mind-blowing climax. His back arched and he gritted his teeth against the pleasure that was almost pain.

It didn't happen. She'd disappeared. His heart rapped hard against his ribs.

"Nick."

"Honey," he croaked, "finish it."

"Nick."

"C'mon, baby. You can't leave me like this." He heard the rapping again. "Somebody's at the door. A cop." Nick opened one eye.

Fuck. He was ready to launch, and there was no way in hell he could zip up his jeans.

She leaned across him, providing some cover but torturing him by inadvertently rubbing her body over his desperate erection. She unrolled the window. His arousal flexed and bowed under the pressure of her weight.

He held his breath.

"Good morning, sir," the cop said. "May I see your license and registration?"

He couldn't move. He couldn't even speak.

"I'll get it," Daisy offered. He closed his eyes and tried to endure the feel of her hand in his pocket. Nick gritted his teeth and hung on.

She gave the documents to the officer. The beam of his flashlight must have picked up the sweat on Nick's face.

"Please get out of the vehicle, sir."

There was no way. He shook his head. "Just shoot me."

Daisy gasped and intervened.

"Officer, as you can see we were, uh, getting a little passionate. It's completely my fault. We got married yesterday in Chicago."

"Chicago?"

"At the Hyatt-Regency on Wabash. Do you know it?"

"No."

"Oh. Well, it was a beautiful ceremony. My dress was this really elegant shade of eggshell with lots of lace, and Nick looked unbelievable in his tux. Well, you can imagine, I mean with his coloring."

"Daisy, the officer doesn't want the details."

"Oh, of course not. I beg your pardon. I wanted to explain we had too much champagne and a little fight and well, we didn't get a real wedding night, if you catch my drift."

Nick rolled his eyes at her.

"The point is we're headed back to Detroit to see family, and we won't be alone again for quite a while, so I started fooling around. That's why Nick can't get out of the car."

The heat in his cheeks surprised him. He'd have figured there was no spare blood left in his body.

The cop handed her the documents and peered at Nick. "Just give me the damn ticket," Nick hissed.

"You need to chill out, son. Marriage is best when you give the ladies what they want. At least that's what Anna tells me."

"Who's Anna?" Daisy asked.

"My third wife. You're newlyweds, so I'll let it go this time. In the future, save this stuff for the bedroom. Or at least the garage. And son, you really should get her a ring. No wonder she was pissed off."

****

It was the cop with his ridiculous comment about the ring that made her finally face the truth.

She didn't want a one-night stand with Nick.

She wanted a whole life with him.

She'd fallen in love with the anti-family man.

The realization felt like a sharp knife sticking

between her ribs, but she couldn't claim it was a surprise. Daisy suspected she'd loved him since the morning he'd walked in on her and Miss Ora. Maybe even since their less-than-memorable conversation seven years earlier.

Despite the name of the wedding boutique, Daisy considered herself a practical person, optimistic but not romantic. If she'd been asked she would have said she didn't believe in love at first sight. But she loved Nick Bowman.

She stared out at the passing cornfields. She didn't bother to second guess herself. Would it have hurt less if they hadn't made love? Probably. But she'd have regretted the missed chance for the rest of her life.

She faced the truth with stoicism. In a perfect world, she'd have chosen Nick as her mate. But even in a perfect world he wouldn't have chosen her.

That was just the way the cookie crumbled.

He looked at her with his devastating slow smile. "I've got to admit," he said, "life with you is never dull."

Chapter Fourteen

He pulled the Jeep into the clearing next to the Malibu.

"If it's all right with you, and the tape's down at the Gray Lady, I'll search the cellar tonight."

"Fine. I'll come down and help you after I change clothes."

He noticed she wasn't smiling.

"Not necessary. I know you're busy."

She shrugged. "I need to do some work at Happily Ever After anyway."

Well, dammit to hell. If she showed up he'd never be able to keep his hands off her or his mind on the blue diamond. On top of that, he'd hurt her feelings. He told himself it was just as well. He needed to get back to L.A. so the time in Mayville would fade from his mind like Brigadoon. He scooped the stuff out of the backseat and carried it into the cabin. Larry twined around his ankles.

"Thanks for going with me," Daisy said.

He hadn't given her any choice. Had he had a choice himself? The interlude in Chicago seemed inevitable.

"Thank you, too."

It was a ridiculous exchange. Thanking didn't come into the past twenty-four hours. Blame, maybe.

"I'm going to take a shower."

She'd meant he was free to go, but the words transported him to the previous afternoon and the most memorable shower of his life. He was instantly hard and furious about it. Furious about all of it. Daisy Budd was not built for a fling, and he'd known that.

"Daisy, we should talk."

She shook her head. "Not now."

Her choked response twisted something inside his chest.

"We could get married."

The shocking words made his jaw drop. It took a full ten seconds before he figured out that they'd come from his own mouth. Did he mean it? He soon discovered it didn't matter.

"No," she said, with a smile. "Thank you." She turned toward the bedroom. "I'll see you later."

Shock turned to fury on the drive back to Mayville. This was all Buzz's fault. His mission from Theo should have been short and simple. Buzz had fucked it up. And where the hell was he? It was time his pseudo brother answered some questions. The anger kept his mind off his ridiculous suggestion and the way she'd rejected it.

****

The warm spray sluiced off her shoulders and massaged her tired muscles. Everything would look better after the shower. She tried to focus on the tasks she needed to complete for the handfast, but she couldn't block Nick's ridiculous suggestion out of her mind.

We could get married.

Somehow that made everything so much worse. If she accepted the one-night stand for the casual sex it was, she could handle it. Once the concept of happily ever after reared its head, the night in Chicago felt tawdry and indulgent and she felt unworthy.

Damn Nick anyway.

She pinned back her wet curls and pulled on a pair of olive green capris and an oversized yellow tunic with fuchsia trim and wished, for the first time, she didn't have to go to Happily Ever After.

When the screen door banged, her heart leaped. He was back.

"Daisy?"

Her stomach clenched, and she wrinkled her nose at the mirror. The day was going downhill like an alpine skier. "In here, Caro."

The willowy blonde stuck her head into the bedroom. Her smooth cap of hair contrasted with the chaos of Daisy's curls. Today it was pulled into a neat knot at the back of her head. She was the picture of elegance in her sleeveless blouse and black capris marred only by the bright patches on her cheeks.

"Where were you last night?"

Daisy sighed and wished she could put this off. "In Chicago. I wanted to see what I could find out about Spuds."

"Spuds?"

Daisy realized Caro was in the dark. She filled her in, half expecting hysterics and surprised at her sister's inattention. The clear blue eyes bored into Daisy's face.

"Were you with Nick?"

She wasn't going to lie. Not to Caro. She braced herself for a lecture. "Yes."

"Oh."

"Oh? That's all you have to say?"

"Have you got anything to drink except kumquat juice?"

"Water."

"I'll get some," Caro said. "Let's sit on the porch."

Settled into the matched Adirondack chairs the sisters stared out at the lake. The storm on the west side of the state hadn't followed them home. The late afternoon sun made even the pine needles shine and the water reflected the image above. Daisy could imagine no lovelier, more peaceful place on earth.

"I hate this place."

Caro's words lacked their usual anger. For some reason that was harder to take.

"I can't remember the last time you were here."

"Seven years ago."

Daisy winced. She hadn't intended to evoke that memory.

"Why won't you stop seeing Nick? You're going to get your heart broken."

"We're just friends." Dang. Another lie. "He's interested in the murder investigation, too." She waited for Caro to notice the slip, but her quick mind was on something else.

"You're just friends?"

Daisy winced at the hope in Caroline's voice. She hated herself for lying to her sister.

"I think you should tell me what you're afraid of."

"He's a bad influence."

"I don't see that."

"How could you? You're a babe in the woods! You've had virtually no experience with other guys."

"I've dated. Some."

"Nobody like Nick."

Daisy couldn't argue with that.

"Please, Caro. Tell me what's wrong. Did you love him? Do you still love him?"

"I can't talk about this, Daze."

"Now or ever?"

"Ever. I need you to trust me. Just this one time."

"You want me to promise to stay away from Nick Bowman, but you won't tell me why."

"Yes."

It wasn't an unreasonable request. She knew she'd spend very little time with Nick in the future. She should have agreed to keep the peace. The Old Daisy would have agreed.

"I can't promise, Caro. I love him."

Her sister went very still. "You mean you slept with him."

"That, too."

"Oh, Daisy."

Daisy listened for anger but heard only grief. She knelt by her sister's chair. "Nothing is going to change, dearest. Nick is going back to L.A., and I am staying here. I would never leave you and Junie, not even if he asked me. He hasn't, of course. And he won't. Please don't be sad."

"Oh, Daze." Caro stared out at the lake.

Daisy wished the beautiful scene could bring her sister peace and comfort.

"I have something to tell you."

Daisy smiled, encouragingly. Caro didn't smile back.

"Isabelle Bowman came into Happily Ever After this morning. She found a report commissioned by her husband and Buzz Bowman. She told me it was a last desperate attempt to save the company."

"Which means a last desperate effort to save the town. I didn't realize things were that bad."

"The expert concluded there was no chance for survival unless the company branches out. The specific suggestion is a prepared food plant and the best, most cost effective location is the Gray Lady property."

"That's not new. Arthur Sneed has contacted me on that twice."

Caroline looked at her, sympathy in the lovely blue eyes.

"The Bowmans have filed a petition for eminent domain. With their connections they'll get a judgment in their favor in record time."

Daisy grimaced. She knew eminent domain was a legal loophole created to allow wealthy corporations or municipalities to buy up private property for the "greater good."

"I'm not surprised. I knew they wanted the property. We'll get a good lawyer, Caro. We'll fight them."

"Daisy, Nick knows about this. Arthur gave him the report. As far as Isabelle knows, he's on board with it."

"I don't believe that."

She didn't want to believe it but it made sense. Bowman's Biscuits and the family meant more to Nick than he'd admit. Even to himself. In a showdown Nick would side with the Bowmans. She searched for a hole in the argument.

"Wait. Why would Isabelle tell you?"

Caro shrugged. "Revenge, maybe? Apparently

Arthur's having an affair with his administrative assistant."

"Mrs. Harter? Impossible."

"Junie heard it from her new best friend Harmony Lime. The point is, Nick isn't on your side."

Daisy didn't reply. What on earth was there to say?

Tears filled Caroline's turquoise eyes. They tugged at Daisy's heart.

"I'll be fine," Daisy comforted her automatically. "I have you and Junie."

"I don't know how to tell you this, so I'll just say it. Jillian Armstrong wants me to work for her."

"Jillian Armstrong the designer? Fantastic! She recognizes your talent, Caro. Oh my gosh, what a break through. I told you so. Oh, finally something worth celebrating."

"She wants me to work in-house. In Chicago." Daisy gazed at the other woman.

"It's a long commute. We can pick the slack up here, and you'll come back on weekends."

"I'm moving to Chicago, dear. Stevie will go with me. Junie wants to go, too. At least for a while."

They were all leaving. Nick had seen what she had missed. Her sisters needed room to spread their wings. They needed to be away from Mayville. Away from her.

"I think it's great." She cleared her throat. "I can't wait to visit when you get all set up."

"You won't have time to visit. Not if you try to run Happily Ever After by yourself. We want you to come, too."

"No." Daisy would not allow herself to think about that. There wasn't a lot she could do for her sisters, but she could give them their freedom. "No. I'll hire some folks to help out. Miss Patience Lanham could use the income."

"Daisy, I know why you wanted the boutique. I know it was meant to give us jobs and to keep us together. I'm sorry things are turning out this way. I just feel that I have to take this chance. I have to go. And I have to get out of Mayville." She got to her feet. "If you want to talk later please come over. I'll be home."

Home. In the cozy house on Fillmore Street. The one she and Stevie moved into less than a year ago. The one they would move out of soon.

Daisy stood on the porch and waved as her sister's tail lights disappeared down Trout Lake Road. It had been a week full of lessons. Her instincts, for example. Couldn't trust 'em. Ditto her judgment. She'd learned she needed to listen to what people were not saying.

And she learned that soon she'd be alone. She wondered why the prospect was so frightening.

****

The plan to search for the cellar hit a snag when Nick arrived at Happily Ever After and found Junie in the midst of a wedding crisis.

"Nick!" She maintained her smile despite the shrill note in her voice. "I'm so glad you're here. This is January Jane Pixley and her mother, Mrs. Pixley."

"January Jane," said the elegant mother. She extended her hand, palm downward. Did she expect him to kiss it? "I named my daughter after myself."

He glanced at the younger woman. Long, brown hair flowed down her back. She wore a tie-dyed shirt with a peace sign, cut-off jeans, and bare feet. A retro hippie.

"You can call me J.J.," the girl said.

"We've got a problem," Junie said. She sounded desperate. "A color problem."

J.J. eyed Nick's gray T-shirt and jeans. "You sure he can help?"

He lifted one eyebrow.

"Do you know Brad Pitt and Jen Aniston? I did the colors for their wedding."

"Are they even married?"

J.J. ignored Junie's muttered question, her eyes on Nick.

"Well, see I want something psychedelic, maybe crimson and chartreuse for my colors. Mother," she made the word sound like "serial killer," "wants to tone it down. She's chosen rose and spring green. The guests will be bored to death."

"I just don't want to incite a riot," Mrs. Pixley said. "Or cause anyone to lose their lunch." J.J. glared at her mother.

"Ladies, ladies," Nick soothed. "We're on the same page. Red and green. It's a matter of degree." He leveled a slow smile at each. He was well aware of the potency of his smile. The atmosphere was charged with a new sexual energy. "Here at Happily Ever After we like to integrate the weddings with nature. Many are held in our courtyard which naturally includes every shade of green including chartreuse." He smiled at J.J. "Our florist can provide a spectrum of red flowers, too, which we can mix and match until you are perfectly happy with the combination."

He went on about nature and colors until their eyes glazed. Either he'd bored them into a coma or seduced them. Six of one, half a dozen of the other. He reached for their hands. "Whatever the final decision on colors they will complement your natural beauty."

"You're good, Nick," Junie said, after the Pixleys' departure. "You may have missed your calling. I'd never have picked you as a colorist."

He grinned at her. "With good reason. I'm color blind as a bat. That argument, though, was about control. I'm an expert on that subject."

His cell phone buzzed and he answered.

"Nick, dear," Isabelle said, "I want you to come to the mansion for dinner." Not again.

He could refuse, of course, and with good reason. The murder made the blue diamond lethal. The mission was no longer a mere tying up of Pops's loose ends. He needed to protect the future of Daisy and her sisters, and it wasn't just a physical threat. The consultant's recommendation to acquire the Gray Lady through eminent domain could destroy Happily Ever After.

Nick needed to convince Isabelle and Arthur not to sue. He repressed a sigh. "I'm on my way."

Chapter Fifteen

In spite of everything, the hot pink sticky note on her computer made Daisy smile.

D—

We had a "drop-in" client. Mon Dieu! A real bridezilla in the making! She and her mom were in a snit about colors but Nick fixed it! (Here Junie had drawn a smiley face.) *The guestrooms are set up with beds, tables, and lamps. Nadine found a recipe for "Batwing Punch," but don't worry—there are no actual batwings in it! I'm making Cauldron Cookies. Don't ask what's in them. You don't want to know! Caro's looking for you. See you a demain.*

Love,

Me

The O in love was heart-shaped and there was a P.S. With Junie, there was always a P.S.

P.S. I almost forgot. Mr. Foote sent over the hearse to pick up a coffin. Apparently Miss Olive told him he could have it. Guess that's one down! As Cherry Ann would say, Huzzah!

Daisy's amusement turned to nostalgia. Dear Junie. She'd always been the reckless one while—at least until seven years ago—Caro had been smart, focused, and driven.

Daisy was the rock. After their mother left and Gran came, both she and her dad had frequently praised her for her practicality, her common sense. What would they say now? She'd ruined everything by trying too hard, holding the girls too close.

She longed for a do-over. Should she have stayed in Grand Harbor? She'd liked being a reporter, but she hadn't felt the same magic during the moments she'd spent with her dad at the Mayville Monitor. Even now she could remember the thrill of clacking keys and the scent of freshly cut newsprint. She suspected the "ink" in her veins was more about the connection with her father than the actual field of journalism.

Family. It always come down to family. She was happiest with them, taking care of them. She was happiest being needed, but she hadn't always considered their needs.

Caro and Junie were entitled to lives of their own. How had she not seen that?

Well, she saw it now. Her jaw tightened. She would let her sisters go and Stevie, too, but she would stay in Mayville. She would build her little business and she would not give up the Gray Lady. She would fight the Bowmans—including Nick—and she would win. She would have her Happily Ever After.

****

Nick found his stepmother in the foyer directing Finch who was attempting to load a gravestone onto a dolly.

"I'm sure Finch has other things to do, Judith.

I'll take that." Finch didn't argue.

"Thank you, dear. And, remember. I'm called Harmony Lime."

Nick refrained from rolling his eyes. "Where's it going?"

"To the mortuary."

"You mean over to Happily Ever After?"

"Hmm? Oh, yes. That's right."

Judith looked different tonight. She'd abandoned her diaphanous robes in favor of black designer jeans, four-inch heels, and a black T-shirt with Yes, Wi-can, spelled out in rhinestones across the front.

"Yes, Wiccan?"

"It's pronounced, 'Yes, We-can.' A take-off on the campaign slogan of somebody or other. I'm certain the bride would prefer to use her own altar, but she and the Grand Wizard travel in a small RV.

Naturally, she'll use her personal theme." Whatever the hell that was. "Naturally."

"Could you move one of the coffins into the old crematorium? That's the bridal suite."

"The newlyweds want to sleep in a coffin?"

Judith's smile, the one that had induced Buzz's father to marry her, spread across her face.

"I don't imagine there will be much sleeping."

Nick tried to block out the image of the high priestess and the grand wizard locked in marital embrace in one of Uncle Randolph's coffins.

"Oh, and Nicky, could you transport a few beds from the homeless shelter to the Gray Lady? The coven members are excited about staying in an old mortuary. Better access to the spirits, you know."

Nick considered the coven house party. It would turn Happily Ever After into Grand Central Station. If he failed to find the blue diamond in the next two days, the event would impede his progress. On the other hand, it would temporarily discourage the treasure-hunting-stalker-murderer. He fought the impulse to shadow Daisy until the danger was past. He'd destroyed their easy friendship with the one-night stand. He didn't want to hurt her more than he already had.

He loaded the altar into the back of Judith Bowman's van, and he sucked in the evening air. The slanted rays of the sun bathed the emerald lawns and the flower beds in a golden light. He remembered the summer evenings out here catching fireflies with Buzz, lying in the perfectly manicured grass to gaze up at the stars. A sense of longing twisted inside. He missed his brother. He missed Pops. His mind drifted to the adventure in Chicago, and he realized, with some surprise, that what he missed most of all was Daisy.

But that was insane. He'd never wanted to be tied down. Long ago he'd made the decision to carve out a life for himself, by himself. It had been the right decision, and he didn't regret it. And yet she'd gotten under his skin. Now he'd discovered that once wasn't enough. Ten times, a hundred times, a thousand times, he thought recklessly, wouldn't be enough. The question was, did he want her enough to give up his cherished independence?

Nick continued to examine the idea until he met Arthur, Isabelle, Judith, and Alice in the front parlor.

The attorney stood by the liquor cart. He held up a bottle of whiskey and Nick nodded. He could definitely use a drink.

Isabelle waited until he'd taken a healthy swallow of single malt.

"Thank you for coming over, Nick," she said.

He thought he detected a catch in her voice, but she looked normal enough, her salt-and-pepper hair combed into its usual neat style, her figure encased in a bright pantsuit. Red? Green? He recalled his performance with the bridezilla-to-be and he smiled.

"You look very nice," he said to his aunt. "Is that spring green?"

Arthur stared at him. "Spring green?"

"I'd call it mint," Alice said.

His sister-in-law, as always, wore a well-tailored pantsuit. He thought the color was some kind of brown. In fact, she looked like a sepia print. Remembering that she was coordinating the hand-fasting, he assured her he would transport the altar to Happily Ever After that evening.

"There's no hurry. Tomorrow will be soon enough," Alice said.

"Tonight, Alice and I are going to collect juniper berries by the frog pond outside Titusville," Judith told him. "It's the only place in the state where those particular berries grow."

Where had that unlikely claim originated? Had some ambitious Wiccan searched every pond, bog, river, and marsh in the state?

"In order to use the berries for the fertility blessing, we must collect them after moonrise," Judith added.

Nick doubted whether the world needed more witches and wizards, but the subject of reproduction triggered his guilt. Had Daisy told him the truth about birth control? He couldn't imagine she'd lie about something like that. He hoped she hadn't lied. He hoped his carelessness hadn't caused an unsolvable problem. Oddly, it didn't seem as unsolvable as it should have.

Nick chafed at the interminable dinner. He needed to get Arthur alone. Finally, the berry gatherers left, and the others removed to Isabelle's small parlor. Arthur poured brandies. Nick could tell from their sober expressions there was more bad news.

He looked at his aunt's unhappy face.

"What is it?"

"I don't know how to tell you, but there is no point putting it off." She glanced at Arthur then back at Nick. "We've had an offer from Amalgamated Grains, and we mean to take it."

"What offer?"

"For the company, Nick. We really have no choice but to sell Bowman's Biscuits."

It was great news all the way around. The sale would solve Daisy's problem, and it didn't matter to him. Except it did.

"No." ," he said. "We're not going to sell."

A shocked silence followed his words. He understood. He'd shown no interest in Bowman's Biscuits during the past seven years despite his one-third ownership. They expected him to be indifferent to the company's fate. Hell, he should have been indifferent.

"We've lost customers," Arthur explained. "We need a complete reorganization and the acquisition of property to even begin to make the company viable. We don't have capital, Nick, and we don't have the leadership."

"Where," he asked, as anger flooded his soul, "the hell is Buzz?"

Isabelle spread her hands and shrugged. "We don't know."

"It doesn't matter." Arthur sounded weary. "Bowman's Biscuits' success was based on the concept of family. There's no family left to run it."

Isabelle slid her hand through her husband's thin arm.

"You are family, dear," she said. "But it isn't fair to dump all this on your shoulders."

Nick's eyes narrowed on his aunt. "Doesn't Buzz's wife know his whereabouts?"

Isabelle shook her head. "She is as baffled as we are."

"Amalgamated has the assets to buy us out," Arthur explained. "They'll keep the name and the signature pink-and-white box, but they intend to drop the piecrust and other non-biscuit products. I don't see them replacing the antiquated equipment. My guess is that within the next few years they'll close the Mayville plant." He sighed. "But the decision is made. We have to sell."

It didn't take much imagination to figure out what would happen to the small town without its largest employer.

"No," Nick heard himself say. "No. I'll take care of this. I will run the company."

The two older people gaped at him.

"What about your racing and your franchise," Arthur asked.

"I have offers for the franchise all the time. I have to finish a couple more commitments then I'll retire. I'd been considering it, anyway."

"Oh, Nick!" His aunt threw her arms around him. "This is just, well, an answer to prayer."

He patted her back. What had he done? He'd committed himself to live in Mayville. He'd put himself squarely in the midst of the dysfunctional family to which he didn't even belong. He'd have no excuse not to marry Daisy Budd if there were any consequences after last night. With a few words, he'd reversed the rotation of the world. At least, his world. His well-ordered existence was about to turn to chaos.

The prospect should have bothered him more.

Isabelle's eyes glistened. "I know what Daddy did to you seven years ago, Nick. I don't pretend to know why, but he always had confidence in you, and I know he loved you."

Nick deliberately erased the image of the confrontation with Pops. The pain no longer mattered. The lack of blood ties no longer mattered. He knew he was a good businessman. He could and would straighten out this family's problems without any emotional commitment. He could still be an island.

****

Oddly, the late afternoon rays of the sun that gilded and warmed the old Victorian made Daisy feel desolate. She knew it was not really the sun at fault, but the mistaken assumptions she'd made and the lonely future she faced. She wandered about the place trying without much success to regain her normal optimism by cataloguing the changes she'd made and the ones she planned to make. Tomorrow things would look brighter. Happily Ever After would become a hive of activity when the Wiccans gathered. A Circle meeting was scheduled for Friday night and a hand-fasting for Saturday.

The cellar drew her in a way it had never done before. Tonight it was less frightening. What, after all, were stacks of old chairs, books, boxes, or even coffins compared with the specter of losing her family? And

Nick.

Daisy knew she was being melodramatic. She was not losing her family. They were merely moving to Chicago. And, as for Nick Bowman, well, she'd never had any claim to him. She was being absurd.

She set to work cleaning up the dead butterflies, depositing the tiny carcasses into one paper bag and the black candle into another. She reminded herself that she alone was responsible for these particular deaths. She vowed never to place another order with the butterfly farm.

When she finished she gazed around the room. She could hardly believe there was a piece of valuable art hidden here, an object that had belonged to a victim of the Holocaust. Where was it? What was it? She shivered as thought of the dreadful injustice of Hitler's Germany and the families who had lost loved ones.

She, Daisy, had no business indulging in self-pity. She would be happy for them as they left; Caro and Stevie and Junie. And Nick.

Nick. She looked around the cellar. There was one thing she could do for him. She could find the blue diamond.

The prospect of a quest soothed Daisy and inspired her. She dug into cardboard boxes and still-full drawers of old bureaus. She sifted through stacks of books and papers. She peered into the roll compartment of a player piano.

She paused, finally, and stood to stretch the aching muscles of her back. That's when she noticed paint-chipped secretary that had been obscured by the piles. She opened the lower doors and gasped.

Daisy focused her flashlight beam and then she

stared at the newfound object for a long time.

The dollhouse, a miniature of the Gray Lady, had been built with exquisite attention to detail. She recognized the scalloped gray tiles, the tall narrow windows, the wide, sheltered front porch and the intricate gingerbread. The chimneys and dormer windows had been placed correctly.

A separation in the front allowed her to open the house to see the inside. The craftsman had duplicated the foyer and winding staircase, the kitchen upstairs, bedrooms and side porch. The large room on the first floor was neither a wedding chapel nor a funeral chapel. Instead it was a parlor that contained Victorian furniture and a Christmas tree decorated with tiny wax candles and miniature knitted stockings on the hearth.

Tears filled Daisy's eyes. The Gray Lady had once been a family's beloved home. She felt an immediate kinship with the dollhouse's creator and a renewed love for the structure. She would not allow the Gray Lady to become a manufacturing plant for Bowman's Biscuits. The house deserved love and she vowed to fill it with happy people, joyous young brides and their families.

Daisy wished she could carry the beautiful creation up to the foyer. It deserved to be seen by everyone who entered the house, but she couldn't lift it. She'd ask Nick to take it up tomorrow. Her heart squeezed. No, not Nick. If she succeeded in finding the blue diamond tonight, she would have no further contact with him. Someone else could carry the treasure upstairs, Jimmy or Quentin or maybe she and Junie could handle it between them.

Daisy blinked away her tears and took one last look at the marvel she'd uncovered and that's when she spotted the dumb waiter. Whoever had built the house had cleverly designed a pulley system to allow the little box to ride up and down between the kitchen and the ground floor. No doubt some Victorian family had installed the mechanism to save its staff from the necessity of using the stairs during parties and entertainments.

In the miniature house the dumb waiter stopped in the parlor. Daisy had seen the waist-high opening in the kitchen but couldn't picture the same in the parlor which was strange because they'd just painted that entire room. Where was the other end of the real dumb waiter? She screwed up her face and closed her eyes and tried to make out the house's architecture. The dumb waiter did not stop in the parlor. Did that mean it continued to the cellar? Her eyes popped open.

She contemplated the wall behind the Secretarysecretary, then shoved and pushed the heavy piece of furniture, one end at a time, until she'd moved it far enough to get up close to the wall. She ran the flashlight's beam over the wall.

At first she couldn't see anything. She edged the big desk back farther and got in closer. Sure enough, there was a faint seam. It sat well off the ground, like a squirrel hole in an oak tree, and it looked as if it had been undisturbed for a long time. Sixty years?

Daisy's heart thudded in heavy beats. Was this where Theo had hidden the stolen treasure? If she pried open the door would she find herself staring at the blue diamond?

There was only one way to find out.

She retrieved a kitchen knife from a box of odd utensils, but the blade was too thick and dull to separate the paint from the opening. A strong sense of urgency kept her from climbing the two flights to the kitchen. She stepped back and stared at the dollhouse. Suddenly she spotted it.

The maker of the dollhouse had thoughtfully provided a set of miniature fireplace tools near the stone hearth in the parlor.

"Eureka." She spoke the word, softly, although there was no one to hear her. After that she lost track of time.

She scraped at the old paint until her hands cramped, then she rested and started again. Every muscle ached by the time she'd loosened the door but more frustration loomed. There was no handle, and she couldn't get enough leverage with the tiny poker. Exasperated, she hit the thing with the edge of her fist. The slight "click" was nearly obscured by her yelp of pain. But she had no difficulty at all in seeing the dark slit between the door and the wall.

She'd done it.

Excitement burbled up inside her. She reached down for the flashlight. A cold breeze brushed against her neck but she had no time to react before the pain exploded in her head.

Chapter Sixteen

Nick stared out at the dark road and wondered at fate.

Seven years after his banishment, he was back in Mayville in the old life. It was as if his racing career and his adventures in L.A. had never happened at all, as if nothing had ever changed and he was once again twenty-three, eager and ready along with Buzz, to be groomed to take over the company.

Except things had changed. There was no Buzz by his side, and no Pops to initiate them. The robust company had rusted in the past seven years. At best it needed an overhaul. At worst it had rotted from within.

And seven years ago he had not misused a local angel unless one counted Caroline Budd, and he did not count her.

He had to find a way to save Bowman's Biscuits, and he had to do it without destroying Daisy.

And he still had to resolve the issue of the blue diamond and the questions surrounding Spuds Langston's murder.

Nick glowered at the road. Had Pops foreseen the complications from his posthumous summons? The answer came quickly. Of course. Whatever else he was, Theo Bowman hadn't been stupid. He'd known his family very well. He'd expected Nick to get snarled in their problems.

171

He'd expected Nick to come back to stay.

The tension seeped out of him and was replaced by an airy sense of euphoria. He found himself in the extremely unfamiliar position of wanting to share his epiphany with someone. But not just anyone.

He wanted to talk to Daisy.

He blinked at the overhead road sign. He'd automatically turned onto the interstate. His lips curved into a smile. Hell.

Nick felt the excitement rise, lava-like inside him as he pulled into the clearing. By the time he reached the screened door his skin felt too tight and a sense of anticipation drove his footsteps. He felt like a damned adolescent. A horny one. An excited one.

He found Larry home alone.

The searing disappointment he felt irritated him. Nick Bowman did not depend on other people. It shouldn't have mattered that she was out. But it did matter. And it worried him.

They still had not identified the murderer.

She had to be at her sister's.

Nick checked the cat's food and water then headed back to town. He wanted to see Daisy badly enough to tangle with the hostile Budd sister, but, he drove past Happily Ever After just to make sure the little red Jeep wasn't there.

It was after eleven and the hulking house was completely dark. Nick felt a flash of relief. He'd have been unhappy to find her here alone. He drove past the carport and glanced at Randolph's old hearse and his heart leapt into his throat when he saw Daisy's car.

Nick slammed on the brakes, jumped out of the car, and sprinted up the back steps. His fingers shook as he turned the knob. The door was unlocked. Damn. He slammed the door open and shouted her name.

The answer came from the cellar. The voice, calm and familiar.

"She's down here, Nick."

He flung himself down the narrow cellar stairs his eyes riveted on the unconscious woman cradled in the arms of a large, blonde male.

An anguished roar filled the room.

His brother's blue eyes widened. "She'll be all right. She's coming around."

****

The male voice comforted her. It sounded like Nick, but she knew it wasn't Nick. For one thing, her hormones weren't rioting. For another there was the scent. It wasn't unpleasant, but it was all wrong.

Daisy lifted her lashes and stared into a pair of clear, sky-blue eyes.

"Buzz."

"You bumped your head," he explained, with a gentle smile.

Her head. Ah. She'd been aware of something throbbing like an outboard motor. It must be her head. She tried to lift it and cried out.

All at once the world shifted, and she reached out to steady herself and stared into a pair of worried eyes, slate-gray eyes. She inhaled and tucked her head into his shoulder. His arms closed around her and she relaxed. The right scent this time. The right man.

"What the hell happened?"

His voice was low, angry, hoarse. She could feel it as well as hear it.

"I saw her car, but the place was dark so I came

inside to check it out. I guess I called her name as I headed up the stairs to the second floor. Anyway, whoever attacked her left the cellar door open when he escaped out the back. I had to decide whether to chase him or check on Daisy." He paused. "She was unconscious when I found her."

Daisy felt Nick's arms tighten around her.

"Can you tell us what happened?"

There was such concern, such tenderness in his voice. She snuggled against him. "I felt a rush of cold air and then a house fell on my head."

Only Buzz laughed. She heard Nick's sharp intake of breath and his harsh, accusatory words.

"How do I know you're telling the truth? How do I know you didn't hit her?"

"Buzz wouldn't hit me," she protested. "He's your brother."

"Step-brother." She heard Buzz sigh.

"I didn't hit her. I'd been keeping an eye on this place, but the intruder must have slipped in under my radar."

"What are you talking about?"

"I've been camped out in the room across the street."

"Why?"

"I was waiting for you. I figured it was time we talked."

"Buzz's right," Daisy said. "You need to talk." Suddenly her eyes popped open.

"Oh my gosh!"

Nick's muscles tightened enough to hurt her.

Only they didn't hurt her.

"What?"

"I almost forgot! I found the blue diamond! At least I found the hiding place. An old dumb waiter sealed up years ago. Oh, and Nick, I found the most beautiful dollhouse."

"Hiding place for what," Buzz sounded puzzled.

"We'll check it out tomorrow," Nick said at the same time. "First, I'm taking you to the emergency room at Clark County General."

She didn't want or need to go to the hospital. "Look in the dumb waiter, okay?"

"Later, Daisy. First we take care of the bump on the head."

She didn't have the energy to make him understand. Instead, she turned to his brother. "Buzz?"

"Sure." He grabbed Daisy's fallen flashlight and headed for the opening in the wall. Second thoughts choked off her excitement. Nick should find the diamond.

"Go with him," Daisy urged. "Put me down."

"Not a chance."

His concern warmed her heart. His fingers, gentle on her sore skull, warmed her blood. She winced.

"You've got a concussion."

"I'm fine. I just need ice. And a good night's sleep."

The gray eyes flashed, and she knew he was remembering the sleepless night they'd just spent together. The blood heated and rose to her cheeks and, for an instant, she forgot everything else. She started at the sound of Buzz's voice. She'd forgotten he was there.

"You won't believe what's in the dumb waiter."

"A blue diamond?"

"Blue diamond? No. Nothing like that. Time magazine's Man of the Year edition from 1938."

Three years before the U.S. entered World War II.

"Who is it," she asked, though she thought she knew.

"Hitler," Nick replied.

"How the hell did you know that?"

Daisy felt Buzz's eyes, but she only saw Nick's.

"Maybe there's a story inside about the Nazi loot."

Nick shook his head. "To be chosen Man of the Year was an honor. Americans didn't know about the Holocaust at that point." Daisy considered that.

"It must be a clue."

"A clue to what? Buzz's exasperation finally reached her. "C'mon you two. Stop mooning at each other.

And let me in on what's happening. Damn Theo to hell."

Nick damned himself, too. He'd involved Daisy in this mess. He should've followed his initial instincts and broken into the place at night. Instead, he'd confided in Daisy, and, curse the woman, she'd acted on her own and last night, she'd been attacked by the murderer. He shuddered at the close call. If she'd turned around and recognized him she'd be dead. Nick shuddered at the close call. His fault. All his fault.

His eyes narrowed at her unnatural pallor. He scooped her into his arms.

"We're going to the hospital," he growled.

"I just want to go home. To the cabin."

Buzz came to stand next to them, and he examined the bump, too.

"I think she's right. With an ice pack and some rest and she'll be as good as new."

"Thank you, Dr. Bowman."

The smile she bestowed on Buzz triggered a hot rush of an unfamiliar emotion. Jealousy? "Could you stay with me?" Nick's arms tightened around her.

"Both of you, I mean. I'd feel safer with both of you at the cabin."

"Both of us?"

She smiled at Buzz. "Why don't you pick up some beer and pizza from the Grainery and follow us home?"

Nick started to protest.

"Please." Daisy widened her eyes. He suspected her attempt to look pathetic was deliberate. She probably wanted the brothers to have a chance to talk.

On the drive back to the lake, Nick scolded her about the folly of searching for the blue diamond alone. He felt badly that she'd gotten hurt and guilty about the Bowmans' plan to acquire the Gray Lady. The one thing he did not regret was what she called their one-night stand and what he'd begun to think of as the start of their life together.

When they reached the cabin Nick carried her into her bedroom.

"Larry," she said.

"He's fine. And full."

She let him remove her clothes and work a nightshirt over her head. He put a hand on each shoulder and peered into her eyes. He studied her pupils. They seemed to match. He wished he could crawl into bed with her, that he could lie next to her in case she woke, but he knew he could not.

****

177

"I'll check on you every hour or so."

"I'm fine."

He heard the screen door open.

"Go talk to your brother."

"Step-brother."

She flashed him an exasperated look.

"Whatever."

"Daisy, there's something we have to talk about."

A new expression appeared in the golden eyes. She looked lost.

"Tomorrow," she said. "The pizza's probably already lukewarm."

"I've got ice," Buzz called from the doorway.

Nick didn't turn to look at him. "Put it in a plastic bag. They're in the lower right hand cupboard next to the coffee."

"Right."

He didn't want to leave but her lashes fluttered and he knew she needed rest. He brushed his lips against her forehead, her cheeks and her lips and only lifted his head when Buzz returned with the ice pack.

"Call if you need me."

"I will. Go. Talk. Settle things with your brother."

"My step-br—" he started to say, but she put a finger against his lips.

He checked on her every half hour. In between times he and Buzz drank the beer and consumed the pizzas then he sprawled in the upholstered chair and Buzz stretched out on the sofa.

"I haven't been here in seven years, but things look the same."

The comment surprised Nick. "I figured you'd be out here every weekend. You loved the place. What changed?"

Buzz's trademark cheerfulness faded.

"Everything. You were gone. I got married."

Ah. He'd almost forgotten Alice.

"What happened with that? Why get married so fast?"

Buzz scraped a hand down his face. He looked much older than his twenty-eight years. His large athletic frame had settled into a plodding heaviness, and wrinkles bracketed his mouth. The blue eyes had dulled.

"It's a long story."

In other words, not Nick's business.

"Let's just say it's been a long seven years, professionally and personally. You've done well."

Nick nodded. "I drove away from here that morning, and I couldn't see my way clear to the next day, but, eventually things worked out."

"I don't know why he did it. Pops never trusted me to run the company. He'd assign me to stuff like company morale or public relations. He sent me to meetings of the grain consortium out in Iowa. I never had real power or even access to the financial situation. Pops did it all. With Arthur, of course."

His brother's words stunned Nick. Theo had designated Buzz as the heir apparent but refused to elevate him to the throne?

"I felt like Prince Charles. I envied you, Nick. You didn't have to answer to anybody, and I was so stuck."

"The grass is always greener."

Buzz stared at him. "Did you miss the family?"

"Not for a damn minute."

Buzz shook his head. A slow, ironic grin appeared.

"You never were any damn good at lying."

Despite the late hour Nick knew it was time to get serious. "What's going on here, anyway? Were you in rehab?"

Buzz sighed. He leaned back on the pillows and closed his eyes.

"When Pops got sick I tried to take over. I figured out revenues were down, so I studied the books and noticed a pattern. In the past year we've lost a number of clients. None of the grocery chains but still, enough to make a difference in our bottom line.

"I called 'em up but couldn't get any satisfactory answers. They'd switched suppliers. Period. The net profit slipped, and I met with the accounting department. Remember Harry Foster?"

"Sure. He's been around forever."

"Not anymore. I wanted to fire him, to bring in one of the Big Four firms, but I didn't have the authority. Then, one day he just disappeared along with a chunk of our ready assets."

"Shit."

"Arthur and I hushed it up. You know the rumor mill in the bread business."

Nick nodded. He knew the power of rumors. They could destroy any business or reputation overnight. He thought of the one-night stand and the risk it had been to Daisy.

"I knew there was something rotten going on, but I couldn't figure out what it was."

Nick understood. He'd felt the same way in Langston's apartment in Chicago."

"I did my best with staff morale, but I was the boy with my finger in the dyke. Our products don't fit the marketplace anymore, the plant's outdated, and our personnel policies need to be streamlined. We need a plant manager on the floor and an outside accounting firm. We need a CEO who's been trained in business. I was a marketing major, you know that. I thought I'd be the face of Bowman's Biscuits while you ran the show. Turns out the company doesn't need a face. We're gonna tank, Nick. Unless we find some capital and expand." He shook his head. "I don't have the heart for this."

The despair in his brother's voice disturbed him.

"There's more, isn't there? What aren't you telling me?"

Buzz sighed. "I'd been hanging out a lot at the bar. One night, after closing at two, I drove past the office. There was a light on in Arthur's window. I should've gone in and investigated, but, I don't know, I never was any good at confrontations. Instead, I checked with Aunt Isabelle in the morning. She said he'd had a late meeting in Ralston and decided to stay over."

"Arthur? You think Arthur's behind all this?"

"I don't know what else to think."

"Good God. He's devoted his life to Bowman's Biscuits and Pops."

"But Pops is gone now. Maybe Arthur figured it's time he got his cut."

Nick couldn't see it. On the other hand, he'd never imagined Arthur would marry Aunt Isabelle either. "What happened when you talked to him?"

A ruddy color appeared in Buzz's cheeks. "I haven't. I decided to quote-disappear-unquote for a while. No one doubted the booze problem. For a while I stayed in Nadine's spare room, and she'd brought me food. Lately I've been in the room across Pine Street."

"What made you move?"

His brother shifted uncomfortably. "It was the drifter. The one who drowned. When he started hanging around young Junie Budd, I checked him out. He was a P.I. from Chicago with a shady reputation. I figured I'd keep an eye on him while I sorted out the business at the company."

Nick stared at his step-brother. "You're interested in Junie Budd?"

"No. No, not in the way you mean. It's just, well, those girls are alone."

"Yeah. Why'd he bill you fifty thousand dollars?"

Buzz sat up, abruptly and the blue eyes widened. "What?"

"Langston." Nick told Buzz about the invoice.".

"No way."

"Yesterday I broke into his office and found your business card. What's the connection between you two, Buzz?"

"Jesus. There's no connection. I don't know. None of it makes sense. I never met the guy. I mean it, Nick."

Nick studied him. "You always used to say that. 'I mean it, Nick.' Whenever you were trying to convince me of something. I'd forgotten all about that."

"I didn't know Langston. There was no reason for him to send me a bill."

"I believe you."

Buzz's blue eyes filled with hope the way they used to when Nick was about to bail him out of some kind of trouble. Nick's heart twisted.

"You find out anything about Bowman's Biscuits?"

"Not much. I can't make head nor tail of the records. I was so damn glad to know you were back."

Nick automatically started to assert his lack of interest in the company, and then he remembered his promise to Isabelle and Arthur.

"I tailed Arthur a few times. He spends about half his nights out at the house on Dollar Lake, where he lived before the marriage."

"And from this you conclude what?"

"If I didn't know better, I'd think he was having an affair. One night I caught a glimpse of a passenger in his Lincoln. Looked like a woman."

Nick nearly choked. Was Isabelle right? Was the buttoned-up attorney, the near lifelong bachelor involved in a liaison with Leilani Harter? It seemed impossible.

"What about your wife? She knows about your clandestine activities, or does she think you're in rehab?"

Buzz closed his eyes. "I don't know what she believes. We don't talk. Haven't for years. When this is straightened out, I'm gonna talk to a lawyer. The marriage was a mistake from the start, and we both know it."

Nick felt a pang of sympathy for the mismatched couple, but Buzz's personal problems weren't his business. He needed to focus on Bowman's Biscuits and the damned blue diamond and the murder. He had a strong hunch they were all related.

Before the estrangement he'd trusted Buzz. He decided to trust him now. He needed his brother's help. He told Buzz about the posthumous letter from Theo and the blue diamond. His brother paled at the tale about Nazi loot, but he listened in silence until Nick finished.

"Nazis, huh? That's why you and Daisy weren't surprised about the Time magazine."

"I think Langston was after the treasure."

"That makes sense. But why drag me into it?"

Nick shrugged. "Maybe he set you up to take the fall."

"Yeah, but why? How did he even know about me?"

"Come on, Buzz. Bowman's Biscuits has a national reputation. Anybody who buys biscuit mix knows the name, and most folks know the family. Theo emphasized family loyalty enough."

"I get that Langston somehow found out about the blue diamond and went after it, possibly using me as a cover, but who killed him?"

"A partner, maybe? Someone who knew enough about the Bowmans and Mayville and the Gray Lady to give him a road map?" They looked at each other.

Such a person had to be someone they knew.

"Then why kill him?"

"Maybe they had a falling out. Or maybe the partner didn't trust him. He smoked a lot of weed."

Buzz fell silent for a moment. "There had to be a partner. Somebody conked Daisy on the head."

Nick's heart jerked and his eyes narrowed. "And that somebody's gonna pay."

"We'll both keep an eye on her, Nick. We won't let her get hurt again. Does this mean you're gonna marry Daisy and stay in Mayville to run the company?"

Nick searched his brother's words for hidden malice or resentment but he couldn't find any. "Yeah. If it's okay with you. That's exactly what it means."

Buzz's grin, the one Nick remembered from a more lighthearted time, spread across his face. "It's okay with me."

Chapter Seventeen

The soft rays of the sun woke Daisy. She felt warm and safe. And excited. She sucked in a breath and inhaled the scent of Nick. Umm. She turned over to touch him, and pain streaked through her head. She let out a moan.

He exploded from the bed. An instant later gray eyes, darkened by concern, peered into hers from point blank range. She stared at the whiskers on his face and ran her fingers over his cheek.

"Nice."

"Never mind that." His voice sounded like the floor of a movie theater after a performance if it could talk. "Does your head hurt?"

"Only when I breathe."

Strong, gentle fingers probed the bump with care. "I'll get some more ice."

"I'd rather have coffee." She smiled at him. "Did you and your brother get a chance to talk?"

A combination snore and snort drifted in from the other room.

She waited to hear him correct her and was pleased when he refrained from saying "step-brother."

"Yeah. We've come to the conclusion you're in danger. I want you to close Happily Ever After until this is over."

She struggled to sit up, and her head throbbed. "I

can't do that. Harmony Lime's coven comes today.

There're a weekend of festivities planned." He didn't argue.

"You knew I'd say that, didn't you?"

"I don't want you alone there, Daisy. Not for a minute, day or night."

Love, as warm as molten metal, poured through her. Nick Bowman was sensitive and caring, a perfect family man. Except he didn't want a family. She had to remember the plan to pursue eminent domain, to deprive her of her house. She didn't want to remember that. She wanted to be near Nick for as long as she could. She knew it wouldn't be long.

"You can stay at the Gray Lady."

"At night, too."

She smiled. "You really want to sleep in an ex-mortuary with a coven of witches?"

"I won't be with the witches. I'll be with you."

She lifted her eyebrows.

"With guests present?"

"I'll sleep on the sofa on the side porch." He held her gaze a moment longer. "I want you to know something, Daisy. When the murder is solved and we've found the blue diamond, I'm not going back to L.A."

Something stirred under her heart.

"You aren't?"

"I've told Isabelle and Arthur I'd stick around to try to save Bowman's Biscuits. You were right, honey. Family's family even when it isn't."

He was staying for his family, for his company. This wasn't about her. Later she'd think about the implications of that. Not now. She found a smile for him.

"I'm pleased for all of you," she said, simply.

He brought her Cocoa Puffs and coffee and helped her into a shower that somehow seemed lonely. She assured him she could dress herself, and soon they were headed toward town.

"We should stop at the hospital."

He sounded like an anxious father. "No need. I'm fine. I've been thinking about something."

She noticed the way his fingers tightened on the steering wheel and she stifled a sigh. He probably thought she was going to make demands.

"Whoever hit me last night must have worked with Spuds and then killed him."

The white hue faded from his knuckles. He was going to allow her to change the subject. Daisy shook off the disappointment.

"That, uh, person, is probably somebody local."

"You mean someone in my family." He sounded remarkably calm. "I agree. In fact, Buzz and I suspect Arthur."

That startled her. "Arthur Sneed? Theo's attorney? Isabelle's husband? But why?"

"We are fairly certain someone is sabotaging the company. It has to be an inside job and, well, frankly, there's no one else inside."

"And the same reasoning applies to whoever's searching for the blue diamond," Daisy said, slowly.

"The two issues have to be connected. Mayville's too small to support two villains."

"But I thought you were the only one in the Bowman circle who knew about the loot."

Nick shrugged. "Arthur had daily access to Pops

for thirty years right up until Pops died. He may have found out at some point."

"I still can't believe he'd have cheated Theo or any of you. And I think he cares about Isabelle."

"Things aren't always what they seem. The Bowmans suck at marriage."

"Not always. Buzz and Alice have been married for years."

Nick shot her a wry look.

"He's divorcing her."

"Oh."

"Hell, Daisy. It's no big deal. Fifty percent of marriages break up in a courtroom. The Bowmans are heavy contributors to that statistic."

She didn't like the cynicism in his voice. "That means fifty percent of marriages make it to the finish line," she pointed out. "There's been divorce in my family, too, Nick, but I haven't given up on

happily ever after."

"No kidding." His voice was dry.

"Don't make fun of me, Nick. I believe in the concept of a happy marriage."

"I believe in the concept, too."

Her head whipped around too fast, and the sharp pain elicited a moan.

He shot her a quick, concerned glance, but his words confused her.

"I hope that's not your answer,"

She touched the back of her head, gingerly. "My answer to what?"

"My proposal, of course. I want you to marry me."

She blinked at him. "My concussion's making me hallucinate."

"No such luck. If you and I are both staying in Mayville, we have to get married. There's no other way to cohabitate in a small town and, lady, I intend to sleep with you."

He delivered the devastating speech while passing another driver, and she stared at his profile.

"I know it's not much of a proposal," he admitted, "but I mean it. Will you? Marry me, I mean?"

She still didn't understand.

"Is this about the Gray Lady?"

He sent her an impatient look and pulled off the interstate even though there was no shoulder and the railing scraped the side of the Malibu. He turned and grabbed her upper arms.

"This isn't about the Gray Lady."

"Then it's about my sisters. You heard they're moving to Chicago and you feel sorry for me."

"Listen to me, Daisy Budd. I never felt less sorry for anyone in my whole life. You've got courage and perseverance and a whole support system here. I'm proposing for one reason and one reason only: I want you, woman." He found her lips and kissed her until they were both out of breath. But neither the thrill of the declaration nor the mounting passion could make her ignore the words he'd chosen.

Want. Not love.

After a moment he ended the kiss, but he stared into her eyes.

"So it's settled," he said, firmly. "We'll get married."

Regret flooded her soul but she shook her head.

"I don't think so."

****

Nick couldn't believe how badly he'd screwed up. Talk about a textbook example of how not to get a woman to marry you. Wrong time, wrong place, wrong circumstances, no knee, no ring. In the moment that counted, he'd forgotten everything he'd ever learned about women, and he'd just blurted out the truth.

I want you.

The problem was the truth contained no romance at all. He might just as well have admitted that happily after for him meant sexual satisfaction. No woman wanted to hear that, least of all a cockeyed romantic like Daisy Budd.

He could have admitted to sympathy about her sisters. He hated to see her hurt by their defection. But he knew she wouldn't see sympathy as a compelling reason either.

She wanted a declaration of love. The word stuck in his throat. In his experience, love was a concept that always led to disappointment. It was something he did not believe in and, as much as he wanted her, he wasn't going to lie.

In the midst of his self-disgust he had to admit to a sliver of relief. Marriage didn't work for the Bowmans. In the end, a man could only rely on himself. Not that she would believe that. She was looking out the window and he glanced at the coppery curls and wanted to thread his fingers through them. He wanted to lose himself in her heat and bury himself in her body. He wanted her so close that no one could hurt her. Not even him.

"Nick?"

Her voice surprised him. "Yeah?"

"That copy of Time magazine. Is there any way

that could be the blue diamond?"

"No." He paused. "It's not worth that much." Her face was too pale under the smattering of freckles and his gut clenched. He pulled into a Stop-n-Go. "Wait here." A minute later he emerged with water and aspirin.

"I don't need it. My head doesn't hurt."

He uncapped the bottle, ripped open the packet, and swallowed the tablets.

"Mine does."

****

The front door of Happily Ever After stood wide open. Nick could see a little old lady, Miss Florence of Flowers by Florence, in the foyer. She had a hanging basket in each hand. Both Caroline and Junie's cars were in the lot next to the hearse as was the sole Mayville police cruiser.

He knew Daisy needed time away from him. She'd be safe here. He stopped the car in front of the house on Pine Street.

"Aren't you coming in to search?"

"Later. I've got some things to take care of. Take it easy this morning and watch your back."

She nodded. "Thanks."

For what? For his half-assed, half-hearted proposal? For involving her in a quest that earned her a concussion? For ruining her reputation?

"You're welcome."

He watched her walk up the path. She really was a sprite. Nick tended to forget her short stature because of her big heart. His own ached. He felt that he'd lost something indescribably dear. He'd have to think about it later. It was time for a word with Arthur. He started the car.

But when he arrived at Bowman Mansion, Finch informed him the ladies were out, and Arthur Sneed was still in bed. It was after nine.

"Still in bed?"

"I believe he got home rather late last night," the butler said.

"How late?"

"I retired at one a.m."

Had he been out with the mystery woman? Or was the woman a beard to disguise his search for the blue diamond and his efforts to destroy Bowman's Biscuits?

Nick resisted the urge to haul the lawyer out of bed and settle this once and for all with his fists.

****

Black and orange roses twined through the trellis arch at the bottom of the courtyard, and vases of black cosmos decorated the stone seat of the Cupid Fountain. Tall sheaves of wheat replaced last week's Renaissance banners in strategic locations around the courtyard.

"Everything looks great," Daisy said to her sisters.

Junie stared at her. "Mon Dieu. You're as white as a sheet, Daze. Did you see a ghost?"

Caroline, busy setting up a table, glanced at the newcomer. "You're upset about Chicago, aren't you?"

"Good gravy, Caro!" In her indignation, Junie forgot to use French. "Why'd you tell her now?"

Daisy wanted more than anything to reassure them. The family break up was her problem, not theirs. "Not at all. I'm happy for both of you. I'm a little tired, that's all." The sound of voices interrupted them. An instant later the ladies from Bowman Mansion appeared at the side gate. Alice Bowman trundled the stone altar on a dolly.

Judith Bowman reminded Daisy of a fruit salad. A voluminous watermelon-colored skirt and lemon yellow poet's shirt were accented by a bold, lime green sash at her waist. A grape-purple pentacle hung on a chain around her neck.

Harmony Lime's bright colors stood in contrast to Alice's tailored black blouse and slacks. The younger woman's pale hair gleamed in the sunlight. Dark glasses concealed the too-close eyes, but Alice's lips thinned in a grim line.

Daisy's heart ached for the woman and her imminent divorce.

Isabelle wore an elegant black sheath with silver jewelry and a determined smile on her face. Daisy's heart squeezed again. The happiness Isabelle had found in her brief marriage would evaporate if Arthur Sneed proved to be the murderer and the mastermind behind the demise of Bowman's Biscuits. So much tragedy waiting to happen.

"We'll need the altar tonight for the memorial service," Alice told Daisy, in a quiet voice. Daisy had forgotten Junie's plans to honor Spuds Langston, a man she still considered her late boyfriend.

"Of course," she murmured. "Do you need anything else?"

"No. We've got plenty of juniper berries and brooms." She smiled at Daisy who smiled back.

"Let me guess," she said. "You're not one hundred percent sold on Wicca."

"I'm more of a chauffeur-slash-witch-Friday," Alice confided. "I don't mind. It takes some of the pressure off Isabelle."

Daisy quelled the impulse to offer sympathy and friendship to Buzz's wife. Alice's sense of privacy was well-known in Mayville.

Another group's arrival ended the short conversation. Daisy shook hands with a tall, silver haired, middle-aged man with chiseled features and an attractive smile, and a plump woman with curly gray hair and lively, intelligent eyes. He wore a polo shirt and khakis, she, a lavender shirtwaist as if they were en route to luncheon at the country club.

"I'm Sarah Glenn Sedgwick, and this is my fiancé, Cedric Carrington." Her musical voice turned tender. Daisy couldn't keep the surprise out of her eyes and Sarah Glenn grinned. "Not what you were expecting, right?"

"You just look so, uh …"

"Normal?" Sarah Glenn chuckled.

"Cedric's a pro over at the Americana Golf Club in Rayburn."

It was hard to believe the golfer was also Grand Wizard of the Celestial Heavens Coven.

Four more women appeared, and Sarah Glenn introduced Prunella Wentworth, a short, squat fortyish woman with long purple hair; Sigrid Cobble, tall, slender and blonde; and Penelope and Regina Watson, plump, fifty, indistinguishable from each other and dressed identically in eggplant pantsuits.

"Penelope and Regina are twins," Sarah Glenn explained, unnecessarily.

"We've always been telepathic," Regina explained, "so Wicca is a natural for us."

"And we love the jewelry," her sister explained. She pulled back the edges of her straight, gray bob to reveal pentagram-shaped earrings.

Daisy and Caroline were left alone when Junie took the guests to their rooms.

"They're a little weird," Caroline commented, "but they seem harmless enough."

Daisy shook her head. "Not so weird. Wicca gives them community, spirituality, and love. The same thing we all want." She smiled at her sister.

"I'm glad they've chosen us to help them celebrate."

Chapter Eighteen

A moment later Daisy and Caroline watched as a slim young woman wafted into the courtyard. Her waist-length, coal-black hair set off a pair of pale blue eyes in a heart-shaped face. Daisy suspected Junie would have described her as an old soul.

Probably in atrocious French.

"Welcome," Daisy said, extending her hand.

Slim fingers were pressed into hers.

"I'm Hecate, the back-up priestess. I'll be officiating at the Circle Meeting and the hand-fast."

Daisy nodded. "My younger sister appreciates your willingness to include the memorial send-off tonight."

"We're pleased to do it," Hecate said. "In fact, the twins have decided to honor their late Aunt Charlotte, too. We will draw down the moon and dispatch them all to Summerland in style."

"Was Aunt Charlotte a Wiccan, too?"

"A Baptist missionary. But our philosophy is all inclusive. After all, we are One in our spirituality."

Daisy suspected Aunt Charlotte and Spuds Langston had two things in common. They'd both been human, and they were both dead. She kept the thought to herself.

Junie called from the back door. "Daze! Miss Olive's on the phone. She wants in on the Memorial Service."

Daisy looked at Hecate.

"The more the merrier," the acting high priestess said.

Junie grinned. "Le mot juste. By the way, Miss Olive's invited the entire congregation of the tuna church."

It seemed as if Spuds, Charlotte, and Ora would have a nice crowd to see them off. This weekend the Gray Lady would be mortuary and wedding boutique combined as the guests and townspeople celebrated the circle of life.

Daisy found comfort in the prospect but they would definitely need more cookies.

****

Nick prowled through the desk drawers and cabinets in Pops's study, but he didn't expect to find much and he wasn't disappointed. If Arthur had sabotaged Bowman's Biscuits, killed Langston, or attacked Daisy in the Gray Lady's cellar last night, he hadn't left any evidence around. But then he wouldn't. The man was smart.

Smart and tired. Nick vetoed his original idea of waking the guy. He couldn't expect the man to confess to a verbal accusation. He needed proof.

Despite the delay, Nick's heart lightened as he drove away from Bowman Mansion and toward Happily Ever After. He realized that life seemed easier, brighter around Daisy. After the hand-fasting, he'd take another shot at the proposal. Meanwhile, there were other things to take care of. One of those involved the woman arranging potted plants on the front porch of the Gray Lady. Caroline was, for once, alone. It was as good a time as any to have this out.

Her exquisite features twisted and the turquoise eyes blazed with hostility as he mounted the porch steps. "What do you want?"

He kept his tone mild. "Why are you so angry at me?"

Her eyes reminded him of a storm at sea.

"I'm not angry. I just want you to leave Daisy alone."

"The way you're planning to leave her alone?"

"Our family is not your business, Nick. I know my sister is low-hanging fruit for a guy like you, but she deserves better. Give her a break and back off." The words stung.

"I'm not out to hurt her."

Caroline's sculpted lips twisted into a sneer. "You've already hurt her. Daisy's not a one-night stand kind of girl."

"Don't you think I know that?"

"You're telling me you didn't sleep with her in Chicago?" Caroline's voice rose. "It's just so typical of the Bowmans. Take what you can get and leave someone else to clean up the mess."

Her words triggered a bolt of pure fury and he grabbed her slim arm. "We're not talking about Daisy here, are we? This is about you and me. What mess did I leave behind? We barely knew one another. If I hurt you seven years ago I'm sorry, but you moved on. Why the bitterness now?"

"You're wrong." She jerked her arm away from him, and he let her go. "This is about Daisy. She seems self-sufficient, but she's more vulnerable than you think. She deserves someone who wants to stick around, someone who loves her. Someone she can love.

She deserves better than you, Nick Bowman." He felt the words like a fist in the gut.

"You're probably right," he told her, recklessly, "nevertheless I am what she's getting. I'm going to marry Daisy."

Caroline swayed, and he moved to catch her before she collapsed. He set her on the front porch glider. After a moment her long lashes lifted. "No," she whispered. "No." No. He felt a stab of pain.

"That's what she said. I'll get you some water." He ran into Daisy in the hallway.

"Hey, Nick. The Wiccans are here. They're nice people."

He noted the sparkle in her eyes and the dewy color in her face. She loved people. and she loved her job. She hadn't built Happily Ever After just for her sisters. He wanted to close his arms around her, to somehow preserve the happiness on her face. Caroline was right. Daisy deserved the best.

"I tried to talk to Arthur, but he's asleep."

"What's next?"

"If you don't need me I'm going out to Dollar Lake."

Her face lit up. "Are we going to break into Arthur's house?"

The twinkle in her lovely eyes lifted his heart.

"Absolutely not."

****

Arthur Sneed's sanctuary eight miles west of Mayville sat on the edge of a round body of water. The tall, thin house reflected both his physical characteristics and his personality. In the years before the rest of the lake property was developed, Arthur had enjoyed complete privacy. The recently added colonials, ranches, and split-levels made the attorney's house stand out like an awkward gosling in a basket of fluffy chicks.

Behind the house was a narrow, dirt lane, a favorite spot of amorous teens. On Daisy's sole trip to the lover's lane, she and her date, Jimmy Crossfield, had played chess. She'd like a return visit, this time with Nick and no game board.

Daisy leaned across him to get a good look at Arthur's house. The hard muscles of his thigh, his intoxicating scent, and his masculine heat combined to stoke a fire in her, and she remembered their adventure on I-94. Was he thinking about that? She sneaked a glance at his face and found his gaze pinpointed on the house, but her disappointment disappeared when his shifting thigh drew her attention to his lap. Ah. On some level he was remembering, too.

Nick parked behind a small grove of trees, and they crossed a small field on foot to reach Arthur's back door. Daisy's heartbeat kicked into high gear. "Did you bring your key thingy?"

He nodded.

"We're getting pretty good at this break-in business, aren't we?"

"Shush."

"Why? Do you think he's here?"

"No. He's asleep at the mansion, but I'd prefer not to draw any attention from the neighbors."

"Good point," she whispered.

She followed him up the back steps to a door six feet off the ground. Her nerves danced with anticipation about the break-in. Or being with Nick. Or both.

He inserted the key, but no satisfying click disrupted the clatter of katydids.

"Fuck."

"What? What's the matter?"

"He's got a computerized lock on it. We'll have to try a window."

They discovered all the windows were well off the ground. Under other circumstances, Daisy would have been impressed with the excellent security measures. She descended the steps and paced the backyard, surveying the basement windows.

"I can get in there," she said. "I'll just break the glass."

"Like hell you will."

"You and I know someone killed Spuds Langston, but the cops consider it an accident. That same someone broke into the Gray Lady last night. We have to do this, Nick. We have to identify this person before he hurts someone else."

She recognized the doubt in his eyes and the distaste. He didn't want to violate the man's property or his privacy. She loved him for that.

"Get back," He he said. He took off his shirt, wrapped it around his fist, and he hit one of the windows with a short, sharp, karate chop. The pane shattered. She started to climb in the window, but he put out a hand to stop her.

"I'll meet you at the back door."

The stainless steel appliances gleamed in the sunlight and the floor, a rich terra cotta tile, glowed.

"Classy," Daisy murmured. "Arthur's got great taste."

She opened the refrigerator door.

"You hungry?"

"The food might give us a hint about what he uses this place for and how often." She surveyed the contents. "I'd say not very. Nothing here but champagne and brie. That seems a little romantic for a man like Arthur Sneed."

Nick said nothing, and they stepped into a short hallway that led to a set of eight stairs. The second floor consisted of a large square room furnished with a few pieces of sleek, light oak furniture and flooded with light. Daisy realized the house, for all its stark, wooden façade included a full complement of floor-to ceiling windows.

"The man likes light," Daisy murmured. "But what on earth does he do here? There are no books or magazines, no television, no clutter of any kind.

No computer."

"And no evidence."

"Maybe it's on the third floor."

He paused to peer into her face. "If you're such an optimist you ought to be able to take a chance on me."

I could if you loved me.

She kept her mouth shut and smiled.

They crossed to another staircase, this one narrower than the first. Nick preceded her up the steps, and his big body blocked her view. She stepped into the room and color exploded all around her.

Stained glass panels hung from the windows that covered each of the four walls. Brilliant, blinding reds and greens, yellows and blues flooded the room and mingled to become purple and pink and orange.

"Oh my god," she breathed. She grabbed his arm for balance. "I feel like I'm inside a kaleidoscope."

When she finally focused on the furnishings, she realized the room was filled with a huge round bed covered with a leopard-skin spread. An enormous flat television screen hung from metal hooks overhead as did an odd, unwieldy canvas apparatus.

"Holy shit," Nick whispered. He stepped to the wall and touched a button. An Amazon curled on a bed in a tiger-striped negligee appeared on the screen while a sensuous drumbeat filled the room.

"Good grief."

"Welcome, lovers." A male spoke but Daisy noticed Nick's attention focused on the tiger-woman who stretched like a lazy boa constrictor. The unseen narrator continued. "Watch and learn as Raymond and Bridget demonstrate the erotic Chinese basket move and other positions guaranteed to enhance your sensual pleasure."

The drumbeat got louder as the Amazon spread her legs and balanced herself on what turned out to be the lap of a tanned, muscular male. Tarzan/Raymond grunted his appreciation at her efforts. He maintained his smile as he thrust upward. Bridget/Jane arched her back and moaned. The gentle sway of the swing made her ample breasts quiver and tighten.

Or maybe it was Raymond's erection.

Daisy gaped at the screen, torn between fascination and disgust. "Do you believe this?"

When Nick failed to answer she glanced over at him. Only a twitching muscle in his rock-hard jaw disturbed his death-like stillness. Daisy's eyes drifted down his body.

It wasn't just the jaw that was rock hard.

****

Nick stared at Raymond and Bridget's pretend, mutual climax. They easily moved into a new position with Raymond on top. In the back of his mind, Nick knew they should leave, but the front of his mind, the part of his brain that governed action, could focus on nothing but Daisy. Desire, hot and urgent, streamed through his body. If he moved, he'd throw Daisy down on the leopard-skin bedspread and bury himself in her tight, hot body. He fought for control while sweat glued his shirt to his torso.

"Notice how Bridget avoids a stiff neck while performing oral sex on her partner," the narrator said. Daisy stared at the screen.

"She does look pretty comfortable," she said.

Nick's body jerked with need.

"This next move is the butterfly swirl. It is one hundred percent guaranteed to produce the world's strongest climax."

"Or what," Daisy quipped, "you get your money back?"

Nick didn't laugh. Every molecule in his body strained with the need for release in the woman next to him.

"Nick?" She touched his cheek in concern.

"You're awfully warm."

He choked. "Hot. Hotter 'n hell."

"Now Bridget will turn onto her stomach," the voice continued. "The love swing allows Raymond to penetrate much more deeply in this position." Under her fingers Nick trembled.

"We should go," he managed to say.

She dropped her gaze to his crotch, and color flooded her cheeks. Jesus. She was turned on, too. "You sure you want to leave?" She hooked her fingers into the waistband of his jeans, and he sucked in his breath. Without breaking eye contact with him, she pulled the tongue out of his belt buckle and slowly, carefully, unzipped his jeans.

He knew her hands would feel the same way they had in the Jeep, and he almost came before she touched him.

"This next position is called the pit stop," the voice said. "It's Raymond's favorite."

Daisy dipped her hands into his open fly and cradled him. She used one forefinger to trace the throbbing vein.

Oxygen. The breath strangled in his throat.

"I think," Daisy whispered, "you're ready to try the pit stop."

They couldn't make love on Arthur's bed. The mental protest did not deter him from stripping off her slacks and panties, or from lifting her onto the bed. He flipped her onto her stomach and slid a hand under her. The feel of her soft stomach drove him over the edge, and he drove himself into her in one wild thrust. God, she felt good. A groan rose in his chest, and his hips battered her.

"I'm sorry," he gasped. "Can't stop."

She pushed back hard, and he groaned again. He gritted his teeth against the pleasure that was too intense to last. His climax rushed at him like a freight train. He came hard, pumping again and again into her body. FinallyFinally, he collapsed on her unable to move, unable to breathe, unable to imagine how it could have happened.

Sweat dripped from his face and hair onto her

neck.

"Daisy."

She made a little sound.

"Daisy?" He placed his palm on the back of her neck. "Did I hurt you, honey?"

She shifted under him until she was on her back. The golden eyes lidded and her slow smile warmed him. She put her arms around him and pillowed him on her soft body. Nick let out a long sigh and lay very still.

Chapter Nineteen

Daisy knew Nick regretted the lightning quick sex. It represented a complete loss of control for a man who valued that commodity over all else. She wanted to reassure him, but his grim expression strangled the comforting words in her throat. Instead, she helped him straighten the bed and they made their way, silently, through the house and the field. She tried to lighten the mood when they reached the car.

"The champagne and brie make sense now that we know what he's using the house for."

"I'm sorry for my aunt," he said, shortly.

Daisy gazed at him, surprised. "Why? What woman wouldn't want a love nest with the man she loves?"

"Arthur's not bringing my aunt out here. He's having an affair with someone else. Isabelle thinks it's Leilani Harter."

Daisy peered at him. "You can't really believe that."

He shrugged. "He's having an affair with someone."

"Dang." Daisy's heart went out to the older woman. After a moment her mind wandered back to the room at the top of the house.

"I wish we could have tried out the sex swing." The car swerved on the highway.

"I'll build us a sex swing after we're married."

She studied his face for a moment.

"If this is about my reputation you can quit worrying about it. I won't be ruined by a brief affair and, in any case, I don't care. My sex life is nobody's business."

"It's not just that. We're compatible, and we're hot for each other. If you think I can live in the same town with you and maintain a hands off policy, you're crazy."

He had a point and she was honest enough to admit it.

"I don't want to end this either."

He glanced at her, his gray eyes on fire. "I want you in my bed. We can't live together in Mayville, Daisy. Not without marriage."

He was right, of course. Still, it wasn't enough of a reason to get married.

"So let's do it."

She yearned to say yes. Was it possible that he just hadn't thought to use the magic phrase? She gathered her courage and asked.

"Do you love me, Nick?"

His pause lasted long enough to kill the eager hope.

"I don't know."

"Thanks," she said, shakily, biting back the bitter disappointment, "for not lying."

"Love isn't everything," he pointed out. "Unless I miss my guess, we just indulged again in unprotected sex. You might just have to marry me."

She winced. Dang.

****

Black cloths covered the three tables borrowed from St. Mary's Star of the Sea. Delicious odors rose from Pyrex pans of chicken tetrazzini, tuna noodle casserole, beans and franks and sweet and sour pork. Jell-O salads and Heavenly Hash joined potato and pasta salads on the tables. There was fresh fruit, cut veggies, chocolate and coconut cakes and plates and plates of Junie's cauldron cookies.

What the guests didn't eat tonight could be used for the hand-fasting feast.

Daisy drove out to the cabin to feed Larry, shower, and change into a gauzy navy tunic trimmed with silver and a pair of jeans. She figured she'd blend in with the night. When she returned, she rearranged the food on the table to conceal the coconut cake from Miss Olive.

Caroline appeared with a bowl of punch. She looked slim and elegant in a black tank top and capris.

She was not smiling but she sounded resigned. "Where've you been?"

"I'm sorry. I should have stayed around to help with the preparations. I went on an errand with Nick."

Her sister's face twisted. "Daze," her voice was gentle, "you can't marry that man."

"Who said anything about marriage?"

"He did. He told me he'd asked. You can't do it."

Can't. Not shouldn't.

"I told him 'no.'" Daisy indicated the full tables and the stone altar set up on the flat grass on the other side of the archway and the trees and bushes jeweled with tiny lights. "Everything looks beautiful. And just in time." Guests appeared at the side gate, and, for a moment, Daisy forgot the troubling subject of Nick Bowman as she admired the imaginative balance between traditional funeral dress and what they imagined was Wiccan attire.

Mayor Hotchkiss and his wife arrived in matching forest green bathrobes embroidered with "His Honor" and "Hers." Quentin wore a Renaissance-style tunic while Cherry Ann had chosen a swimsuit halter top and a pair of pantaloons ala I Dream of Jeannie. Miss Olive wore her customary funeral dress but she'd added some silver jewelry. Isabelle wore a red kimono while Arthur had on a dark, gray business suit. Alice appeared in dark slacks and a sweater. Junie's toga had been a pink bed sheet in a previous incarnation.

Daisy's heart flooded with affection for the people of Mayville and their attempt to connect with the newcomers.

"Daisy!" Junie yodeled. "You look très jolie. How do you like my outfit?"

Daisy's gaze drifted over the feathers stuck in Junie's ponytail band. "Pocahontas meets Bewitched?"

"Ah ciel! The precise look I was going for. Have you seen Nick?"

She'd done a lot more than see him. Fortunately, Junie seldom waited for an answer.

"Wait until you see Harmony Lime."

Nick's stepmother arrived moments later in a white, Victorian wedding gown with long tight sleeves and a hooped skirt. Her hair drifted down her back and kohl emphasized her large eyes.

"I can't decide whether she looks more like Cleopatra or Morticia Addams," Daisy said.

"He, on the other hand, looks simply gorgeous." Junie sighed and nodded at Nick. The man wore a khaki shirt and ancient blue jeans that hugged his powerful legs. Daisy silently agreed with her sister.

Physically, Nick was every woman's dream.

"I think you should marry him."

Daisy gaped at Junie. "What?"

"He told me he asked. Why wouldn't you marry him? It's obvious you've got the hots for him. Why not marry him and have your own happily ever after?"

Daisy looked up to see Caroline within earshot, a tight expression on her beautiful features. "Merde," Junie muttered. "Caro's jealous."

Daisy shook her head.

"What other objection could she have? I mean, he's Nick Bowman. Where's the bad? And you need someone around, Daze, since we're going to Chicago."

Hecate drifted past, wisps of white lace dripping from the arms and hem of her long dress. "It's time," she said, "to cast the Sacred Circle."

Daisy found a spot on the grass. After a few moments she felt the hair stand up on the back of her neck, and she knew Nick had come up behind her. He smelled like male and sex and heaven. She forced herself to focus on Cedric dressed in a white cape and Hecate beside him.

The Wiccans began to chant and soon the townspeople joined in.

Prunella's voice rose above the whispers. "As the sun sets, so our friends have left us. The water of our tears like the salt water of the sea, and the water of our mothers' womb, blesses this Circle."

Daisy blinked at the lovely words. Maybe Wicca wasn't crazy at all.

"I call the South," Hecate continued.

Sigrid's voice rose. "As life is a day, so our friends

have passed into the night. The first of our life, the memories and courage, the strength given to us by our friends bless this Circle."

Nick's hand on her back felt comforting and warm. She suddenly understood the reason for funeral services and other rituals. The sense of community did not make letting go any easier, but it did make it possible.

Daisy glanced at her sisters. She had to let them go. She inhaled a deep breath of evening and felt something inside her relax.

"I call the East," Hecate said.

"As all that falls shall rise again, so our friends will be reborn," Harmony Lime chanted.

"And the North."

"As the Earth forms us so our friends shall return to the earth."

The familiar voice startled Daisy.

"Our Mother feeds us, and clothes us. She gives us everything and in the end she takes our bodies back," Alice said.

"Our Lady, you are the Goddess as are all women," said Hecate. She did not appear to be addressing anyone in particular but, rather, the universe as a whole. "You give birth. You feed the children from your own body. And you take them back for a new birth. World without end, eternal creation."

Daisy felt a cool breeze and realized Nick had moved away from her. She spotted him next to Junie. They made a stunning picture, Junie's fairness contrasted with his dark mystery. It was how Nick and Caro must have looked together all those years ago. They looked right. Nick and Daisy would look all wrong.

The dusky sky turned to royal blue and finally indigo as individuals spoke of the recently departed.

Penelope spoke of her aunt, Charlotte Mumford, a woman who liked to crochet and play slot machines. Junie spoke of the man she remembered as Adrian Smith and the way his eyes crinkled when he was amused.

Miss Olive mentioned Ora's allergy to coconut, her love of music, and her lifelong desire to be buried in a rosewood casket along with her parents and twin. Tears pricked the backs of Daisy's eyelids.

When they'd finished, Hecate stepped into the center of the circle. This time she spoke directly to the dead.

"We are with you," she said, "here to help you with your deaths. Our lives are formed of many others and we form other lives in turn. We honor your lives, and we honor your deaths. They are part of us."

Our lives are formed of many others.

It was true. Love wasn't just a bond of blood. It was everywhere. Nick had taught her not to hang onto her relations. She wished she could teach him to trust his. Isabelle and Buzz cared for him and Harmony Lime, in her own way. Mostly, Daisy knew how Theo Bowman had felt about his eldest grandson. He'd loved him enough to let him go, enough to bring him back.

She felt steady gray eyes on her and she exchanged his glance. Her heart brimmed with emotion.

"And now we praise the Goddess," Cedric intoned, "and the Great Horned God, through whom we are reborn. Raise your arms and feel the power of mysticism. It is time for the dead to travel to Summerland. We wish them happiness on the other side of the veil."

****

While the guests descended on the food-laden tables on one side of the garden, Isabelle, Arthur, and Harmony Lime joined Nick near the fountain.

"It was a nice tribute," Isabelle said.

"Yes. Doesn't Cedric make a wonderful Grand Wizard?"

"Certainly," Isabelle agreed. "Of course he is the only male in the coven."

"He did a fine job," Arthur said.

"He gets his power directly from the Horned God," Harmony Lime explained.

Arthur could have been the horned god himself, Nick thought. Was it possible that infidelity was his only crime? But if that were so, who was behind the sabotage of Bowman's Biscuits? And who had attacked Daisy in the cellar of the Gray Lady? The questions circulated in his brain, but he could find no answers. He realized, suddenly, that he was standing next to Alice. He smiled at her.

"You had a major role tonight," he said. "Does that mean you're a card-carrying member of the coven?"

She laughed, lightly. "I have more of a guest pass. I don't mind helping out. The send-off seems to give people a sense of closure."

Nick nodded. He felt a sharp jolt of sympathy for his soon-to-be-ex-sister-in-law. He wondered if she knew about Buzz's plans. He heard her voice again but it was directed at Arthur and it was tinged with concern.

"You don't look well," she said. As she spoke the older man grabbed his chest and struggled for breath. Isabelle hurried to his side.

"Nick," she shouted, "call 911."

"No, don't fuss, my dear," Arthur gasped. "I'm just tired. Need a cold drink and, perhaps, a chair."

Nick helped him to sit. A moment later Alice handed Arthur a glass of lemonade. Even after a long drink, the man's face resembled rice paper.

"Let me drive you to the hospital," Nick said, in a low voice.

"No," Arthur's voice was weak but firm. "I'll be fine. I just need a good night's sleep."

"Perhaps it's your ulcer," Alice suggested, anxiously.

"Ulcer?" Nick noted his aunt's surprise. He would have bet his best racer that Isabelle didn't even know about an ulcer but Alice knew. Did Buzz have any idea how entwined his wife was in the life of his family?

Arthur shook his head. "Suspected ulcer. I think not. I believe I'd like to leave if it's all right with you, dear," he said to his wife.

Nick stared at the attorney. Arthur Sneed had always been a dry stick, as loyal as he was polite. It was nearly impossible to believe he was either an embezzler or a murderer. It was equally impossible to imagine him in the trapeze embedded in Leilani Harter. He helped Arthur to his feet and said he'd accompany him home.

"Isabelle and I can manage."

"I'll go with them," Alice reassured Nick. "Don't worry. He'll be fine."

A moment later Nick's cell phone buzzed.

"Hey," his brother said. "I'm in the cellar rooting around for the damn blue diamond. It's hotter 'n hell, and I'm thirsty."

"You want beer?"

"Make it pop."

Nick spotted Daisy slicing the coconut cake while using her body to protect it from Miss Olive. She was safe enough with half the town out here. He grabbed the soda for his brother and headed for the cellar.

Buzz took a long gulp before he spoke. "You get a chance to talk to Arthur?"

"He's ill. Aunt Iz just took him home."

"I can hardly believe he's mixed up in this."

Nick nodded at his brother. "There's no proof of it, yet, but I did uncover a secret." He omitted the personal details but gave Buzz a brief description of the sexual playpen at the top of Arthur's house.

Buzz stared at him. "Arthur Sneed?"

"I know."

The door at the top of the stairs opened. When Nick realized it was Caroline Budd, he felt a wave of disappointment compounded by irritation. He felt a sudden, violent urge to see Daisy.

"Caroline," Buzz said. "Long time no see."

It was a typical Buzz greeting, but the man's voice contained an odd, strangled quality.

The woman's already tight lips thinned. She nodded but turned her attention to Nick. "I want to know why Junie's telling everyone you and Daisy are engaged. You said she'd turned you down."

His eyes narrowed on Daisy's sister, and he lost his tenuous hold on his patience.

"I intend to change her mind."

Caroline's face filled with anguish.

"Please don't. You'll destroy her. You'll destroy us all!" She turned away from him and ran up the stairs, slamming the door behind her.

Chapter Twenty

The townspeople and the Wiccans bonded over their shared potluck supper. First they discussed the recently deceased, but the conversations drifted to crafts, spelunking, spell-casting, the economy, retirement, and grandchildren.

The full moon appeared at twilight, and the picnickers carried their folding chairs to the field outside the courtyard where someone had set up a brazier and lit a fire. The early evening's sacred circle morphed into an old-fashioned campfire.

Sigrid began to chant. Everyone joined in and laughter erupted when Mayor Hotchkiss tried to harmonize. The chanting turned to "Row, Row, Row your Boat," and "Green Grow the Rushes, Ho" and "Blest Be the Tie That Binds."

Daisy watched with a sense of contentment that she knew she owed to Nick. Sure, he'd knocked her off balance and created turmoil in her heart, but he'd also taught her to realize how much she belonged here in Mayville. How much she loved it. Almost as much as she loved her family. Almost as much as she loved him.

She wished she could help him see that he belonged here, too. Not out of a sense of duty or even lust but because he was a Bowman. She toyed with the possibility of marriage. Could it work with love only on one side? Yes, she decided. She'd make it work. And, maybe someday he'd let down his guard enough to love her back.

Something of her thoughts must have shown on her face because when he sat down next to her on the concrete lip of the Cupid fountain he slid his arm around her waist.

"Why aren't you with the crooners?"

She rested against him, leaned her head on his shoulder. "I was waiting for you."

His arm tightened around her.

"If the offer stands I want to marry you."

"What changed your mind?"

She told him the truth. "I think we can be happy."

"Ever after?"

She smiled. "Why not?"

He pulled her against him and hugged her hard enough to bruise her ribs. In that moment, Daisy felt a jolt of pure joy. Everything would be all right.

Finally, he released her and kissed her hand.

"You've made me very happy."

She grinned. "There's something I have to tell you."

"Sure, honey."

"When you dated Caro, I had a crush on you."

He said nothing and she laughed. "I know you don't even remember me, but I never really got over you."

"So you've still got a crush on me." He sounded pleased.

She laughed again and shook her head. Then her face sobered.

"It's not a crush anymore. I'm in love with you, Nick. I think you should know."

His big warm hands cupped her cheeks, and his lips met hers.

She told herself it would be all right.

His big, warm hands cupped her cheeks and his lips met hers

She told herself it would be all right.

Relief was a tsunami inside him.

She'd promised to marry him.

The stars winked like jewels in the velvet sky. The earth smelled of summer and cut grass. The sounds of the singers warbled on the breeze. Nick pulled his woman against him and rested his chin in the froth of curls on her head. He felt a sense of blessed peace. For the first time in seven years, he felt no bitterness or anger or grief or even any detachment. Just a quiet sense of wellbeing. And it was all due to this woman.

He couldn't wait for the guests to disappear.

He couldn't wait to touch her again, to hear her cry his name. He couldn't wait to hear her whisper the magic words.

I'm in love with you.

****

After the townspeople drifted back to their homes with their empty dishes and a warm sense of camaraderie and Wiccans retired to their rooms, Daisy strolled around the back courtyard picking up litter and tidying up the chairs and tables.

Junie arrived too late to help.

"Where's Nick? Shouldn't he be helping you?"

Daisy refrained from pointing out that, unlike Junie, Nick was not on the payroll.

"He went up to the mansion to check on Arthur."

"Oh."

Junie straightened a chair. "Daze, thanks for tonight. The send-off for Adrian felt like closure."

Daisy hesitated, unsure whether it was time to reveal Adrian's identity. In the end, she didn't have to make the call.

"I know Adrian wasn't his real name."

"You do?"

Junie nodded. Her blonde ponytail bobbed. "It was Spuds something-or-other, and he was a private detective from Chicago. He was here for a reason, wasn't he? Something in the cellar?"

Junie's laughing blue eyes were sober but calm. She'd deduced the truth, or part of it. Junie Budd was growing up. Daisy decided to trust her with the rest of the secret.

"We think he was after a piece of art that was stolen from a Holocaust victim during World War II."

"Stolen by whom?"

"Theo Bowman."

"Oh. Poor Nick."

"He got a letter after his grandfather's death. Theo said the blue diamond was hidden in the Gray Lady's cellar. He asked Nick to find it and return it to the rightful owners."

"I thought you said it was a piece of art."

"We're not sure what it is. Blue diamond could just be a code phrase."

Junie looked thoughtful. "Or maybe the treasure really is a blue diamond."

Daisy nodded. "That could explain why we haven't found it yet. The proverbial needle in a haystack."

"Do you think Adrian meant to keep it for himself?"

Daisy searched her sister's face for signs of distress but found none. "Either that or he expected a payoff. We're fairly sure he was working with somebody."

"You were right, Daze. Adrian was a loser."

Daisy felt a wave of satisfaction. Junie's taste in men was maturing, too.

"Daze? I'm not going to Chicago. I'll stay here with you."

"There's no need, Junie. I'm not going to be alone after all. I'm marrying Nick."

Junie squealed and grabbed her in a bear hug. "I'm so glad! It's just like a fairy tale! Prince Charming comes to Mayville to meet his Cinderella."

Daisy touched her sister's soft cheek. "Is that all you have to say?"

"Uh, tres bien?"

"That's my Junie."

The Wiccans sorted out the rooms with Sarah Glenn and Cedric downstairs in the former crematorium and the rest of the ladies dispersed among the remaining bedrooms. Junie decided to sleep in the large closet next to the porch. Once everyone was settled, Daisy changed into a nightshirt and took the porch sofa. The vinyl cushions squeaked when she stretched out, and she wrinkled her nose. Probably just as well Nick had decided not to come back to the Gray Lady. There was nothing left but the floor.

Still, she missed him.

Weariness engulfed her, but she didn't fall asleep. A week ago she hadn't thought further than the next mortgage payment. Now it seemed her future was charted and defined in a way she couldn't have imagined and the key players had all changed. The glow in her heart and the absolute sense of rightness assured her it wasn't a mistake even though the Budds had never excelled at marriage.

It came down to partner choice, Daisy decided. Her pretty mother had grown bored in the small, Michigan town. Caro and Junie had married on short acquaintance. This was different. Even though Nick hadn't wanted to settle here. Even though he and Daisy had known each other for only a week.

Daisy ignored the echoes of Budd family failures.

Her marriage to Nick would be different from Budd and Bowman marriages of the past. This time would be a victory for both families.

Drowsiness set in disturbed only by an occasional thunk as Junie rolled into the wall next door. Daisy set her mental alarm clock to oh-dark hundred and fell asleep wondering where Nick was sleeping and whether he was dreaming of her.

The hot breath on the back of her neck answered the first question. Breath and teeth and the now familiar Nick-scent mixed with whiskey and industrial-strength testosterone.

His weight pressed her down into the squeaking cushions.

"I want you, honey." She shivered at the feel of lips against her neck. "I've wanted you all night. Had to come." His boozy laugh was thick. "Got to come again. Know wha' I mean?"

Panic stirred in Daisy's stomach. She wondered if she'd suffocate in the vinyl before she died of humiliation. The house was full of witches. His lusty words scattered the panic, and the rough texture of denim against her bare legs triggered her desire. Strong fingers slid under her belly, stormed the beach head between her thighs, and stroked her.

"Oh God, you're wet."

She heard his breathing roughen and quicken. With his front plastered against her back, she felt the rat-a-tat-tat of his heartbeat. Daisy forgot all about the awkward circumstances as his thick erection replaced his talented fingers. He triggered her climax as he drove himself into her with a gut-deep groan. The pillow muffled her scream. He held her in place as he thrust harder and faster until she couldn't breathe or think, until she came again and again. She knew he was close when his hand tightened and his body stiffened and his teeth bit the side of her neck. All at once he collapsed and growled his satisfaction into her hair. For a few seconds she didn't know where his body left off and hers began.

The uncontrolled passion should have frightened her, but she reveled in it. It was heavy, uncomfortable, awkward, stifling, heaven.

She wanted to whisper she loved him, but it didn't matter. He already knew.

"Daisy?"

She didn't understand. Nick's gasps told her he hadn't yet caught his breath. How could he speak?

"Daisy? Are you all right? I thought I heard a noise."

It wasn't Nick. It was Junie. Good grief. She arched up to free her mouth.

"It's the wind, honey. Go back to sleep."

"Daisy?" The voice was only a few feet away, and Nick was still embedded in her body. Daisy prayed it was too dark to see anything.

"What's going on?"

Male fingers dug into her flesh, and Nick let out an annoyed grunt as he lifted himself off her.

"Merde!"

"Daisy, dear?"

Daisy groaned at the sound of the second, more mature voice. They'd wakened one of the witches. She prayed for a miracle but knew she wouldn't get it. The overhead light came on as she struggled to pull down her night shirt.

"Gracious goddess." Daisy winced but Miss Regina wasn't looking at her. The older lady's eyes were on Nick's open fly. "How marvelous! A love tryst!"

Daisy was aware of Nick clumsily trying to zip up. She tried to block him from view and divert the guest's attention with an awkward apology.

"Miss Regina, I just don't know what to say."

"I'm Penelope and there's no need to say a thing. I understand perfectly."

"You do?"

"Of course. Tonight's a full moon. A night for romantic love."

Daisy wasn't sure the mating on the sofa could be characterized as "romantic love," but she didn't question her luck.

"L'amour, toujours, l'amour," Junie added, wickedly.

"Mother Nature will always have her way," Penelope said. "A full moon is a sign of fertility. I wouldn't be a bit surprised if a new soul enters your life nine months hence."

"Oui, oui!" Junie clapped her hands. "I'm going to

be an auntie. Again!"

By the time the Wiccans gathered for breakfast some hours later, Nick had disappeared. Daisy only wished she could have done the same.

Prunella passed a shallow plate filled with fluffy scrambled eggs to Sigrid.

"I understand some of us missed all the excitement last night."

Apparently discretion was too much to hope for.

"These blueberry scones are delicious, dears," Sarah Glenn said. "Could I have the recipe?"

"Il n'est rien," Junie said. "I tweaked a recipe from the back of the Bowman's Biscuit Mix box."

Prunella was not to be diverted.

"Such a virile young man," she sighed. "I quite envy you."

"Nick is Daisy's fiancé," Junie put in.

"That's lovely, dear," Sigrid said, "but as pagans we require no labels and we make no judgments. We believe in the natural. And there is nothing as natural as mating."

"Sig, you're embarrassing Daisy," Sarah Glenn admonished.

"Love is a wonderful thing," Sigrid protested. "Don't you agree, Cedric?"

The Grand Wizard choked on his toast.

"We were snug as a bug in a rug last night," Sarah Glenn said. She cast a sympathetic glance at Daisy. "And since it was the former crematorium, we had the advantage of nice thick walls. I don't see Hecate this morning. Did she oversleep?"

"I believe our acting high priestess made a conquest, too," Prunella said. "That red-headed police officer."

Jimmy? Had Jimmy spent the night with the girl with the old soul? Daisy shot a glance at Junie. Her younger sister did not seem perturbed.

"A full moon," Sigrid said. "Few can resist a sign from the goddess."

The back door opened and closed, and Daisy gritted her teeth. She'd hoped Nick had enough sense of self-preservation not to come back this morning.

"Perhaps you would like to be hand-fasted today along with Sarah Glenn and Cedric," Miss Regina said.

"Or they might prefer a traditional wedding," Sigrid chimed in. "Either would be lovely."

"Or perhaps Nick will whisk you off to Las Vegas," Miss Penelope said. "He seemed in something of a hurry."

Footsteps crossed from the top of the stairs and everyone turned to greet the newcomer.

"Good morning, Caroline," Sarah Glenn said. "You look lovely today."

With her gleaming blonde hair in a loose topknot on her head and a white, lace sundress, Caro did look like an angel. A very white-faced, very distressed angel.

"Daisy, could I have a word?"

No one could miss the tension in Caro's voice.

"Of course." Daisy excused herself from the table and rose.

"Oh, Daisy dear, I must tell you I invited the good friends who shared the circle with us last night to attend the hand-fast," Sarah Glenn said. "I hope that's all right. Cedric and I felt such a cosmic connection with them."

"You invited them all?" Daisy couldn't hide her

dismay.

"I didn't mean to add to your responsibilities. I assured them it was potluck again."

"No, that's fine. Everyone's welcome."

She followed Caro out to the courtyard. The concrete surround on the Cupid Fountain was still cool but the sun reflected off the water and the air was filled with the scent of honeysuckle and the chirps of insects. She watched her sister try to bring her emotions under control.

"They think you're going to marry Nick Bowman."

Daisy sighed. The hand-fasting would take all her focus today. She'd hoped to put off this confrontation.

"They are right. I agreed to marry him last night."

Caro's breath hitched. "It's because of Chicago, isn't it? Because Junie and I are deserting you."

Relief washed through Daisy. She grabbed her sister's cold hand. "No, no. You're right to leave, and I'm okay with it. This is different. He asked me, and I said yes. I care about him, Caro. It has nothing to do with you."

Tears welled up in her sister's eyes. The sight tore at Daisy's heart.

"Don't cry, honey," she whispered. "It will be all right. Everything will be okay."

Sobs shook Caroline's slim frame and Daisy gathered her sister in her arms.

"It won't be okay," Caro said, shakily. "It will never be okay, and you're wrong. This has everything to do with me. I'm sorry, Daze. I know you care about him, but you simply cannot marry Nick Bowman."

Daisy heard the honest misery in her sister's words and she held very still, bracing herself for a blow.

"Why can't I marry Nick?"

"Because," Caroline sobbed, "because he is Stevie's father."

Chapter Twenty-One

Nick showered at the cabin and changed into a fresh pair of jeans and a T-shirt he pulled out of the suitcase in the back of the Malibu.

All his T-shirts were dull, dark colors, black or gray or olive. Those colors, he thought, no longer reflected his state of mind. Maybe he'd try yellow or forest green or psychedelic pink. The world was bright and welcoming and it smelled like a rose. No, not a rose. A daisy.

He'd never forget the look on her face last night when she realized they had an audience. He flushed slightly, remembering Miss Whatever-her-name-was's view of his unclothed crotch. Well, hell. It'd be a good story for the grandchildren.

Nothing bothered him today. Not the unsolved murder or the failing company or the as yet unrecovered Nazi loot. He'd always thought he'd known what he wanted in life. He'd been wrong. He couldn't wait to start his life with Daisy. He couldn't stop grinning.

He heard an irritated meow and glanced at the creature wrapped around his ankle.

"Sorry," he muttered as he searched for the can opener and a fresh can of tuna. "How'd you like a new home," he asked Larry. "Not the mausoleum but somewhere else. Maybe we'll buy the house on Dollar

Lake." There'd be worse ways to spend his time than with Daisy up in Arthur's sex swing.

The cloud of contentment followed him to Bowman Mansion where he greeted Finch then made his way to the breakfast room. It was seven-thirty, the time the household always sat down to breakfast. There was only Alice at the table.

"There's something I'd like to tell you," she said, after he'd helped himself to coffee and food. He nodded. He found it difficult to meet her eyes. The width between them had to be mere millimeters less than average and yet he felt almost cross-eyed when he faced her.

"I am going to see a divorce lawyer. I hate to break up the family, but I'm afraid I can't stay married to a man with a drinking problem."

The declaration startled him. Apparently she didn't know Buzz intended the same action. Nick wondered why she was telling him.

"I'm very sorry," he said. "Does my brother know?"

"You mean your half-brother, don't you?"

Nick realized he didn't. Buzz was his brother. Always had been, always would be. He said nothing.

"I won't serve papers until he's back from rehab. Since you have returned as the head of the family, I thought I should tell you first. Isabelle will be devastated."

He lifted an eyebrow. "What about Buzz?"

She seemed to have no answer for that.

"I assume you've wrestled with this for some time, so I won't attempt to talk you out of it. I will certainly do whatever I can to make certain you're comfortable."

The words sounded cold and businesslike. She nodded without smiling, but Nick didn't miss the gleam of malice in her eye. Under the surface of this quiet, unassuming woman, Buzz's wife for the past seven years, was a cauldron roiling with angry emotions. She reminded him of himself when he'd left Mayville, and he wanted to warn her to let the fury go, that it would eat at her soul, but he couldn't find the words. And, besides, they were only words.

Alice would have to find peace in her own way.

"How is Arthur this morning?"

"I believe he's still in bed. The summer has exhausted him."

Damn. Another visit in vain.

Isabelle appeared a moment later. She'd dressed in a gauzy tie-dyed caftan, bright plastic beads, and there was a gardenia in her hair.

"As you can see, I'm already dressed for the hand-fast. Good morning, Nicky, dear."

"How's Arthur?"

"He had a restless night, poor dear." Isabelle did not sound distraught. Maybe she was just grateful to have her husband beside her in bed. "He promised me he'd sleep in so he'd be fresh for tonight's festivities."

Isabelle paused to take a sip of the coffee.

"I have some news," he told his aunt. "I'm going to marry Daisy Budd."

Smiles wreathed Isabelle's pleasant face. "Of course you are, dear. After that business last night. you really have no choice." Damn the confounded grapevine.

"This has nothing to do with last night. I want to marry Daisy."

232

"I can't blame you. She is not the family beauty, but she has a huge heart."

He imagined how many times Daisy had heard that remark. Not the family beauty.

"In any case she will make a wonderful CEO's wife." Isabelle smiled at him but the expression faded as she glanced at her niece-in-law. "Just as you did, Alice, dear. We have all appreciated everything you've done for the family."

There was something in Isabelle's voice. Did she know Buzz intended to divorce Alice and vice versa?

Alice smiled, neutrally, and got to her feet. "Will you excuse me? Harmony Lime devised some sort of a nun's robe for me to wear to the festivities." She closed the dining room door behind her.

Nick looked at his aunt. "How long has Judith plagued her with Wicca and Zoroastrians?"

"I don't believe Alice minds," Isabelle replied, thoughtfully. "She has never really recovered her spirits after the loss of the baby."

Nick stared at her. "What baby?"

"Alice was pregnant when she and Buzz married. I thought you knew that."

"No." The information explained a lot, though. He felt a wrench of sympathy for both Alice and Buzz. Mostly for Buzz.

"After the miscarriage they never conceived again. Not surprising, really."

"What do you mean?"

"Only that they have never seemed well suited and I've always suspected Buzz of regretting the marriage."

Nick eyed her with admiration. Not much got past Aunt Isabelle. He wondered how she had failed to find

233

out about Arthur's home away from home.

"What about you and Daisy? I know it isn't my business, but I hope you will have a family."

He grinned at the prospect of a small stubborn daughter with flame-colored hair and incurable optimism. "I'll give it my best shot."

He got to his feet compelled by a sudden urgency to get back to the Gray Lady.

"I have something for you," Isabelle said. She led him into her small morning room and handed him a large, bound book.

"Take a look at this when you get time. I think you'll find it interesting."

****

The townspeople started to arrive in midafternoon. Despite overhead rumblings, the sky was still clear and it seemed the weather would hold.

Daisy wore a butter-hued, ankle-length sundress, sandals, and a crown of daisies fashioned by Stevie and Junie. She fixed what she hoped was a cheerful smile on her face and concentrated on keeping it there. While she helped prepare the tables for more home-cooked food, Daisy mentally reviewed the situation. There had been no way to avoid this heartache. Nick had always affected her like a tidal wave. She'd have fallen in love with him even if she'd known about Stevie. She'd been lucky to have these few days with him, and she knew she would cherish their memory in the lonely years ahead.

Lonely years? Her heart twisted as she pictured countless Thanksgiving dinners with Nick and Caro and their growing family. It would hurt but, eventually, the pain would dull. And there was the one small comfort:

Nick hadn't known about Stevie. As soon as he learned the truth, he'd do the right thing.

She'd stake her life on it. And he would learn the truth—soon. She'd made Caro promise to tell him.

Daisy lifted her chin and straightened her spine.

Caro would marry Nick and Stevie would have a father and she, Daisy, would create a new life for herself at Happily Ever After.

"Good morning, Daisy," boomed the mayor, who had dressed, once more as Henry XIII. "Many felicitations to you on bagging the whale."

Daisy thanked him and set about greeting the other guests including Debbie Popple costumed as Bewitched's Endora.

"You got your signals crossed, girlfriend," Debbie teased. "You were supposed to fix me up with Nick Bowman, not get engaged to him yourself, but listen, no hard feelings. I'll probably meet somebody at your wedding. Maybe you could invite that TV reporter,

Cory Aspen, from Detroit. I hear he's single."

Daisy recalled the cocky, obtuse newsman. "What a shock," she murmured.

Cherry Ann had chosen to wear her Juliet wedding gown, and she resembled the bride of Frankenstein while Quentin arrived in a white monk's robe. It seemed he'd solved the problem of lunging.

"Chief Sharkey said Quent looks like a KKK member," Cherry Ann confided. Her husband's brow furrowed.

"Ridiculous. Anyone can see that I'm Galadriel from Lord of the Rings."

"Wasn't Galadriel a girl?" Daisy spoke without thinking, and Quent glowered at her.

"Elves are known to be asexual."

Cherry Ann giggled. "I don't know about that, dear. How would they get more elves?"

Daisy thought, not for the first time, that Cherry Ann's sense of the absurd was a good balance for Quent. Caro had been much too somber for him. Pain gripped her heart. Caro had married the eccentric professor only because she was pregnant. No wonder Quent had never behaved as a proper father to the little boy. Poor Caro. Poor Stevie. Poor Quent.

The ladies from Bowman Mansion arrived accompanied by Arthur Sneed who looked paler than usual in his brown business suit. Had Nick had time to confront him with the allegations? She thought not.

She wished she could soften the blow of Caro's revelation. He'd be shocked and, well, she didn't know whether he'd be upset. Probably. But, in spite of appearances, he had never really been a Prodigal Son. He hadn't left his family with a light heart, and Daisy knew he wouldn't leave his family again.

"Quelle delight!"

Junie's voice pierced her consciousness, and she noticed that her sister had tweaked her ice blue Renaissance costume into appropriate handfast attire by adding a magic wand.

But it wasn't her sister's fairy-like beauty that stopped Daisy's heart.

Junie had Nick Bowman by the hand.

"I've brought you un cadeau," she said. "He's not wearing a costume, but you've got to admit he's perfect."

Nick didn't give her a chance to answer. Concern flared in his gray eyes as he studied her face.

"What's wrong, sunshine?"

"I'm just a little tired."

"Naturalement," ." Junie chuckled. "All that l'amour."

A horrified scream jerked Daisy's attention to the Cupid Fountain where a child teetered on the concrete surround. As everyone watched, paralyzed by horror, he swayed, lost his balance, and plummeted into the water.

Nick wasn't the closest spectator, but he had the quickest reactions and reached Stevie first. He reached into the fountain, scooped the child up with one arm, and carried him onto the lawn like a soggy football then he tossed Stevie in the air a few times until the boy's cries of fear became shrieks of pleasure. Gradually conversation resumed among the guests as they watched Mayville's bad boy set the child on his feet and take one of his hands while Caroline Budd grabbed the other. The trio headed to the house together, a dark haired man, a blonde woman and a tow-headed boy. Father, mother, child. A perfect family.

Daisy's initial sense of horror gave way to relief as, all around her, people praised Nick Bowman's quick actions. Several people called him a hero, and she nodded her agreement.

Luckily it was time for the ceremony.

Hecate summoned the guests to the circle and everyone followed her, pied piper-like under the white arch twined in red roses, white lilies, and green snapdragons. The flowers, chosen with care by Daisy and Miss Florence, reflected traditional handfast colors.

Sarah Glenn looked elegant and serene in an embroidered tunic worn over an ankle-length skirt. Cedric had foregone a polo shirt and khakis for black trousers and a loose, collarless shirt of a rich, burgundy.

He offered Sarah his arm and patted her hand. His distinguished middle-aged face radiated affection as the couple journeyed to each of the compass points on the circle where they received blessings and gifts.

Daisy tried to listen, but her heart was upstairs in the Gray Lady. At this very moment, Caro was undoubtedly uttering the words that would change all of their lives. Daisy willed Nick and her sister to accept the truth and to embrace it.

Sarah Glenn's vows made Daisy tremble with emotion.

"From the moment we met," she told her intended, "you have understood me and supported me. You have enriched my life is so many ways as we've walked a path together. You always see the goddess in me. I promise to always see the god in you."

Cedric paused for a long minute. "I love you, Sarah Glenn. And I always will."

Tears coursed down Daisy's cheeks, but from the gulps and sniffs she heard, she knew she wasn't the only one affected by the groom's simple declaration. True, unadorned love touched everyone. She forced a smile. It was, in its way, a comforting thought.

Chapter Twenty-Two

Fate, Nick realized, had provided a perfect moment to find out why Caroline Budd hated him so much. He waited for her to help her son change his clothes. After Stevie blasted out of the house Nick took Caro's arm.

"I'd like to talk to you."

She didn't want to be with him. The tension in her arm revealed her resistance, but he knew she wouldn't bolt. He'd just fished her son out of the fountain, and she would pay her debt. After all, she was a Budd. Before he could come up with another way to ask what the hell her problem was, she asked him a question.

"Were you happy in California?" It was a start.

"I wasn't unhappy. I set goals and met them."

"Why did you come back to Mayville, Nick?"

He knew it was too late for lies. She was going to be his sister-in-law. Daisy loved and trusted her. He'd trust her, too. He told her about the quest for the blue diamond.

Caroline's blue eyes searched his face. "Why didn't Theo ask Buzz to find it?"

He shrugged. "Daisy believes the letter was an olive branch, that Theo used it to lure me back into the family and the business."

"Is that what happened?"

He chuckled. "Pretty much."

"Daisy's got good instincts about people. Most of

the time."

Nick studied her. Was their battle over? No.

She'd calmed down, but there was still something in those turquoise eyes. Turmoil. And tears.

"Caroline," he said, catching her hand.

"You love her, don't you? Oh, no, please don't tell me. I'm just,"—she tugged her hand away from him—"I'm just so sorry." She fled down the corridor and out the door.

He let her go but he frowned, thoughtfully. She was still distressed, but, for once, it seemed he was not the source of her anxiety. So what was? What was her secret? He promised himself he would find out.

The notes of a recorder informed him that the hand-fast was under way. Nick sprinted down the hallway. He didn't want to miss another moment with Daisy.

****

At the end of the ceremony, the hand-fasted couple jumped over a broom, a pagan custom that symbolized crossing the threshold to a new life together.

Warm, strong hands at her waist made Daisy inhale deeply. Nick. Had he been behind her all the time? How had she not sensed him? Smelled him? A pang of sadness hit her. Their connection was already weakened.

"I liked the ceremony," he murmured into her ear. "Maybe we should do a hand-fast, too." Her heart twisted. Caro hadn't told him.

She flashed him a bright smile.

"You were Batman."

He shrugged off the compliment.

"More like the Old Man and the Sea. I fished out a

minnow." His light tone matched hers, but the gray eyes looked puzzled. "He seems like a great kid. We should order one just like him."

Tears collected behind Daisy's eyes, but she held her smile. "He is a great kid. Look, I've got to get back to the tables."

She felt his eyes on her as she crossed the lawn and she knew he was confused. It would all become clear later, as soon as Caro told him the truth. When she reached the table, she glanced back and saw that he'd walked over to where Arthur Sneed stood next to the honeysuckle bushes. She willed her sister to go talk to him, but Caro appeared to be very busy with the food. Daisy knew she couldn't let this go. As soon as the dust cleared, Daisy would talk to her again. Nick had to be told about his fatherhood and soon. The doomed engagement had to end before Daisy lost her sanity.

****

Arthur's dizziness held off until after the ceremony. He sat in a chair provided by his wife and willed himself to do what he knew he had to do.

"I'll get you a plate, dear," she said.

The thought of food made him nauseous. What he needed was Dutch courage.

"I'd prefer a drink."

Tonight he would talk to Nick. His conscience was torturing him. Anything, including personal and financial ruin was preferable to one more angst ridden, sleepless night.

Someone pressed a glass into his hand, and her touch reacted on him like electroshock. Damn. Damn, damn, damn. Anger rushed through his system. Anger that she had that effect on him. Anger at his own helplessness. This would end now. Tonight. He drank down the lemonade then turned to his wife.

"I'm going inside to use the facilities," he said. He patted her hand when she offered to go with him. "No, dear. Stay and enjoy your friends. I'll be fine."

Arthur inhaled the scent of freshly cut grass and the fresh night air. He heard the friendly voices around him, the eager laughs, and he wished he had the right to enjoy the evening. But he didn't. He hadn't for some time. He longed for the moderation and control that had characterized nearly all of his sixty years. Damn. He should never have married. He should have stuck with his bachelor ways, his coin collection, his reading. He should have let Isabelle remain a friend. He knew it was the marriage itself that had opened the door to sensual delights and, ultimately, destruction. He should have left that door closed.

****

Nick stood in the shadows of a honeysuckle bush and followed Arthur's progress toward the house with his eyes. He read the tension in the stoop of the older man's thin shoulders. Arthur Sneed was a man at a tipping point. Daisy was right. Tonight was the time to confront him.

Arthur disappeared through the back door. Was he planning to take another look around the cellar? Nick slipped his cell out of his pocket and punched in his brother's number.

"Arthur's in the house."

"Good. Time for a summit. Think he's heading to the cellar?"

"One way to find out."

****

The cellar door was closed and there was no sliver of light but Arthur knew she was down there. It was not merely that they hadn't found the diamond. She preferred the dank, spooky underground. She was a creature of the dark.

After the injury to Daisy Budd, he'd told her the search was off, but he knew she wouldn't heed him. She would use her wiles to bend him to her will, and she would expect to succeed. Why not? Her wiles had already made him abandon every principle by which he'd once lived.

This time it wouldn't work, but he dreaded the confrontation. A wave of self-disgust struck him. If he'd been any kind of a man, he'd have rejected all this—her—long ago. If he'd been any kind of a husband, he'd have confessed long before now.

She'd ensnared him, bewitched him. He'd been a damned fool. It was too late to save his integrity or his marriage. It was not too late to call off the madness.

Arthur opened the cellar door and found the vast room lit by a single candle.

The air, cool and musty, carried a sense of doom, and his poor eyesight blinded him to what awaited. When he reached the bottom step, he found her reclined on a blanket. For once her sensuous body reminded him of a serpent sunning itself on a rock. She held out her hand, and, with some reluctance, he dropped down to the blanket next to her.

"This isn't exactly our aerie, but it'll do."

Aerie. For some reason Arthur thought of Hitler's mountain retreat at Berchtesgaden. A rather apt analogy. He, too, had destroyed everything in his path. Everything good. A shiver racked his body. This was it.

Tonight he'd break her hold.

"It's over, Alice."

She said nothing, and he peered at her. Could it be this easy?

"I mean it. I'm going to tell Nick what I've done. And Isabelle, too."

"You'll go to jail."

"I know. I'll keep your name out of it."

"Not much chance of that." Her voice was low key, the sensible Alice he'd known for seven years. Where was the devil who'd led him around Hell for the past months? But that wasn't fair. He was the devil. He had no one to blame but himself.

She leaned close to him, and her nearness had the usual effect. His blood raced even as he sensed the menace in her, felt the revulsion mixed with the raging lust. He didn't move as she manipulated his belt and zipper. He shuddered, hating her touch and needing it, caged by a terrible helplessness and self-loathing.

"No more."

She ignored him. She squeezed and massaged him until he hardened, until he groaned.

She'd destroyed his illusion of himself as a civilized, evolved man. He knew the truth now. He was nothing but a lump of primordial ooze, a horny old man.

"Well, Arthur?"

His arousal throbbed with need, and he thrust himself into her hand, silently imploring her to continue. She stroked him, teased him, drove him to beg for it. She loved to hear him beg.

He heard a door open and close, but he couldn't open his eyes. He heard Alice's breath. Was she going to blow him or the candle? "Please," he muttered, "please, please."

She squeezed him once more and he erupted, his hoarse cry barely audible. He felt so tired. So incredibly tired.

****

There was no light in the cellar. Either Arthur had developed radar, or Nick had guessed wrong.

Shit.

He paused on the step, aware of that same sense of wrongness he'd felt in Langston's office. And then he inhaled a whiff of smoke. He reached back to warn Buzz to keep quiet. Was this a trap?

He continued down the steps. At least Daisy wasn't here. He and Buzz should be able to handle one sick old man.

He flicked on the overhead bulb when he reached the final step. The dim light illuminated a strange tableau. Buzz gasped. "Alice."

Her voice was lazy and laced with contempt. "Welcome to my web said the spider to the flies."

Nick stared at the pistol in his sister-in-law's hand.

"What the hell's going on?" Buzz sounded confused. "What're you doing down here in the dark? Where did you get the gun?"

"I'll answer your questions if you tell me where you've been for the past fifteen days."

"You're the partner," Nick said, his eyes narrowing on her, the truth hitting him. "You're the one who hired Spuds Langston and killed him. The one who tried to set Buzz up to take the fall. You're the one who left the letters and butterflies and hit Daisy. You're the mastermind."

Buzz pushed past Nick to confront his wife.

"Is it true?"

"You were never as clever as your brother. Except once."

"But why?"

"I might as well ask you why you married me then left me alone night after night after night." Alice's voice was calm, deadly. "What I don't understand is why you stayed married to me."

"Aw, Alice. You know it was never any good."

"You took seven years of my life, and now you're going to pay for it."

Her voice was calm and dispassionate. There was no discernible malice in it, just determination. Nick knew they were in trouble.

"Of course. I knew you'd eventually destroy Bowman's Biscuits on your own. I didn't want to wait that long to see the Bowman family groveling in the dirt."

"But you're a Bowman."

"You're such a fool."

Nick stared at Arthur's prone body. His eyes were closed, his face, chalky.

"What did you do to Arthur," he asked.

"A slight sedative. He has the same chance to survive as the rest of you. Just give me the blue diamond and you can live. Otherwise—," she waved the pistol, "—I'm afraid I have no choice."

There was no chance. Even if they could produce the Nazi loot, she couldn't afford to let any of them leave the cellar. Nick started to edge closer to her. If they could keep her talking, distract her long enough for him to knock the gun out of her hand, they might have a chance.

"Alice, sweetheart, if this is about the baby, I..." She cut off the unformed question.

"There was no baby."

Buzz's jaw dropped. "No baby? But the doctor's report, the miscarriage."

"All faked. I knew you'd fallen for someone else, that it was a matter of time until you'd dump me. I had no intention of losing out on the Bowman's wealth, so I lied about a baby. And you were such a chump. You believed it. Playing Sir Galahad never pays off, Buzz. It's something you should remember."

"I don't think it was about the money," Nick said, suddenly. "I think you wanted Buzz to love you, and he didn't."

He realized his mistake when she cocked the pistol in his direction. She was distracted only by the sound of the cellar door opening and a voice. "Caro? Are you down here? We have to talk." Daisy. Goddammitall to hell.

"Get out of here," he yelled at her. Naturally she ignored the command.

"Nick?" He heard her light footsteps on the stairs.

"What's going on down here? Why are there no lights? Is Caro with you?"

"Please join us," Alice said. She moved the single candle into position to make the gun visible to the newcomer. "We're talking about old times."

Daisy gaped at the small group. Her glance fell on the older man on the floor.

"What's the matter with Arthur?"

"I drugged him."

Daisy moved toward the gunwoman.

"You were Spuds's partner, weren't you," she said, slowly. "You killed him, didn't you? I'm guessing he wanted to find the blue diamond and sell it on the black market, but you weren't interested in the money. This was all about revenge."

"What're you talking about?" Buzz asked her.

"It's classic," Daisy went on. "The woman scorned. Oh, Alice, it wasn't worth it. You didn't need a man's love to be fulfilled. You're smart and competent. You could do anything on your own."

The gun hand quivered, but Alice's voice remained calm. Nick continued to inch toward her, but he could no longer think clearly. Anxiety clouded his judgement. Damn the interfering little witch. Why couldn't she have stayed upstairs, out of harm's way? He willed her to move behind him.

"I loved him, and he was about to leave me. I tricked him into marrying me, but it was never any good. Now you'll pay." Her gaze shifted to Buzz. "You and your whole family. I want that treasure, and if I don't get it in the next sixty seconds, I'll start shooting. You—," she pointed the gun at Daisy, "—will go first."

Nick's heart thundered in his chest.

"They'll hear you upstairs."

"I don't think so. Everyone is outside, and I've got a silencer. Well? Do you have the diamond?"

"Alice," Buzz begged, dropping to the floor in front of her, "you don't have to kill all these people. Come with me. I'll take care of you. I'll make sure you have everything you want."

"Tempting as that offer is," she said, dryly, "I'm afraid it's too little too late. I'm going to assume no one has the diamond and therefore, your fates are sealed but there is something I want you to know."

The woman was obviously enjoying her moment in the spotlight. If only they could prolong it, Nick thought. He was about eight feet away from her. If he could move within six feet he'd have a good chance of flinging himself at her, catching her by surprise and taking the only bullet she'd be able to squeeze off.

"Quentin Crisp is not the father of Caroline Budd's child," Alice said.

Nick felt Daisy's eyes on him, but he didn't move his focus from the woman with the gun.

"The kid was conceived that night at the cabin," Alice went on. "His father is my loving husband."

"No, no that's not right." Daisy's voice was agitated. "It isn't Buzz. Stevie belongs to Nick." Her voice sounded nearer. "I'm sorry you had to find out this way," she said, in a softer voice, "but it's true. Caro told me."

The anguish in her voice and the words themselves startled Nick enough to break his concentration at least for an instant.

"He's not my son, Daisy. I never slept with your sister."

"I don't believe you," Daisy said. She didn't even hesitate. "My sister wouldn't lie."

Pain slammed into him. She chose to believe her sister. Once again he learned the painful lesson; blood is thicker than water. You'd think he'd learn.

"Nick's right," said Buzz. He rubbed the back of his neck. "And Alice is right. Caroline and I were together that night. I never told anyone because I was ashamed. She was Nick's girl. I don't know why she didn't tell me about the baby."

"It was because you were married," Alice said. "To me. And we were 'expecting.'"

"Oh God," Daisy groaned. "I'm so sorry, Nick." Had she changed her mind? It didn't matter. The words had no effect on him. He hardened his heart against her. If they ever got out of this cellar, he was on a plane back to L.A. Relationships and family were not for him. He'd finally gotten the message.

"I think that's enough confession time," Alice said. She got, lithely, to her feet. "I'm leaving now and, as you can imagine, it would be very awkward for me to leave witnesses. When they discover you're all dead except Arthur, they'll believe he's gone over the edge. They won't be wrong."

Nick knew he was too far away but at least he could divert her.

She put both hands on the pistol. "Oh, and I've changed my mind about the order. You'll go first," she said.

She aimed at Nick just as he hurled himself toward her. Time seemed to expand as he waited to hear the small, deadly pop and feel the searing heat of the lead as it ripped through his flesh. She could hardly miss at this distance. Out of the corner of his eye he saw that Daisy was moving, too. He saw her scoop up the candle and fling it at the gunwoman's head. He heard the "pop," but he felt nothing. Had Alice shot wide? And then suddenly Alice was shrieking as flames raced through her hair. She dropped to the floor as the fire quickly caught the dry boxes nearby and dropped onto her clothing.

Nick yelled at Daisy to get out of the cellar as he knocked the gun out of Alice's hand and tried, without success, to put out the fire.

"I can't," she yelled, "Alice shot Buzz."

Nick's gut twisted as he smothered the fire with his body. Buzz. He held onto the shrieking Alice, as he gazed helplessly at his unconscious brother. And then the cellar door opened. Caroline ran down the steps, her face white, her eyes huge.

"Call an ambulance," Daisy shouted, but Caroline didn't seem to hear her. She dropped to the floor and cradled Buzz's head.

"Never mind," Daisy said as she pulled a cell phone out of her pocket. "I'll do it."

Chapter Twenty-Three

All the excitement was over. The Wiccans were gone and Happily Ever After was closed. Alice Bowman languished in a burn unit in a New York hospital. Meanwhile, Arthur Sneed remained at the Bowman Mansion under Isabelle's care. She'd said she believed in her vows and that she'd decided to forgive him. The police believed he had not been involved in Spud's murder and the two Bowman brothers, now CEO and director of marketing, had yet to decide whether to prosecute him for sabotage of the company.

The bullet that had hit Buzz Bowman had grazed his skull, and, after one night in the hospital, he was back home. Within a few days, he and his brother began to strategize about the future of the company.

The few people who knew about the Nazi loot had concluded it was a hoax. Junie provided all of the details for Daisy during her daily call or visit. Caroline called daily, too, anxious to find out whether Daisy was ready to talk about what had happened. She wasn't ready to talk. She needed time alone she'd told everyone. The truth was, she was hurt by Caro's lie, but she was devastated by her own reaction to it.

She sat for hours in the Adirondack chair on the cabin's porch and watched the summer days slip into evening. She'd decided to sell the Gray Lady to the Bowmans if they still wanted it. She was unqualified to run a wedding boutique much less to be a bride herself. She knew nothing about trust or love.

Nothing.

When push came to shove, when the chips were down, when it was critical to believe the man she loved, she hadn't. She'd apologized that night. And the day after and Nick had accepted those apologies with a kind of distant formality. She had let him down in the worst way possible. She had chosen her family over him just the way Theo had done.

He would never really forgive her, but it didn't matter. She would never really forgive herself.

Daisy stared out at the lake and watched it change colors to match the sky. Soon the Gray Lady and the cabin would go back to the Bowmans. Soon her sisters and Stevie would move to Chicago. Soon she would have to think about her own future.

But not yet.

****

"You found anything yet?" Buzz pushed himself back from his desk as the brothers took a break from their daily work trying to restructure Bowman's Biscuits. "Down in the cellar, I mean."

"Nope." Nick didn't tell his brother he'd stopped looking. He'd spent every evening of the past week in the Gray Lady's cellar, but he hadn't been searching for the phantom loot.

"It's been seven days," Buzz said, with a sigh. "I don't think Caroline is ever planning to talk to me." "Give her time," Nick advised.

"I don't want to give her time. Hell, I've had a son for seven years. It's time I got to know him. It's time he got to know me."

"What're you planning to say to her?" Buzz stared at his older brother.

"I'm going to insist that she marry me."

"She's planning to move to Chicago, you know."

"Well, she can just change her plans. Or, she can leave the boy with me. It's certainly my turn."

Nick chuckled, humorlessly. "You might want to use a more conciliatory approach."

"What about you? Are you still going to marry? Daisy?"

"No."

"I think you're a fool."

Nick's eyes narrowed, and his fists clenched.

"You love each other. She set Alice's hair on fire to try to save your skin. So what if she believed her sister over you? It was natural."

"I know. They're sisters. Blood."

Buzz frowned at him. "It was natural because she's trusted her sister all her life. She's known you what, seven days?"

Nick shrugged. "Blood's blood."

Buzz gazed at him for a long moment, then he cursed and jerked open his desk drawer. He pulled out the scrapbook Isabelle had given Nick.

"What're you doing with that?"

"Aunt Isabelle suggested I get you to look at it."

"Later. We've got a company to save."

"This is more important." He handed it over, and, reluctantly, Nick began to flip through the pages. It was full of newspaper clippings, report cards, and snapshots of birthday parties and dances, football games, and prep school and college awards, programs and tickets and ribbons that he and Buzz had won as youngsters. There was an entire section on his racing career.

A lump formed in Nick's throat but he swallowed it. He looked over at his brother.

"So? What's the big deal?"

"Don't you get it? Theo treated us both the same. You were as much his grandson as I was."

"Then why did he disinherit me?"

"I spent a long time puzzling over that," Buzz admitted. "He knew, everybody knew that you'd make a better CEO for Bowman's Biscuits, but he sent you off and kept me around to screw up. I think he didn't want you to take the job out of a sense of duty. I think he wanted you to have your own adventure, pursue your own dream, but, at the same time, he wanted you to come back to Mayville."

Nick stared at the photographs of himself as a child.

"That's what Daisy said."

"That's probably why he devised the story of the Nazi loot. He knew that one day he'd have a powerful reason to summon you back. He knew you'd come. He knew you wouldn't turn your back on the family and he was right."

Nick was silent.

"Theo didn't play favorites with us, unless you count the fact that he had more confidence in you. It isn't fair to judge Daisy by the same standard. She didn't expect her sister to lie."

"But she expected that from me."

Buzz shook his head. "That wasn't even about you. It was about her and Caroline." He paused. "Junie says she just sits out there at the cabin staring at the lake. Don't you think she's suffered enough for doubting you? Don't you think you've suffered enough?"

Nick leafed through the scrapbook for another minute as his brother's words washed over him and the terrible sense of betrayal eased. The need to punish Daisy faded, banished by the much more compelling need to be with her, to take care of her, to love her. If he didn't do something, quickly, he faced the rest of his life without her.

****

Three days later Nick drove out to the lake. He found Daisy on the porch in one of the Adirondack chairs facing the lake. Larry occupied the other. The cat protested, briefly, and then permitted Nick to take his seat.

"Hey," he said.

"Hey, yourself." She didn't smile.

Nick felt a sharp pang as he peered at her face. It was thinner and without its customary animation. Because of him?

"Got any kumquat juice?"

"Help yourself."

He studied her for a moment. She was physically present and polite enough, but she wasn't really there. Would his words make a difference? He was suddenly unsure.

"You know I keep thinking about how you'd have handled Caroline's situation if you'd been in her shoes. Not quietly, that's for sure. You'd have hunted the guy down with an air rifle." She glanced at him.

"Maybe. You never know how you'll act in a situation until it happens."

He picked up one of her hands. It was cold and unresponsive. He chafed it, absently.

"My expectations were unreasonable. You'd never had a reason to doubt your sister, and you were convinced she'd told you the truth about Stevie. It wasn't a great moment to try to think things out, either, what with Alice's gun pointing at you. I want you to forgive me."

"There's nothing to forgive you for," she said.

"Then forgive yourself. I don't want you to think about this anymore. I want to get on with our lives. You agreed to marry me, and I'm gonna hold you to it."

She turned to him and the golden eyes gleamed with unshed tears.

"I'll do it again."

"What?"

"I'll doubt your word. Don't you see? Trust is everything. It is to me, and I know it is to you. You trusted Theo—believed in him—for more than twenty years, and then he sent you away. I said I'd marry you, and then I let you down."

Nick got down on his knees to get closer to her.

"It isn't the same thing. And, anyway, I've decided you were right. Isabelle gave me a scrapbook that Pops put together. It's clear he thought of me as his grandson. You were right about that."

"I'm glad you've made your peace with Theo, but I still can't marry you."

He lifted her cold hand to his mouth and pressed his lips against her knuckles.

"Why?"

She stared at her hand. "I thought it would be enough, trust and liking and, you know, the attraction."

"And it isn't?"

"No. Not for me. Happily ever after isn't just a

comforting concept to me. During the past few days when I had to face the fact that my sister lied to me and that I failed you, I realized that a marriage needs more than just trust. It needs love." He held her hand against his cheek.

"Our marriage will have love. You love me. I knew it that night in Chicago. Somehow I can't see you going to bed with a guy you don't love." He watched the color seep into her cheeks. "And I love you, too, Daisy. I think I loved you from the moment I heard you trying to reason with Quentin about his codpiece. Let's put the past week behind us. Let's start a life together. Now."

She looked at him, steadily.

"You never wanted to marry, Nick, you told me so yourself. What if you suddenly realize you don't want to be tied down? That you miss your old footloose life? I think we should wait, think this over for a while."

He held her hands and peered into her eyes. He knew she wanted to believe.

"Wait right here," he said, getting to his feet.

Her eyes widened. "You want the kumquat juice now?"

"Just wait here."

****

She watched him jog to the Malibu and open the trunk. She couldn't believe he was still driving the rental car. It felt as if he'd been back in Mayville for years. She couldn't believe he'd said he loved her, but the longed for words hadn't jolted her into stratospheric bliss. She'd told him the truth about her reservations. They'd been together a week. He'd been on his own so much longer. He might have proposed for so many reasons. He probably felt he owed her marriage after their shared, unprotected intimacy. He might even believe he wanted to settle down and raise a family but would he feel the same way tomorrow? Next week? Next year?

Daisy wrapped her arms around her waist and shivered. She didn't fully trust her own instincts anymore.

He returned a minute later carrying a large, cardboard box. As he lowered the sides of it she could see it was the dollhouse she'd found in the cellar, the miniature version of the Gray Lady. Its fresh paint gleamed in the sunlight, and she noticed the rooms were freshly painted and filled with tiny furniture—and people. There was even a Christmas tree in the parlor.

"It took hours for us to restore it," Nick said, "but it was worth it."

"Us?"

"Caroline and I worked on it every night this week. We sanded and painted and talked about you, about how important you are to each of us. We wanted you to have the miniature house."

"Because you plan to raze the real one?"

"No. It's partly to show our support for Happily Ever After."

"And what's the other part?"

His cheeks turned ruddy as if he were slightly embarrassed.

"It's a symbol. I want a home with you. A life. A family. And I wanted you to know I can be a handy guy to have around the house."

This time the happiness hit with full force. Daisy cried out and flung her arms around Nick's neck. "You are a handy guy," she said, her words muffled by his shirt, "a handy guy and an essential guy. I love you so much."

His lips found hers before all the words were out of her mouth, and neither of them spoke for a long, long time, not, in fact, until the Mendelssohn melody filled the air.

Daisy slipped the cell phone out of her pocket.

"Happily Ever After," she said, breathlessly, "This is Daisy."

"Elias Foote here. Over in Titusville? You know that rosewood casket you sent me?"

"Miss Ora's coffin?"

"No, t'other one. Fer the one that ain't dead yet."

Miss Olive's. "Of course."

"My wife was vacuumin' the inside, and she couldn't get the lining to lie flat in the cover. Seems someone put an envelope in there at some time."

"An envelope?"

"Yeah, it's got Mr. Theo Bowman's name on it. Thought you might want to give it back to the family."

A thrill of excitement worked its way up Daisy's spine.

"Thank you, Mr. Foote. We'll be right over." She hung up and looked at Nick. "It was in the coffin. Theo hid it in an envelope in the lining of the coffin. It's been there for sixty years. Do you think it could be the blue diamond?"

"Only one way to find out."

"You don't sound very excited."

He chuckled and held her hand over the bulge in his jeans. "You are mistaken."

Half an hour later, they climbed into the Malibu and made the trip to Titusville.

"I can't believe Theo took the risk of hiding the treasure in the lid of a coffin," Daisy said, as her excitement mounted. "What if Miss Ora or Miss Olive had died sometime in those sixty years? Your Uncle Randolph would have buried the treasure with them."

"Uncle Randolph was probably in on it. He and Pops came back from the war together. Anyway, we don't know for sure that it is the treasure. Could be a deed to the house or old tax forms or nothing at all."

"I know it's the blue diamond," Daisy said, smugly. "This is a day for happy endings."

He reached for her hand and lifted it to his lips.

"I can't argue with that."

They retrieved the worn envelope from the mortician, who seemed a little disappointed that they didn't open it in his presence. Back in the Malibu, Nick slit the flap, and Daisy held her breath while he upended it in his hand and shook. A piece of folded paper slipped out along with a velvet drawstring bag. Nick handed the bag to Daisy. She worked the strings free and shook the contents into her hand. It was a ring. A heavy silver man's ring.

Daisy's eyes widened as she examined it. A silver-mounted pedestal formed a swastika. At the center sat a diamond as large as a robin's egg and as blue as the summer sky at the center. She peered inside the thick band and found the initials A.H.

"Adolf Hitler," Daisy breathed.

"The letter's dated June 5, 1952 and signed by Pops," Nick said. He looked at Daisy and began to read it aloud.

"In July of 1945, the survivors of my platoon were looking for souvenirs in the Führerbrau. I happened to find a metal box partially submerged in water from a burst pipe. In it I found this ring. I knew it was valuable both because of the diamond and for its historic significance, but, unlike the stolen paintings, it could not be returned to the proper owners. It would become the property of the German government which, at that time, was non-existent. I decided to protect the ring until it was time to return it to a restored Germany when the time was right."

Nick stopped to look at her and Daisy thought she'd drown at the warmth in his gray eyes.

"The right time was when he wanted you back in Mayville," she said. "He saved the ring for your quest."

Nick pulled her across the seat and into his arms. The ring bounced out of her hand and into the well of the car but neither of them made a move to retrieve it. He cupped her face in his big hands.

"In the end," he murmured, "Pops was a hero. He gave me you."

Daisy smiled just before he kissed her. Eventually they'd have to figure out to whom the ring belonged, but that could wait. Right now she just wanted to kiss and be kissed and bask in her very own happily ever after.

A word about the author...

Ann Yost is a former newspaper reporter and freelance humorist. The mother of three grown children, a daughter-in-law and a brand new son-in-law, she lives in Northern Virginia with her reporter husband, Pete, and Lucy, their golden retriever.

www.annyost.com

~*~

Other Ann Yost titles
available from The Wild Rose Press, Inc.

ABOUT A BABY
EYE OF THE TIGER LILY
THAT VOODOO THAT YOU DO
HE LOVES LUCY
THE EARL THAT I MARRY

www.ingramcontent.com/pod-product-compliance
Lightning Source LLC
Chambersburg PA
CBHW070901180626
46817CB00003B/870